SPECIAL MESSAGE TO READERS

THE ULVERSCROFT FOUNDATION
(registered UK charity number 264873)
was established in 1972 to provide funds for research, diagnosis and treatment of eye diseases. Examples of major projects funded by the Ulverscroft Foundation are:-

- The Children's Eye Unit at Moorfields Eye Hospital, London
- The Ulverscroft Children's Eye Unit at Great Ormond Street Hospital for Sick Children
- Funding research into eye diseases and treatment at the Department of Ophthalmology, University of Leicester
- The Ulverscroft Vision Research Group, Institute of Child Health
- Twin operating theatres at the Western Ophthalmic Hospital, London
- The Chair of Ophthalmology at the Royal Australian College of Ophthalmologists

You can help further the work of the Foundation by making a donation or leaving a legacy. Every contribution is gratefully received. If you would like to help support the Foundation or require further information, please contact:

THE ULVERSCROFT FOUNDATION
The Green, Bradgate Road, Anstey
Leicester LE7 7FU, England
Tel: (0116) 236 4325

website: www.foundation.ulverscroft.com

In addition to her novels, Fay Cunningham has had a number of short stories published in women's magazines. Her particular interest is forensic science, and the part a forensic artist plays in helping to solve a crime. Fay was born in north London and moved several times before settling in Essex, where she now lives with her husband and a very old cat.

SLEEPING DOGS

Gina Cross is a forensic artist for the police. She teams up with Adam Shaw, an investigative journalist, to find Nathan Fox, a school caretaker, involved in the mystery of a child's death twenty years ago. Fox had found something that incriminated three of the students, but then he'd disappeared. The students are now grown up: one is a renowned plastic surgeon, one a politician and the third is a lawyer. But now Fox is back, and no one is safe — and she's not the only one hunting Fox. When Gina's friend is kidnapped and held hostage, anything, including murder, is on the cards.

Books by Fay Cunningham
Published by The House of Ulverscroft:

SNOWBOUND
DECEPTION
LOVE OR MARRIAGE
CRY BABY
DREAMING OF LOVE

FAY CUNNINGHAM

SLEEPING DOGS

Complete and Unabridged

ULVERSCROFT
Leicester

First published in Great Britain in 2009

First Large Print Edition
published 2013

The moral right of the author has been asserted

Copyright © 2009 by Fay Cunningham
All rights reserved

A catalogue record for this book is available
from the British Library.

ISBN 978–1–4448–1602–0

Published by
F. A. Thorpe (Publishing)
Anstey, Leicestershire

Set by Words & Graphics Ltd.
Anstey, Leicestershire
Printed and bound in Great Britain by
T. J. International Ltd., Padstow, Cornwall

This book is printed on acid-free paper

Prologue

She sat cross-legged on the grubby mattress, her hands together, her head bowed. She remembered the prayers her parents had taught her, singing them silently in her head.

The room had one small window, too high for her to reach, the glass frosted. Faded wallpaper covered the walls, pale rosebuds twined with yellowing ivy. The room was small, but she had a bed and a chair, and they had brought her food. Strange little tubs and pots in a bag. Curry and poppadoms.

When they came for her she was ready. She had been put in a large bath and the woman had scrubbed her with a ball of scratchy fabric, prizing her hands away to rub a soapy cloth between her legs. Her hair was clean and shining, falling below her waist. She had been given a new dress to wear, and the woman had put socks and shoes on her feet. The man came into the room and stood by the woman to look at her. He was short and fat and smelled of cigarette smoke.

'We'll get our money back on this one,' the man said. 'She only looks about eight years old.'

This was the family that had paid for her. This was the freedom her mother had promised. This was England.

A man came to collect her and drove her to a big house. He took her to a room with a large bed and told her to wait. Someone would come and tell her what to do. 'No one will hurt you if you do what you are told,' the man said.

In the house where she had lived before, in another country, her mother had hidden her from the soldiers. She was told to crawl beneath the house and not make a sound. The soldiers' boots stomped and strutted above her head, and through cracks in the worn wooden floor she could hear the men shouting and laughing. Once, she thought she heard her mother scream. After a while they went away.

'They would have hurt you,' her mother said.

Now she sat on the side of the big bed and waited. No one would hurt her if she did what she was told.

1

The bones were laid out on a table, grouped the way they were found, using photographs taken at the scene. Gina Cross held the skull gently, running her fingers over the ridges of the eye sockets and the forward projecting cheekbones.

'Not European,' she told Reagan. 'Asian, I would think. A young female.'

He nodded. 'Pathology reckon about eleven or twelve years old. Small for her age. The bones have been there twenty years or more, hidden in silt at the bottom of a pond where animals couldn't get at them. There may be more; we haven't sifted the pond thoroughly yet.'

Gina touched a bone with her gloved hand. Such small bones. Had the child fallen in the pond and drowned? Had there been a search all those years ago? A line of policemen moving across the fields, searching for a child they would never find. She looked around the spare, sterile room. There were no windows, and it felt claustrophobic in spite of the cooling fans. This was no place for a child.

'What else did you find in the pond?'

Reagan had been leaning against the wall but now he pushed himself upright and came to stand beside her. 'Not a lot. An old shopping trolley, bricks, maybe rope or sacking. All the things you need to dispose of a body — or just a load of stuff people throw in ponds. You tell me.'

Detective Inspector Reagan looked more like a farmer than a policeman. He was a big man with a ruddy face and keen blue eyes, and sometimes his pronounced Suffolk accent made him sound slow, but Gina knew how quickly his mind could work when necessary. He treated a crime scene like a jigsaw puzzle, carefully sorting the pieces until he could put the whole picture together.

Still holding the skull, she turned back to the table. They might just be old bones but they were the bones of a child, a child whose life had ended twenty years ago in a dirty pond in the middle of a field.

'How was she found?'

'A crowd of those do-gooders, environmentalists or whatever they call themselves, cleaning up the countryside. Someone was bright enough to recognize a human bone when they saw it and report it to us.' Reagan stared morosely at the table. 'The pond'll have another trolley in it next week.'

Gina shook her head, smiling. 'Ye of little

faith.' She stood the skull back on the table and squatted down in front of it. She closed her eyes for a moment, then picked up her pad and started sketching. The face small and heart shaped. Tilted almond eyes. Hair like a dark waterfall, falling almost to the child's waist. Gina had no genetic background to go on, so she could have been wrong about the hair, but she didn't think so.

The young police officer who had been standing on the other side of the room walked over to watch Gina draw. He had trouble associating this petite young woman with a pile of old bones. Gina Cross was dressed in loose navy shorts and a sports top, her dark hair tied in an untidy knot on top of her head, her bare shoulders tanned to warm copper. Not at all like the pale-skinned forensic experts he was used to.

'Is that what you think the little girl looked like?'

Gina looked up from her pad. Did he think she was guessing? 'No, Officer McIntyre, this is what I know she looked like.'

He frowned, peering over her shoulder. 'What is it you do, exactly?'

The fact that she could do more with her pad and pencil than most forensic artists was none of his business. 'I put the flesh back on the bones,' she told him.

Gina had been working as a freelance forensic artist for the Castlebury police force for over two years, but she would always be an outsider. Her sketches were far better than any the computer could produce — and that was the problem. Gina couldn't explain her talent, and the one thing the forensics team hated above all else was the unexplainable. She finished her drawing and tore the sheet from the pad, handing the sketch to Reagan. 'Do you know how she died?'

'The pond's deep and the sides are slippery clay. If she fell in, there'd be no way out. There's nothing to tell us exactly how she died. We'll probably never know for sure. Some of the bones will be missing, lost somewhere in the pond or moved by animals or fish, and there's been wear over the years.' He picked up a long bone. 'There are teeth marks on this one, see? It was sticking up out of the muck at the edge of the pond and something had a chew on it, probably a rat.'

She looked at the bones on the table. The child deserved more than that. 'I hope you find out what happened to her.'

Reagan looked at the drawing again. 'I hope so too. Hang on while I photocopy this, then you can have the original back.'

He offered her a lift home but she refused. She had been about to take her usual Sunday morning run when he picked her up and she was still wound up, still annoyed at the scepticism she had seen on the face of the young officer. She ran faster than usual until sweat beaded her face and pooled, hot and wet, under her arms. She hoped a hard run would take her mind off the dead child, but it didn't.

After the long run up through the park she sat on a bench at the top of the hill to get her breath back. She had lived in Castlebury all her life. It was a nice, medium-sized East Anglian town, wearing its rows of Victorian houses like a comfy old cardigan, but recently the town had undergone a face lift. Now bright new houses climbed the hill and blocks of expensive apartments bordered the river. Change for change sake, her grandmother would have called it. Whatever they did to modernize the town, Castlebury would always be ancient.

By the time she got home it was almost midday. The old Victorian house she lived in had once been a shop and the big bay window at the front made it perfect for a studio. The flat above the shop was furnished with old pieces from her grandmother's house mixed with a few new bits she had chosen herself, the dark antique furniture complementing the white walls and bright rugs on the polished oak floor.

She climbed the outside stairs to her flat and made straight for the bathroom. After a call-out by the police, she needed to shower and change. A ritual cleansing that never quite managed to remove the smell of death from her skin and hair. She wanted to scrub like a surgeon, clean her nails, floss her teeth and run a flea comb through her hair. Sometimes she had to resist the urge to burn her clothes.

She stripped and stood under the shower, letting the hot water cascade down over her head and face until she began to feel clean again. Wrapped in a towel, she went in search of food, and a few minutes later she was sitting at her small dining table, eating cold macaroni cheese straight from the carton.

She spread the sketch of the little girl in front of her, wondering if there was still a parent somewhere waiting for a child who would never come home. The pond was in a field with only a few houses nearby, the nearest village a good three miles away, and twenty years was a long time. Reagan had given her some good advice: don't get involved with the dead. But he didn't see the dead the way she did. Today he had seen a pile of old bones — and she had seen a child.

After she finished her lunch she logged on

to her internet connection, Googling missing persons. The website with the most hits was some sort of people finder called Parent Track. She decided that would have to do and downloaded her sketch of the child, together with a message asking if anyone had information about a little girl who had gone missing twenty years ago. Don't get involved, Reagan had told her. Easier said than done.

Two weeks later, the same day Megan turned up for work with a black eye, Gina got a reply. She tried to remember to check her personal email every morning, but she had been busy, and the message had been sitting in her in-box for over a week.

I need to speak to you. I have a photo of the child. Jessica Fox.

Gina had never really considered what she was going to do if someone actually answered. This was the time to walk away. All she had to do was pick up the phone and pass the woman's name to Inspector Reagan. But she didn't. She typed in the phone number of the studio. If the woman phoned back, she would tell Reagan then.

By the time she got downstairs, the door to the studio was unlocked and Megan, her nineteen-year-old assistant, was already at her desk. The girl didn't look up. 'Y're right?' she mumbled.

A long time ago Gina had deciphered this to mean 'Are you all right?' which was evidently some sort of greeting and didn't require a reply.

Megan had worked with Gina from the day the studio first opened. Only sixteen then, she had been chucked out by her mum and left to fend for herself. Without a job and with nowhere to live, she had moved into a council flat with a boyfriend only a little older than herself.

'I've got no GCSE certificates,' she told Gina, 'but I can answer the phone, and I'm good with numbers. I really need this job, Miss Cross — my boyfriend spent the rent money and we're going to be chucked out.'

A big girl at the best of times, Megan was now heavily pregnant and Gina was finding it increasingly difficult to cope with the enormity of her assistant's stomach. At some point, Gina was sure, the whole thing would just pop like an overblown balloon.

This morning Megan was wearing draw-string trousers and a cropped top that left her protruding belly exposed to the elements. Her long, straight hair was a mix of dark and light brown with streaks of red, but that changed as often as Megan could afford the spray-on colour. Her flip-flops were bright pink and her toenails black. Megan kept her head down and Gina looked at her assistant suspiciously. Megan wasn't exactly shy.

'What's the matter, Megan?'

The girl looked up sheepishly. A red mark slashed across her cheek-bone and the beginnings of a bruise darkened the skin under her eye. It looked painful.

'How did you do that?' It was a rhetorical question. Gina was pretty sure she knew exactly how Megan had got her black eye.

'Walked into a door.'

Gina filled the kettle at the little sink and turned it on without speaking.

Megan sighed. 'Gary came back.'

'He did that to your face?' Gina waited a second to calm herself down before she spoke again. 'Why?'

'I got mad at him. It was my fault.' Megan raised her shoulders in a shrug. 'I should remember to just shut up until he sods off again.'

Gina spooned instant coffee into large mugs, topped them up with boiling water, and handed one to Megan. Then she got milk out of the little fridge. 'And when will that be?'

Megan shrugged again. 'It's his flat and his baby, Gina. He has a right.'

'No, he doesn't.' Gina tried very hard to keep her voice even. She felt sick to think

Gary had knocked Megan about again. 'He doesn't have any rights. He gave up his rights the first time he beat you up and walked out on you. For God's sake, Megan, you know what he's like. I thought he'd gone for good this time.'

'So did I.'

'So what are you going to do?'

Megan dropped her hands to her stomach protectively, swinging backwards and forwards in her swivel chair. 'Wait for him to go again. He won't stay long, he never does.'

The rest of the morning was taken up with paperwork, Gina making a point not to mention Megan's slowly blackening eye. In the afternoon Gina had an eighty-year-old woman sitting for a portrait. The family wanted something to remember the old lady by, which seemed a bit like asking you to write your own epitaph. The old woman insisted on talking all through the sitting and accompanied her little anecdotes with a lot of hand waving, which made sketching her difficult. By closing time, Gina was dead tired. 'Do you want to stay with me tonight?' she asked Megan.

Megan shook her head. 'I'll be fine.'

Gina was worried Megan wouldn't be fine at all, not if Gary was still in residence, but she couldn't exactly force the teenager to stay with her. Just as they were closing up the shop, the telephone rang. Gina picked up the phone and nodded at Megan to go. The girl slipped out and closed the door behind her.

'Hello? Gina Cross Studios.'

For a moment there was silence on the other end of the line. 'Did you get my message?' The woman sounded nervous. 'My name is Jessica Fox. I have a photo of that little girl.'

For a moment Gina couldn't think what the woman was talking about, then she remembered the missing persons website and the message.

'Oh, yes. Thank you for phoning. Do you know who she is?'

'No, I don't know anything about her. I found the photo with my mother's things.' There was another pause. 'My mother died a few weeks ago. Of cancer.'

'Oh, I'm sorry to hear that. So your mother had a photo of the little girl?'

'Or possibly my father. I don't know. I've never seen the child before. She's not English, is she?'

'I'd like to see the photo,' Gina said. 'I have an art studio in Castlebury. Do you live locally?'

'Angel Green, about six miles from town.'

'I'll be here all evening. I live in the flat

above the studio. If you want to bring the photo over, perhaps we can work out who she is. If not, later in the week will do.'

She gave the woman the address, locked up and climbed the stairs to her flat. There was no hurry, she told herself. The child wasn't going anywhere.

2

By eleven o'clock Gina had decided the woman wasn't going to turn up. The temperature had picked up again and even after a cool shower she slept fitfully, every tiny noise bringing her out of a shallow sleep. It was too hot, even with all the windows open. When the phone rang just after six she was almost glad.

Inspector Reagan made some insincere remark about being sorry to wake her and then told her they had found another body.

'Bones again?' she asked, sitting up and pushing her sweat-damp hair out of her eyes. Not another child. Please, not another child.

'No, this is a burnt-out car, still hot this morning, with the driver burned to a crisp in the front seat. An accident, I'm sure, but we need to identify the driver as quickly as possible.'

She took a deep breath. She didn't want to do this. It was too soon after the last one. She wanted to spend the morning in her studio, drawing people who were still alive.

Reagan listened to her silence. 'We've already got forensics on the scene but they haven't got a lot to work with. We could do with your help.'

'I'd rather not.' She was freelance, damn it! She didn't have to look at a barbecued body if she didn't want to. 'Forensics don't like me; they think I get in the way.' She knew there was another reason the forensic team didn't want her around. She spooked them.

'Never mind, then. Sorry again if I woke you. The driver ran into a tree last night on one of the little back lanes outside town, probably drunk. We won't know for sure until we get the lab report back but I want to notify any relatives as soon as possible.' Reagan paused. 'Anyway, not to worry. Thanks for your help, by the way.'

Gina got up and staggered groggily to the shower. It wasn't one of those over the bath things but a proper walk-in shower cubicle she had paid to have installed when she bought the house. As far as she was concerned, it wasn't a luxury but a necessity. This morning the water was hot and heavy on her head, pounding away any lingering tiredness. She dried herself quickly and slipped into her running gear, giving up on her hair. Still damp and curly, it defied all her efforts to tidy it up. In the end she just bundled it all together on top of her head with an elastic band.

She ran half her usual route through the park and began to feel guilty. She was the only person who could do what Reagan wanted — give a quick identity check on the victim. She slowed to a jog, watching a fat squirrel climb a tree, while she fished her mobile phone out of the pocket of her shorts. Thinking Gina had food, the squirrel came back down the tree, chattering at her crossly as she raised the phone to her ear.

'How are you getting on?' she asked Reagan.

'No further, really. We haven't moved the body yet and until we get the results of the dental check and everything else, it could be anybody, male or female. The car is a Renault Clio, the registration indecipherable. This one really went up.'

Gina was annoyed with herself for being so weak-willed. Why couldn't she just say no and mean it? 'I'll come if you send someone to pick me up. I'm running through the park, so tell them I'll be at the bottom gate in about ten minutes.'

By the time she got to the lower gate a police car was already waiting. As she climbed in she looked around worriedly, hoping no one she knew was watching. It must look as if she was being hauled in for questioning.

The lane where the burned-out car had

been found was completely blocked by two police cars and the forensics van, the smell of cooked meat still lingering. The lane was narrow, with only room for one car at a time and no passing places. It was a lane someone would have to drive along with very great care. The bank on one side was dotted with trees and one large tree had a car embedded in its trunk. As she climbed from the police car she saw a couple of young police officers standing well back, looking as if they were having trouble keeping down their breakfast. She slipped the protective covers over her trainers, trying not to breathe too deeply, and put on the gloves someone handed her, even though she had no intention of touching anything.

It was only a little past eight but already hot, the hedgerows and banks steaming in the early morning sunshine. Birds and small animals had retreated from the fire, and the only sounds were the crunching of crisp vegetation underfoot and the strange tapping and scraping from the forensic team. Gina crouched down and slid under the blue and white tape, ignoring the hostile looks from the people in white coveralls. She was here to do a job, the same as they were.

The burned-out shell of the car stood on an irregular patch of bare earth, brown twigs sticking up where bracken had been. The front of the car was buried in the tree, the trunk of the tree scorched, the lower leaves crisp and brown. Someone in a white bunny suit smudged with soot was turning over the earth beside the car with a stick. As she moved closer, she saw the outside of the car was blistered, but flakes of paint still remained. One of the technicians was collecting paint flakes and dropping them into a bag. The front of the car was smashed in, the door on the driver's side open, the driver's body bent forward, knees pulled towards the chest and hands curled into claws round what was left of the steering wheel. Gina had worked with forensics long enough to know that intense heat shrivels muscles and tendons, forcing limbs and fingers into a flexed position. A blackened seatbelt buckle sat between the charred thighs like a sporran. The clothes had mostly gone, leaving burnt strips of cloth fluttering like bunting. The face was fixed in a grimace that was almost a smile, the mouth open in either a scream or a last gasp for air.

Gina stepped back and took several deep breaths, trying to breathe through her nose and stop the smell turning to taste on her tongue. She knew how the stench of burnt flesh lingered, clinging to clothes and hair, and refusing to leave without a sickening reminder that lasted for days. The atmosphere around the car was thick and oily, heat from the still-hot metal distorting the air like a mirage. A policeman in uniform was rooting in a ditch beside the car. He suddenly shouted and held something up above his head.

'I've found a woman's handbag.'

Reagan appeared from nowhere. 'Let me see.' Pulling on gloves, he took the bag and opened it, frowning at Gina as she moved closer. From what she could see, the bag was good quality black leather with a designer insignia embossed on the flap. The leather was dirty but not burned. Reagan reached into the bag and took out a matching purse. 'Some cash and notes and a couple of credit cards.' He glanced at Gina. 'Looks like we don't need you after all.'

The officer who had found the bag looked back at the ditch. 'If it's the driver's handbag, how'd it get in the ditch?' In the ensuing silence the young policeman looked embarrassed. 'I just wondered why it wasn't burnt up in the car.'

'It probably got thrown out of the car by the impact.' Reagan carried on rummaging in the bag. 'Tissues, lipstick, usual women's rubbish.' He unzipped a compartment and pulled out a driving licence. 'I've got her picture and her address. She was twenty-five years old and lived a couple of miles back up the road.' He looked back in the bag. 'Hang on a minute, there's something in an envelope.'

Gina couldn't understand the expression on Reagan's face. He walked towards her and held an old-fashioned Polaroid photograph under her nose. The photo was badly faded and bent at the corners, but it was still possible to make out the face of a child, a pretty little girl with dark skin and tip-tilted eyes. The face of the little Asian girl looked back at Gina, the hair just as long and just as dark as she had imagined. There was a sad acceptance in the dark brown eyes, as if the child knew her life was almost over.

Gina looked up at Reagan. Trying to keep her voice steady, she said, 'I don't know anything about this.'

Reagan dropped the photo into an evidence bag. 'So why is your name on the front of the envelope?' He looked at Gina expectantly.

Her throat was suddenly dry. 'A woman named Jessica Fox phoned me to tell me she had a photo of the child.'

'Now why would she do that?' Reagan put up his hand. 'Not now, I need a pathology report before I can be sure of anything. See me in my office tomorrow morning.' He gave Gina a look that was meant to put ice in her veins. 'Early.'

She watched Reagan's departing back, and when he didn't look behind him she moved towards the car. She walked round the vehicle and stood staring at the open door, chewing her bottom lip. The door bothered her. If Jessica Fox had been trying to get out when the car caught fire her hands wouldn't still be on the steering wheel, and if she was unconscious and someone else had opened the door, why hadn't they pulled the woman to safety? And how about the handbag? Would Jessica Fox have been driving with the bag on her lap? If it had been on the floor or on the passenger seat it seemed unlikely it could have ended up in the ditch.

The intense heat had melted a gold ring on the woman's right hand, turning it into a teardrop that hung from the blackened bone like a piece of Dali sculpture. A single gold earring lay amidst the debris on the floor. All that remained of a life.

Taking a quick breath, Gina looked at the charred features and saw the woman's face. It had once been a pleasant face, not pretty but friendly, with a determined tilt to the chin. Now all that remained was open-mouthed shock that death had arrived so suddenly and so unexpectedly.

3

Gina arrived at the police station the next morning not quite at the crack of dawn but still too damn early. She had work to do and she could have told Reagan everything she knew in one sentence at the scene of the accident. Having to appear at the police station was a punishment. After a lot of manoeuvring, she managed to squeeze her little red Metro between two police cars, daring anyone to stick a ticket on her windscreen.

The old police station had been in the centre of the town and easily accessible, the entrance lobby always full of stray dogs and American tourists asking the way to the castle. The man behind the counter in the old building had been more easily accessible, too. The new building was a circle of black glass and chrome with no visible entrance and nowhere to park, about as inviting as a black hole, but perhaps that was the idea.

She approached the desk apprehensively. She didn't want to be here. She was still trying to get over the fact that a woman she had spoken to only a few hours earlier had burned to death on a quiet country lane, probably on her way to the studio.

'Detective Inspector Reagan. He's expecting me.'

The man didn't look up from his computer screen. 'Take a seat.'

The seats were hard plastic, so slippery it was impossible to sit still and so high her feet didn't touch the floor. She felt like a naughty child waiting outside the headmaster's office. With nothing better to do while she waited except twiddle her thumbs, she studied the posters on the wall. How to cope with burglars, sexually transmitted diseases, drug addiction, rape; posters for missing children, missing people, even missing dogs and cats. For a moment she imagined a place where all the missing people were stored like lost property. Hand over a ticket and get your missing child back.

Reagan kept her waiting fifteen minutes. He frowned when she walked into his office, waving her to a slightly more inviting chair. 'What do you know about the woman in the car you didn't tell me yesterday?'

'I put the sketch of the little girl on the Internet, that's all,' she said defensively. 'I thought someone might know who she is, and then I got a phone call from the woman in the car, Jessica Fox. She said she had a photo of the child, so I gave her the studio address and told her to bring it round to my flat.'

'The driver of the car hasn't been positively identified yet.'

Gina just looked at him. 'Do you know what made her crash?'

'The lane's particularly narrow on that bend and because of the recent heat the surface was dry and dusty. She may have been going too fast, or had a few drinks before she left home. Or she may have met something coming the other way. We won't know until we finish checking the area.'

Gina had a sudden vision of skin like black leather stretched tight over a grinning skull. 'Her body was terribly burned. Could someone have thrown petrol over her and set her alight deliberately?'

'Now why would you think that? The car probably had a full tank of petrol and once it caught fire anything inside would have burned more fiercely because of the enclosed space. The woman's clothes would have acted as a wick and body fat can actually boil, did you know that? That's why there wasn't a lot of her left.'

Gina was silent for a moment, her hands clasped tightly in her lap. That was more information than she needed. 'Was she already dead when the car caught fire?'

Reagan opened the folder and turned a page of the notes. 'Yes. Broke her neck when the car hit the tree. The burns were post mortem.'

Thank God for that, thought Gina. 'I know her name was Jessica Fox, but who was she? What do you know about her? She didn't tell me anything on the phone.'

Reagan turned another page. 'Jessica Mary Fox. Twenty-five years old. Worked as manageress in a boutique in the village and lived with her mother. The mother died two months ago. Cancer, I think.' He sat silent for a moment, reading the notes. 'The father, Nathan Fox, disappeared twenty years ago. The daughter started looking for him after her mother died. She was posting messages on the Internet, begging him to get in touch.'

'The father went missing twenty years ago? The same time the child died?'

'Could be coincidence.'

Gina looked at Reagan sceptically. 'You once told me you don't believe in coincidences. Besides, Jessica Fox had a photo of the child she found with her mother's things. That's a rather big coincidence.'

Reagan smiled his ruddy farmer's smile. 'Stranger things have happened. Don't forget we're working on rough estimates here. The child died about twenty years ago, give or take a few years, but we have no way of pinpointing the exact time Mr Fox disappeared. The wife never reported him missing.'

Which was strange, she thought. Why would you not report a missing husband?

She wrote out a statement for Reagan, promised him a printed copy of the message on her computer, and then walked back to her studio, enjoying the sunshine but not the traffic. When she walked into the studio Megan was at her desk and she was pleased to see the marks on the girl's face had faded, probably down to some rather skilful work with a foundation stick. When they took a break for lunch, she told Megan about her visit to the police station.

'Why would the Fox woman drive her car into a tree?' Knowing Gina would want coffee, Megan unplugged the electric kettle and took it over to the little sink in the corner. 'She must know all the dodgy corners on that lane. Besides, it was dark, and if something had been coming the other way she would've seen the lights.' Megan held the kettle under the tap, waiting for it to fill. 'I know you feel bad about the little kid, but she died a long time ago, and now the Fox woman is dead as well, so it's all sorted, isn't it?'

'I asked Jessica Fox to bring the photo to me.'

'So it's your fault she hit a tree?' Megan carelessly pulled up her shirt and scratched her stomach. 'God, it doesn't half itch sometimes.'

Gina shuddered. She hated it when Megan did that. 'No, I'm not saying it was my fault, but the Fox woman was bringing the photo to me because I asked her to, so I feel partly responsible. Besides, she was all on her own. Her mother died and her father left her.'

'Like your father left you.' The kettle turned itself off and Megan reached for the jar of instant coffee. 'I just think you shouldn't get mixed up in this,' she said. 'The little kid died a long time ago. You can't bring her back.'

Gina knew she couldn't bring the child back, but the little girl's death was still a mystery and she didn't like leaving mysteries unsolved. If Jessica's father had nothing to do with the child's death, why had he gone missing about the same time the child died, and why hadn't his wife reported him missing? And wasn't it a little odd that Jessica Fox managed to run into a tree on the very night she was bringing a photo of the child to the studio? There were just too many coincidences.

She tried pumping Reagan, but he wouldn't give her any more information apart from telling her they were contacting all Jessica Fox's known relatives and the investigation was still ongoing. Police gobbledegook. She felt frustrated. She couldn't think of anything else she could do but she hated giving up so soon. The fact that Jessica's father was missing had stirred up old memories and opened old wounds. According to Reagan, the man had left without a word when his daughter was only eight years old. What kind of man does that to a child?

It was Megan who pointed out the notice in the local paper stating that a funeral service for the woman who had burned to death in her car would take place the following week. Gina knew the one time you could be sure of getting all the family together in one place was at a funeral. Someone was bound to recognize the dead child. All she had to do was find something suitable to wear.

4

The funeral was a sad little affair. Jessica had few friends and even fewer family, a straggle of bemused mourners with nothing to connect them except the dead.

Gina put a small basket of late spring flowers with the others outside the chapel, bending down to read the attached cards. A wreath from Aunt Jane, pink roses from Maggie, a bouquet from Andrew — still with the Tesco label on — and a small pot of African marigolds without a card.

Several people nodded politely to her and she nodded back, but still no one spoke. She knew their silence was a mark of respect, but Jessica was only twenty-five, and Gina hoped if she died young someone would organize a going-away party and have a few laughs.

The little stone chapel where the service took place was set in carefully clipped lawns, gravestones lying like white bones in the grass, flowers wilting in marble urns. She remembered a graveyard in Hawaii she had visited with Simon, where people had left fruit, toys, and cans of beer by the graves, tributes that were more use to the dead, surely, than a faded bunch of flowers. The service was mercifully quick, but as the coffin disappeared from sight Gina wondered if cremation had really been the best option for Jessica Fox.

She watched people filtering out of the chapel. Most of them didn't seem to know one another and looked slightly embarrassed. A woman stood undecided, as if she couldn't remember why she was there, and a tall man in a long black overcoat was in such a hurry to get away he almost knocked Gina over. She thought the overcoat was a bit excessive on a warm day, but perhaps it was the only thing he had in black.

She eventually found Jessica's aunt, a plump, motherly lady who lived in Kent and hadn't seen her sister or niece for several years. There had been three sisters, but now Jane was the only one left.

'I kept meaning to visit,' she told Gina. 'I broke my ankle just before my sister's funeral, so I had to stay home. Now this . . . ' She waved her hand helplessly, fighting back tears. 'Why do we always leave everything until it's too late?'

Gina shook her head. She had felt the same way when her grandmother died. So many things left unsaid. She took the sketch of the child out of her bag and unrolled it. 'Have you ever seen this child? She died twenty years ago.'

Aunt Jane shook her head. 'That's a good drawing, though, really lifelike, and she looks so sad. Who was she, poor little thing?'

'That's what I'm trying to find out. Your niece, Jessica, had a photo of her, so someone in the family must have known her.'

'Foreign, isn't she? I don't remember anyone mentioning a foreign child. Do you think she was adopted or something?'

The thought hadn't occurred to Gina, but it was a distinct possibility. 'Who would know?'

Aunt Jane looked around. 'The old man in the wheelchair. Uncle Ron. He's over eighty. Knows the whole family, and he likes to gossip.'

Uncle Ron was sitting in the sun while he waited to be loaded into a car and driven back to his residential home. He said he was enjoying the outing, although it was mainly funerals he went to now. Once he started talking, Gina had trouble keeping up.

'He was a real hard worker, Jessica's dad. He kept those grounds looking spick and span all year round. He had one of those big ride-on lawnmowers he used to swan around on like the king of the castle, and he was happy to go out in all weathers, trimming hedges and cutting back bushes. Nice young man he was. His wife, she was nice, too. I never will understand why he left her.'

'Grounds?' Gina said. 'What grounds?'

'At the school. Nathan was the caretaker. They had a little house in the grounds and the little girl loved it there. Shame they had to move.' The old man shook his head. 'I never will understand why he just packed his bags and left.'

'Little girl?' she asked hopefully. 'A little Asian girl?'

'Goodness me, no. No foreigners at that school. No, I meant little Jessica. The poor little lass loved living at the school, she loved all that space to run around in. It's sad to see the young ones go before us old 'uns.'

Nodding sympathetically, she asked, 'Do you know who's paying for the funeral?'

'Young Jessica inherited the house when her mother died, but it's to be sold now. I reckon there'll be enough for this and quite a bit left over. It'll go to Jane, I expect, the rest of the money.'

Gina glanced across at Aunt Jane as the woman wiped away a tear. First she had lost her sister to cancer, now her niece had died in a terrible accident, and there was no way she could make up for all the years she hadn't found time to visit. Life is far too short to do all the things we know we should, Gina thought, but we still get stuck with the guilt. She walked over to say goodbye.

'I've got to go and clear out the house sometime in the next few weeks,' Aunt Jane said. 'Not a nice job, but it's got to be done. If I find anything to do with your little foreign girl, I'll let you know.'

'I really want to find out who the child is. Jessica told me she found the photo with her mother's things. Do you know why Jessica's father suddenly disappeared?'

Aunt Jane frowned. 'Now that's a mystery if ever there was one. Claire never seemed that bothered. You'd think she'd be devastated, her husband suddenly leaving without a word. We were quite close then, but she didn't ask for my help. I don't know where she got the money to buy a house, but she just moved out of the caretaker's cottage with Jessica and bought a house in that little village. Jessica thought her father was dead.' Jane looked tearful again. 'I wish I'd kept in touch. I feel as if I abandoned her. But Claire was such a strong person, she never seemed to need anyone's help — and she never told me how ill she really was.'

By the time Gina left, the car park was almost empty, except for a man leaning against the side of an open-top car, a low green sporty thing with spokes on the wheels and a soft top folded untidily in the back. The man looked as if he was waiting for someone, and Gina was about to get into her own car when he started walking towards her.

He hadn't been inside the chapel or she would have noticed. He was quite noticeable. He was dressed in jeans and a wrestler-back vest, with leather sandals on bare feet and a denim jacket hanging from one shoulder. As he got closer she could see he was at least six feet tall. A snake tattoo curled round his left bicep and his hair was cropped short. Almost army, but not quite.

'Hi,' he said. 'I thought I recognized you. Gina Cross, isn't it?' She waited, her hand on the door of her car. He held out his hand. 'I'm Adam Shaw.'

Gina kept her own hand firmly on the door of her car.

A slight smile curled the side of his mouth and he dropped his hand back to his side. 'I brought flowers to the funeral.'

'The marigolds.'

'I met Jessica once; she seemed a nice person.' He looked down at Gina and she wished she'd worn heels. 'I saw you inside and I wanted to talk to you, but if I tell people my occupation they usually run screaming for the nearest exit. Can we manage with just a name for the moment?'

'You must be an undertaker.'

He shook his head, handing her a business card. 'Journalist. I mostly do freelance work.'

Much worse than an undertaker. 'What exactly do you want, Mr Shaw?'

'A few minutes of your time.'

She dropped the business card in her bag and was just about to make a rather sharp reply when she caught sight of something moving out of the corner of her eye. A figure had been standing in the shadow of the chapel and was now moving quickly towards a lone car parked at the very end of the car park. She turned as fast as she could, but not fast enough — the man had his back to her and was climbing into the car. He was driving a large black 4×4 of some sort and she tried to see the registration number, but the car was at an angle, moving away from her fast. Turning on to the main road, the car disappeared, screened from her sight by a large hedge. Mr Fox, come to his daughter's funeral? Wishful thinking. She had no way of knowing what Jessica's father looked like and the man in the car could have been anyone.

She realized Adam Shaw was still talking to her and she hadn't heard a word he said. 'Sorry?'

'I said perhaps we could have a drink, or a

coffee or something. I'd like to ask you some questions about Jessica Fox.'

'I don't talk to journalists.' She knew she was being rude but if he hadn't been standing in her way she might have got a better look at the man in the car.

'Perhaps we could share information, Miss Cross. You work for the police, I believe. A psychic artist or something.'

Another newspaper reporter had called her that once and she was still trying to live it down. 'You used the wrong word, Mr Shaw. I'm a forensic artist.' She frowned at him. 'How do you know I work for the police?'

Adam Shaw gave her a lazy smile. 'I'm an investigative journalist, Miss Cross. I investigate things.'

She climbed into her car and slammed the door, looking at him through the open window. 'And that's exactly why I don't particularly like you, Mr Shaw.'

He put both hands on the bottom of the window and bent down so his face was level with hers. His eyes were a particularly intense blue, unusual with his dark hair.

'Why are you here, Miss Cross?'

'You should be able to find that out quite easily, Mr Shaw. You're the investigative journalist.'

He smiled again, pushing himself upright.

'Yes, but I'm not psychic, am I?'

Gina drove home far too quickly, a late rush of adrenaline making her hands shake on the steering wheel. Journalists had caused her nothing but grief in the past, and this was no exception.

Megan looked up as she came into the studio. 'How'd it go? Did you find out anything?'

'How much I hate journalists.' Gina kicked off her shoes. 'Some piss-arsed little prick who thinks he knows it all.'

Megan grinned, heaving herself up out of her chair. 'Coffee?'

'No, beer. Have we got any left?'

Megan peered in the fridge. 'Two Stellas coming up. You sound as if you need one.'

Gina drank straight from the bottle, letting the cold beer soothe her temper. 'No one knows anything about the Asian child. Nathan Fox, Jessica's father, worked as a school caretaker before he vanished. When he left, his wife moved to the village with little Jessica. An aunt is going to clear out the house in a few days and promised to let me know if she finds anything, but otherwise it was a dead end.'

'So who was this little prick of a journalist?'

Gina knew she had been stupid to let the man get under her skin. 'He was over six feet tall, which makes him a big prick, and I don't want to talk about him.'

Megan gave her a curious look, but let it go.

Gina had two urgent portraits to finish and that kept her occupied until it was time to send Megan home and lock up. She changed into her running gear and ran her shorter route round the park. The funeral had made her miss her early-morning run and she felt guilty if she didn't exercise at all, but the run did nothing to loosen her knotted muscles and now she had a headache as well.

She showered and changed and then used the Internet to look up Adam Shaw. She was surprised to find the man had a whole page to himself. Military police, a police negotiator, and a war correspondent for *The Daily Telegraph* before going freelance. Now his speciality seemed to be politics. So why was he at Jessica Fox's funeral?

She managed to get rid of her headache with a supermarket gourmet meal and a couple of glasses of wine. Then she logged on to the web page to delete her sketch of the little girl, but changed her mind at the last minute. What harm could it do to leave the sketch on there a few days longer? If Aunt Jane didn't find anything at Jessica Fox's house, someone else might have an answer to the mystery.

She took a sip of her wine, thinking she probably drank too much, but she didn't smoke, and sex had been a rare occurrence since she broke up with Simon. DIY, she found, wasn't nearly as much fun. Mind you, she thought, sex with Simon hadn't been much fun either. Simon had wanted a Stepford Wife, someone in a frilly pinny with a hot meal waiting when he got home from work, someone to clean his house and bring up his children, a servant rather than a companion. At one time she had considered the three years she spent with Simon as wasted years, but they hadn't been. She had learnt a lot.

She was sitting staring absently at her computer screen when her ISP told her she had one new email message.

We need to talk. Adam Shaw.

She angrily deleted the message. She didn't want to talk to him. The last journalist she had spoken to assured her he was only interested in promoting the work of the forensic team in Castlebury, but the article had turned into a witch hunt, literally, with her as the quarry, and she had no reason to believe Adam Shaw would be any different.

She got up from the computer and

wandered over to the window of her living-room. The old Victorian house had small windows upstairs, but the ground floor, with its large bay window at the front and French doors on to a small courtyard at the back, gave her more than enough light for an art studio. She looked down on to the street below. She had parked her own car round the corner near the outside stairs to her flat, but a large black car was parked directly under her window. From above it looked huge.

About the same size as the car that had left the funeral in such a hurry.

5

Driving from Essex to Suffolk the following morning, Gina still felt uneasy. The sort of feeling you had when you went to pay for something and couldn't find your purse. She refused to believe she had any sort of sixth sense, but the feeling of disquiet stayed with her all the way to Felixstowe.

She had been asked to identify a body that had been in the sea for some time. The local police had a list of people missing in the area, but salt water and marine animals made identification difficult. She didn't mind helping the police, but a body that had been in the water for a while wasn't the prettiest thing to have to study at close quarters. She tried to visualize the face before the ravages of aquatic carnivores and putrefaction had taken hold, wishing she'd accepted the mask she'd been offered.

'He's old,' she told the officer in charge of the investigation. 'I don't know, sixties, seventies — it's not easy when someone's been in the water that long. He was tall and thin with a long, bony face. Gaunt.'

'Senile?' one of the officers asked. 'Did he

know what he was doing?'

Gina wondered why they thought she could answer a question like that. If everyone thought she was some sort of clairvoyant, it was no wonder she got treated with scepticism. She handed over her sketch and was about to leave the crime scene when her mobile rang. She apologized and moved away from the stink of the body, unable to hold her breath and talk at the same time.

'Gina? It's Adam Shaw. Glad I managed to track you down. Look, I really do need to talk to you. An exchange of information could be helpful to both of us. If you're coming from Felixstowe you'll have to leave the A14 at Ipswich, won't you? Meet me at the Little Chef and I'll buy you lunch.'

She wondered who had told him she was at Felixstowe. Someone at Castlebury police station no doubt. She managed to swallow the instant refusal on the tip of her tongue. She really would like to know if he knew anything about the child — or Nathan Fox, for that matter — but all she wanted to do right now was drive straight home and take a shower. She still had all the forms to fill in that went with her identification sketch, she stunk of dead fish and dead bodies, and the last thing she was thinking about was food.

'I'll be late,' she told him. 'I won't get back

to Ipswich until about two o'clock.'

'All the better. By then you'll be hungry and need a break. I'll text you my mobile number. If you get held up, give me a ring, otherwise I'll see you about two.'

She was about to say something, but he'd hung up. She had half a mind to drive straight past the restaurant, but Shaw had been right, by the time she turned off the A14 on to the A12 she was really hungry and the thought of a big pot of coffee, plus a certain amount of curiosity, made her drive into the restaurant car park.

Adam Shaw was sitting at a table by the window. He watched Gina get out of her car and then hesitate with her hand on the car door, as if she might get back in and drive away again. Convinced her curiosity would get the better of her, he smiled to himself as he saw her square her shoulders, shut the car door, and drop the keys in her bag.

She was wearing a loose sports shirt over tight, stretch jeans, trainers on her feet. Her chocolate curls were secured on top of her head with a scrunchy, but tendrils had come free and hung like tiny corkscrews in front of her ears. She brushed them aside impatiently as she pushed through the door and scanned the tables.

She had forgotten how attractive he was.

Not good-looking, exactly, but with a sense of purpose, as if he knew exactly what he wanted. He waited for her to sit down and then pushed the menu towards her. Still hungry, she asked for coffee and the all-day breakfast. Adam ordered more coffee and a burger and chips for himself, put his elbows on the table, steepled his hands, and studied her thoughtfully.

'First of all, what haven't you told me?'

She needed coffee before the Spanish Inquisition. 'Like what?'

'Like what you do for the police. Why they call you out to look at a body, presumably to draw it. There are such things as cameras these days. Why do they need you?'

'That's a lot of whys, Mr Shaw. I thought this was an exchange of information, not quiz night.'

Adam Shaw sat back in his seat. 'Tell me what you do, Gina. Tell me what you do that's so special.'

'You don't want to know, Mr Shaw,' she said, as the waitress arrived with their order. 'Not while you're eating.'

He smiled slowly. 'My name is Adam, and stalling isn't going to get you out of this one.'

'I'm a forensic artist, Adam. I draw dead people. I do what a good computer programme can do — but sometimes I do it faster.'

Blue eyes scanned her face. 'I dug up an old newspaper article about you.'

She scowled at him. 'The one where they call me a witch? I thought for a while I was going to be burned at the stake.'

He gave her an amused grin. 'Don't they drown witches? Throw the poor woman in the river and if she floats, she's a witch, but if she drowns — oops, sorry, we made a mistake?'

She smiled in spite of herself. 'Something like that, but we all have talents we take for granted — things other people can't do. My grandmother could pour flour straight from the bag into the mixing bowl, and if she wanted six ounces, she'd have exactly six ounces. A woman I worked with could pick exactly twenty sheets of typing paper off a ream without counting them. Some people remember faces, others can find things that are lost. I can't do any of that — but I can tell what a person looks like from a 100-year-old skull. That's how I found out I can do things other people can't.'

She took a sip of her coffee, surprised to find he was listening without the expression of disbelief she had been expecting. 'We were shown a skull in a history lesson at school and told to draw it. Everyone else drew the skull, but I drew a face. I got teased about it for months. The teacher said I mustn't let my imagination run away with me.' She paused. 'Sometimes I still don't know whether what I'm seeing is real or just my imagination. My grandmother told me to keep it to myself, not tell anyone what I could do, but Castlebury doesn't have a forensic artist and when Inspector Reagan asked if I could help out on a freelance basis . . . ' She shrugged. 'As I said, I only do what a good computer programme can do.'

They ate in silence for a few moments and then Adam asked, 'What did the police want you for today?'

'A body in the river. It'd been there some time so it wasn't very nice, and I was probably no help. Most of the time I have to guess. I can only really help if the police already have an idea who the person is, and then I just confirm what they already know.'

'And they believe you?'

'Inspector Reagan does. He knows what I can do and what I can't. He doesn't think I'm a witch or an alien.'

Adam looked at her thoughtfully, tilting his head first to one side and then the other. 'Witch, definitely. Aliens have different ears.' He poured himself a second cup of coffee. 'So why were you at the funeral of Jessica Fox?'

'Jessica phoned me to tell me she had a photo she found after her mother died. I asked her to bring it to me at the studio. On her way to me she hit a tree and was burned to death in her car. The least I could do was go to her funeral.'

'Why did Jessica Fox want you to look at a photograph?'

She was getting fed up with his questions. 'People often bring me photographs so I can sketch the subject. I'm a portrait artist, Adam. That's what I do.' She put her knife and fork together on her empty plate. 'Now you,' she said. 'Exchange of information, remember?'

'I'm doing an article on Robert Cauldwell, our local politician, and Fox was a caretaker at Cauldwell's school, but Jessica Fox had no idea where her father was. He disappeared off the face of the earth. Most people leave a paper trail of some sort, but with Nathan Fox there was nothing, which was very strange.'

'A lot of people disappear,' she said. 'I would have thought it was quite easy. Illegal immigrants do it all the time. The government has no idea how many people are in this country at any one time, and if Fox went abroad he probably just hopped on a ferry and got lost in the shuffle.'

'I agree it can be done,' Adam said. 'Not as easily as you seem to think, but it can be done. The big question is — why did Nathan

Fox disappear? He had a job he evidently loved, a wife, a child, and no major debts that I can find, but he just walked out, never to be seen again. It just doesn't add up.'

'His wife didn't report him missing, so she must have known why he was leaving. Maybe he was running away from something. Maybe he did something. Killed someone, or robbed a bank.'

Adam looked at her speculatively for a moment and then shrugged. 'Again, there would be records. If there was a murder or a bank robbery and Nathan Fox went missing at the same time, the police would have been looking for him. They weren't.'

Gina decided to put some more of her cards on the table. Adam Shaw could get at police and newspaper records more easily than she could. 'Do you know anything about a child who went missing around that time? A twelve-year-old Asian girl? Because that was the photo Jessica Fox was bringing me. The police found the bones of an Asian child in a local pond. They'd been there twenty years. I put a sketch of the child on the Internet on the off chance someone might recognize her, and Jessica Fox found a photo of the child with her mother's things.'

'And you think Nathan Fox might have killed the child?'

'I don't know, but there must be a connection between Nathan Fox and the child, mustn't there, if he had a photo of her, although I can't imagine a man killing a little girl when he had a daughter of his own.'

'How old did you say the dead child was?'

'Eleven or twelve, probably, but small for her age. She would have looked a lot younger.'

Adam stood up. 'If she'd lived, she would still have been several years older than Jessica. Maybe Fox travelled to Asia before Jessica was born.' He picked up the bill, waving away Gina's offer of payment. 'I'll do a bit more digging. I doubt this has anything to do with my political article, but it's intriguing, all the same.'

'I'd like to find out who the child is,' Gina said. 'And what happened to Nathan Fox.'

Adam Shaw smiled. 'I'll see what I can do.'

It was just starting to rain, heavy spots that heralded the beginning of a summer storm. Gina sat in her car for several minutes with her windscreen wipers going, watching Adam struggle with the soft top of his little green sports car. Eventually he got it secured to his satisfaction and raised his thumb in triumph. His shirt and trousers were soaked. Was that really fun? she wondered.

6

If Gina had expected the next day to be any better, she was due for a disappointment. Her ten o'clock sitting didn't turn up, but Megan's boyfriend did.

'What do you want, Gary?' she asked, before he had a chance to say anything.

He was dressed in his dealer gear, a leather jacket that came to his knees and a black shirt over pale grey chinos. He was five feet six inches tall and looked like a bad imitation of The Fonz.

Gary sat on the edge of Megan's desk. 'Smile, Gina. Frowning gives you wrinkles.' He grinned at her. 'How about a cup of tea?'

Megan got up to fill the kettle and looked appealingly at Gina. Please don't make a fuss, the look said. Gina could never work out why Megan didn't mind being hit round the face. 'What do you want, Gary?' she asked again.

'I'm a messenger. Someone asked me to come here and deliver a message.'

Megan put a mug of tea on Gina's desk and handed the visitor's mug to Gary. Gina picked up her tea. 'What message?'

Gary smiled. 'What's it worth?'

'I'm sure you've already been paid,' she said coolly. 'There is no way you would come here with a message for me unless you'd been paid to deliver it.' All the same, she was curious. Why would someone send Gary with a message when the studio phone number was in the book?

'It's not written down,' Gary said. 'I had to remember what to tell you. Something to do with a picture of a kid. He said to tell you to come to the HiLo bar in Ipswich tonight, before ten, because he's got some information for you.'

Gina heard Megan's intake of breath and frowned at her. 'Who told you?' she asked Gary. 'Who gave you the message?'

He shrugged. 'Some guy called Andy Crabtree. He goes there all the time. Knows everyone.'

'How did he know you know me?'

Gary pretended to look puzzled. 'Sorry, didn't quite get that.'

'Don't piss me off, Gary. You know exactly what I mean.'

'Hey,' Megan said mildly.

Gina sighed. 'Look, Gary, just finish your tea and go, OK? You've given me the message, so just go.' She almost told him to leave Megan alone, but changed her mind. She'd been equally protective about Simon, always making excuses for him when he put her down in public, or told her she looked like a tart. There's none so blind as those who won't see, her grandmother used to say. After Gary had gone she opened the fridge and took out a couple of bottles of beer. She felt she needed one. She popped the tops and handed one to Megan.

'Someone knows something about the little girl. That's good, isn't it?' Megan studied Gina's face worriedly. 'Isn't it?'

'I don't know.' Gina took a swig of her beer. 'Should I go to a bar to meet someone I don't know? And is Gary telling the truth? He's always got a secret agenda of some sort.'

'No, you're right. You can't go on your own. I'll come with you.'

'Thanks, Meg, but no, you won't. Besides, I probably won't go.'

She closed the studio that evening and went up to her flat, still wondering what to do about Gary's message. Part of her wanted to forget the whole thing but somewhere inside her a small stubborn streak told her she couldn't. A child had died, and there must be a reason no one had ever looked for her or reported her missing. Maybe this Andy could tell her who the child really was and solve the problem once and for all. In the end she decided meeting someone in a crowded wine bar couldn't be that dangerous. And if Gary had been making it all up, she would just have a wasted drive to Ipswich.

She checked her emails, deleted most of them, microwaved a meal, had a shower, and was trying to decide what to wear when the phone rang. It was Adam.

'Sorry, Adam, I'm just going out.' She held up a cotton dress that looked slightly the worse for wear. Was there time to iron it?

'When can I see you again? I've been thinking. I need to know who you spoke to at the funeral, what they told you . . .'

'Adam, I'm in a hurry right now. Phone me tomorrow.'

She put the phone down before he could argue and looked at her watch. It was already 9.30, no time to iron, so it had to be jeans and a T-shirt. She used one of her best velvet bands to pull her still-damp hair back off her face and changed her trainers for high-heeled sandals. That would have to do. She was about to pick up her car keys when the doorbell rang. She opened the door a few inches, wishing she had a spy hole, or at least a chain.

'Sorry to disturb you, but I really do need to talk to you.' Adam Shaw stood on her doorstep looking not the slightest bit sorry. He was carrying a bottle of wine.

'I'm just going out.'

'So you were telling the truth. I thought it was a brush-off.' He looked her up and down as if he were inspecting a rare breed of cattle. 'You look taller. Can I come in for a moment?'

'No.'

'Are you always this hostile, or is it just me?'

'I'm really pushed for time.'

'No problem.' He walked past her into her living room and handed her the wine. 'I'll only keep you a minute.'

'Adam, I don't have time to talk now. I'm going to Ipswich to meet someone who has information about the child, and I'm already late, so you'll have to leave.'

She watched in amazement as he picked up her handbag and dropped her car keys and her mobile phone inside. 'Do you need a jacket? No, it's warm. We'll take my car, it'll be quicker. You can bring me up to scratch on the way.'

Furious, she snatched her handbag back. 'Hang on a minute . . . '

'You said you're already late and you're wasting time. It's a half-hour drive, and if you don't come with me I'll just follow you.'

Which was probably true, she thought, and it might be safer to have someone with her when she met Andy Crabtree. Swallowing her irritation, she followed Adam out of the door.

He kept the top down and drove fast up the A12, straight over all the roundabouts, heading for Ipswich Butter Market. When they reached the town centre, Adam ignored all the car parks, parking illegally in a side road and waiting with obvious impatience while she climbed out. As soon as she was on her feet he slammed the car door and walked off, moving so fast on his long legs that she had to trot to keep up with him. Angry and out of breath, she followed him into the wine bar.

'Who are you supposed to meet?' Adam said.

She looked around, getting her breath back. 'Someone called Andy Crabtree.' She felt completely out of place. All the girls were in their teens, wearing jeans and crop tops, the obligatory belly-button studs on full display. A glance at the men made her realize it was getting more and more difficult to decide who was straight and who was gay. Thank God she'd come with Adam, otherwise she would have been the oldest person in the room. Adam found a table in a corner and she sat down while he went to get the drinks. Almost immediately a young man dropped into the seat opposite her.

'Hi, I'm Andy Crabtree. You must be Gina Cross. I know everyone else in here.'

Andy Crabtree had blond, highlighted hair and looked like a member of a boy band. He was wearing skin-tight black jeans and a white shirt unbuttoned enough to show off his abs. Gina was sure he was wearing mascara.

Crabtree glanced over at the bar. 'Is he your boyfriend?'

'No, he's just someone who came with me.' She looked across the room where Adam Shaw was weaving his way towards them with two glasses of lager. In this just-out-of-the-womb environment, he looked positively ancient. 'What do you know about the Asian child?'

Crabtree fidgeted on his chair. 'Nothing. It was some old guy, said to get a message to you, said you're looking for a child, said he'd be here tonight.'

She looked around. 'Is he here now?'

'No, but he might still come in. It was later when I saw him.' Crabtree was tapping nervously on the floor with his foot. He stood up as Adam got to the table. 'I'll let you know if the man turns up.'

'Crabtree?' Adam pushed a glass of lager towards Gina and sat down opposite.

She nodded. 'Nervous as hell and upset

58

because you're with me. He evidently expected me to come on my own.'

'If he finds out I'm a journalist he'll be even more upset. Most of this lot look as if they're using. What did Crabtree say?'

'Some old guy gave him a message for me. I don't know any old men.'

'Anyone over twenty is old in this place.'

The noise level was so high it was almost impossible to talk, and after an hour Gina looked at her watch and stood up. 'He's not going to turn up now, is he?'

'Not if he's as old as you think.' Adam took her arm to steer her to the door. 'This place won't really get going until after midnight. It's not for old men.'

Andy Crabtree caught up with them as they were going out of the door. 'Sorry about wasting your evening.' He asked Gina for her phone number and she gave him the studio number. 'Just in case I see the guy again,' Crabtree told her. 'So I can let you know. It's sod's law, isn't it? He's been in here every night until now.'

Which was very strange, Gina thought, if the man had asked to meet her.

7

They walked to the car in silence. Although the evening had started out warm, it was cooler now, and she wished she had brought a jacket. They were halfway home before she realized they were being followed.

'I think . . . ' she began nervously, looking over her shoulder.

'We're being followed. I know.' Adam pulled on to the outside lane and put his foot down. The car behind them did the same. 'What kind of car is it?' he asked Gina. 'Can you see?'

She turned round in her seat. The other car was right behind them and she couldn't see much past the headlights. 'Something with one of those bull bar things on the front. It looks like a tank.'

'Hang on,' he said.

He wrenched the steering wheel left at the next slip road and swung into a narrow lane. It had a wicked S-bend, but the little car stuck to the road like glue. The one following stayed with them. He accelerated hard as the road straightened out but the car behind was catching up. She saw the bridge over the river in front of them, the lights of the village, then the big car slammed into the back of them and the little sports car swerved across the road, grazed a brick wall, and almost tipped over. Adam tried to steer a straight line but the wheels had stopped gripping the road. The car spun in a slow, almost graceful circle and bumped down a slope into the river. They were still going quite fast and a tidal wave of water swept over the open car, drenching Gina. She gasped, swallowing dirty river water, the cold literally taking her breath away. She coughed, trying to spit out bits of God knows what.

Adam climbed out first, swinging a long leg over the side of the car. 'It's quite deep,' he said. 'Be careful.'

For a moment she couldn't move. She was sitting up to her waist in water, adrenaline still pumping through her veins, and she was beginning to shake with cold.

'If you stay there you'll go into shock and get pneumonia. Besides, the guy in the big car might come back.' He reached down beside her and undid her seatbelt. 'Stand up and climb on the seat.'

For God's sake, couldn't he give her two minutes to catch her breath without barking out orders?

He caught her as she stood and lifted her

easily on to the bank. At that moment a large black car came hurtling back down the road towards them. For a second she thought it was going to plough into the river and finish them off. Instead, the driver slowed and looked towards them for an instant before accelerating off towards the bypass.

'Did you see the driver?'

'No, not properly.' Christ, she'd been so shit scared she hadn't seen anything except the car bearing down on them. For a moment she had been sure she was going to die.

'Damn. Neither did I.'

He gave her a little push to keep her moving, but she stopped, catching hold of his arm. 'My phone. It's in my bag.'

'It'll be full of water. It won't work.'

'Yes it will.' She found she'd lost a shoe. Damn heels — her trainers wouldn't have come off. 'The phone's in a special case that's supposed to be waterproof. Megan gave it to me last Christmas.'

He waded to the car and came back carrying her handbag. Most of the things in the bag were ruined, but the phone was still safe in its plastic case, the screen glowing reassuringly when she pressed the menu button. He took the phone from her. 'I'll call a taxi. You're shivering.'

'We've got to notify the police. We were almost killed.'

'I'll call them in the morning. There's nothing they can do tonight except keep us hanging about. We'll wait at the top of the road for the taxi.'

'Why can't we wait here?'

'Because the guy who pushed us in the river may come back again and I don't want to be sitting here like one of the local ducks when he does, OK? Besides, walking will warm you up.'

She took off her other shoe and tossed it in the river, allowing herself to be led, dripping, up the road. She trod on a stone and yelped, the pain almost overriding the cold. She looked at Adam but he didn't say a word; he just marched on, leading her along like a naughty child. Trotting to keep up with him was becoming a habit. Then she trod on another stone.

'Slow down, damn it! I'm all wet, I've got bare feet, and someone just tried to kill me.' She sniffed, fighting back furious tears.

He kept walking. He knew how cold and scared she was, but he had to keep her moving. 'If someone had wanted to kill us, we wouldn't be alive. That was just a warning. Wait here if you want. I'll get the taxi to come and pick you up.'

She wiped her face with both hands, No use looking in her bag for tissues. 'I'm OK.' She was warming up a bit and her clothes had stopped dripping. By the time they got to the top of the road a taxi was waiting for them. If the taxi driver was surprised by their appearance he was too polite to say anything. He took one look at them, opened the car boot, and produced a plastic sheet that he laid carefully on the back seat. He probably couldn't care less if they wanted a late swim with their clothes on as long as they didn't make his seats wet.

Gina sat shivering on the plastic sheet until they pulled up in front of her studio. She didn't offer to pay for the taxi and she didn't remember even saying good night. Adam made the taxi wait until she had climbed the outside stairs and opened her door, then he raised his hand in a wave, but she had already gone inside.

She made herself take a hot shower and stood under it until some feeling began to return to her hands and feet. She put her brain on hold, refusing to think about what had happened. There would be plenty of time for that in the morning. Wrapped in a towelling robe, and with socks on her feet, she got into bed and huddled under the duvet. It was a warm night, but right now she was so cold she couldn't imagine ever being warm again. She thought fleetingly of Adam Shaw, still in control, even with his shirt clinging to his body and his shoes squelching as he walked. Then she slept.

The next morning she awoke to her alarm clock bleating on the bedside table. She usually woke up before the alarm went off, and it took her a moment to remember what had happened the night before. She was still wrapped in the robe, but sometime during the night she had kicked the duvet on to the floor. She went to sit up and only just stopped herself screaming, the pain in her ribs making her think every one of them must be broken. She crawled out of bed with difficulty, hobbling across the room like an old lady. The mirror showed a bruise slanting across her breastbone like a plum-coloured stripe and she knew there would be no running that morning.

When Gina walked into the studio Megan looked at her curiously. 'Why are you walking funny?'

'We got shunted off the road last night. The seatbelt bruised my ribs.'

Megan's eyes opened wide. 'Are you hurt?' She stopped for a moment to frown. 'Who's we?'

Gina sighed. She didn't think she'd broken

anything, but she was beginning to wonder. Even sighing hurt. 'It's a long story,' she said, lowering herself gingerly into her chair.

Once she had the details, Megan looked worried. 'It's a wonder you're not really badly hurt. Both of you could've been killed. Are you sure your ribs aren't broken?'

'No, I'm not sure. I don't know how it would feel if they were, but I'm sure it would be worse than this. I was luckier than Jessica Fox,' she added soberly.

'No one knows why Jessica went off the road and hit a tree, do they?' Megan looked at Gina thoughtfully. 'If you and the reporter had both been killed coming home from a wine bar, everyone would have thought he'd drunk too much and misjudged the corner. The police would have thought that, too, wouldn't they?'

'You mean Jessica might have been shunted off the road deliberately and that's why she ran into a tree? No, that's ridiculous. God, I need some coffee.'

Megan added milk to the coffee she had already poured and then stood quite still in the middle of the room, her hand on her bulging belly. 'Did you see it move?'

'I don't want to see it move. The thought of something moving around in your stomach is quite revolting.'

'No, it isn't, it's great. There's a little person in there. How can you not be interested?'

'Easily.' Gina took the mug of coffee Megan handed her. 'If someone gave Jessica's car a push, maybe she wasn't meant to be killed, just warned off, like me.'

'Or maybe you were meant to be killed, but got lucky.'

'Gee, thanks for that. I feel much better now.'

'Will you promise to leave it alone, then? Not meet any more strange men in bars or at funerals?'

'I promise,' she said, and she really meant it at the time.

8

Unexpectedly, Gina had a peaceful night's sleep and put on her running gear as soon as the alarm went off. If she didn't run, she was going to stiffen up.

The weather was still beautiful, with a cloudless blue sky arching like a dome over the flat Essex countryside. A hawk hovered above the riverbank looking for breakfast and eddies of mist danced on the water like wayward ghosts. In broad daylight, on a truly glorious morning, it was difficult to imagine anything nasty lurking in the bushes.

Back in her flat, she showered and changed, ate a bowl of cereal, and went down to the studio. Light was flooding in through the big bay window at the front and Megan had already opened the French doors on to the little courtyard garden. It was tempting to sit outside, soaking up the sun, but she resisted and got stuck into the job of finishing the portrait of the old lady, which took her up until lunchtime. Determined not to miss lunch again, she'd sent Megan next door for sandwiches. She was trying to decide between seafood cocktail in malted bread and chicken with stuffing in granary when she got a phone call from Andy Crabtree.

'Have you seen the old man again?' she asked him, handing the sandwich boxes to Megan.

'Er . . . not exactly.'

'Well, have you or haven't you? It was a wasted journey last time, and I'm a bit busy right now.' She frowned at Megan, who was lifting up the top slice of bread to peer in the sandwich.

'I just wondered if we could meet again sometime. I didn't get a chance to talk to you the other night and there's something I need to tell you. I've been asking questions and I heard something really weird last night.'

Gina thought it might be a good idea if Andy Crabtree stopped asking questions.

'I'm sorry, Andy, but I've decided not to go any further with this. Thanks again for your help, but let's just leave it now, OK?' She put the phone firmly back in its rest and took the remaining sandwich from Megan. Seafood. Oh well, it saved her having to make a choice. 'That was Andy Crabtree,' she said, taking a bite.

'I thought it was. What did he want?'

'He's been asking questions. I told him to stop. I don't like being followed, or dumped up to my neck in the river, but I don't want anyone else to get hurt.'

'Have you thought this Crabtree person might be trying to chat you up? You need something to take your mind off dead people. It's two years since Simon dumped you. You should be seeing other men.'

'Simon didn't dump me, I dumped him. Crabtree's years younger than me and I'm sure he's gay. Besides, I can make my own decisions about men, thank you very much. I don't need help.'

'You make really bad decisions about men,' Megan retorted. 'Simon was a wanker. He may not have hit you, but he made you feel bad about yourself. That's worse.'

'Probably,' Gina agreed. 'That's why I don't want to get in that situation again.' She had a sudden vision of Adam Shaw. When he walked out of the river, his wet shirt clinging to him, he had looked uncannily like Mr Darcy from the movie *Pride and Prejudice*.

Megan started on the second half of her sandwich. 'I left you the seafood one because it has crabsticks in it, and I don't know what a crabstick is. What's inside that sandwich didn't come from any crab I've ever seen.'

Gina looked at her sandwich curiously and then took another bite. 'It tastes fine.'

At that moment the studio door opened and a customer came in asking about a sketch in the window, a sketch Gina had done of her grandmother. It had been copied from an old photograph, showing a stubborn-looking girl in her early teens with long, straight hair and an obstinate look in her eye. There was a vague family likeness, but there the similarity ended. Gina had inherited her father's Latin genes, giving her a tangle of dark curly hair and eyes the colour of black coffee.

'That sketch isn't really for sale,' she told the customer, a heavily built man with thick black hair and bushy eyebrows. 'It's just to show the sort of work I do. I could do you something much more personal if you like, copy a family photo, or perhaps you'd like to arrange a sitting . . . ' Her voice tailed off. Something was surfacing at the back of her mind. She couldn't remember faces unless the face was actually in front of her. Now it was.

'You shouldn't put a picture in the window if you don't intend to sell it. Putting it in the window usually means you're offering it for sale.'

He had an accent but she couldn't place it. 'With the frame, the sketch is priced at £500,' she told him, hoping to put him off.

The man smiled at her pleasantly. 'I'll take it,' he said.

Megan had been watching the interchange

silently. Once the man had gone, the picture grudgingly but carefully wrapped, Megan punched the air with her fist.

'Five hundred pounds for your grandmother! Wow! He must be mad. What did he want with a picture of your grandmother? I know you said you'd never sell that drawing but £500 will pay the electricity bill for another month or two, and you can always copy her photo again.'

'Shut up, Megan.' Gina took a breath. 'I recognized him.'

Megan's eyes opened wide with surprise. 'Fox?'

'I don't think so. It was the man who shoved Adam Shaw and me off the road. I only got a glimpse of him in the dark, but it was definitely the same man, and probably the same one who drove away in such a hurry at the funeral.' She sank into a chair. 'I'm not often wrong, am I?'

Megan clutched her stomach. 'Did he know you recognized him?'

She nodded slowly. 'I think so. That's why he came, I expect, to see if I recognized him.'

'Knowing it would scare the shit out of both of us if you did.'

'So it was an all-win situation for him, wasn't it? If I didn't recognize him, no problem, but if I did, he knew I'd be too scared to do anything about it while he was here. Now he's gone there's no point.'

'But you'd recognize him again?'

'If I see him again — although he won't look like that next time.'

'Do a sketch of him so we can give it to the police. To Inspector Reagan.'

'I can't remember what he looked like, Megan. You know I have trouble remembering faces if they're not right in front of me. I remember his expression, the look in his eyes and all that, but he had plugs in his nose to make it look bigger and he was wearing a wig, a toupee sort of thing. I bet he changes his appearance all the time, otherwise he wouldn't have come here.'

'Unless he plans to kill us both.'

'That would be stupid.'

'Yes, but does he know that?'

'What he doesn't know is that if I see him again, whatever he looks like, I'll recognize him.'

'Then let's hope he doesn't find out, cos then he will kill us.'

Gina looked at her pregnant friend worriedly. 'I didn't mean to get you involved in this.'

Megan shrugged. 'Not your fault, and the scary man isn't really interested in me. It's you he's after.'

Gina smiled. Megan had a great way of making her feel better. 'So what do we do now?'

'Tell Inspector Reagan.'

'The man came into my shop to buy a picture,' Gina said. 'They can't arrest him for that. And I can't prove he shunted us off the road. Even if I could, and even if Reagan believed me, the man could say it was an accident.'

The phone made her jump. She picked it up absently. 'Hello?'

The voice on the other end of the phone was breaking up, difficult to hear. 'I've got a bit of trouble. I'm coming back to the studio.'

She took the phone away from her ear and shook it. 'Who is this?'

'For fuck's sake, Gina. It's Gary.'

Normally she would have hung up — Gary in trouble was something she didn't want to know about, but this time he sounded frightened. She put her hand over the phone and looked at Megan. 'It's Gary. He's coming back here. He's in some sort of trouble.'

Megan went back to her typing. 'He's always in some sort of trouble.'

Gina put the phone back to her ear just as Gary shouted, 'You've got to help me, Gina. It's your fault I'm in this shit.'

She put the phone back in its rest before

she lost her temper. 'He's blaming me. He says it's my fault.'

Now Megan looked up. 'How could it be your fault?'

'I don't know.' She was beginning to wish she hadn't hung up quite so quickly. 'Perhaps it's got something to do with the message he brought me.' The message was the only thing she could think of that involved both her and Gary.

An hour later Gary still hadn't turned up.

Megan looked completely unconcerned. 'Don't worry about him, Gina. He's always telling me he's coming over and then sods off somewhere else. If he does come, it's an hour later than he said.'

But Gina did worry about him. Had she done something to get him into trouble? Maybe even put him in danger? She still felt on edge when she closed up the studio. 'Do you want to go and get a drink somewhere?' she asked Megan.

'Sorry, can't tonight, I've got an ante-natal class at the hospital.' She picked up the small rucksack she used as a handbag and slung it over her shoulder. 'I've met some real interesting people there. Cindy Cauldwell, the politician's wife, she goes, and that girl from the local radio station, she's due to drop any minute. It's a bit like one of those

'Celebrity Get Me Out Of Here' things.'

Gina locked up and climbed the outside stairs to her flat, still uneasy about Gary. Perhaps he'd changed his mind and gone back to Megan's flat, rather than come to the studio. It was all very well for Megan to tell her not to worry; Megan hadn't heard the panic in Gary's voice.

★ ★ ★

She slept fitfully until a dream woke her. A man in a big black car was chasing her and she was running across a field towards a pond, knowing she was going to fall in and drown. As the water closed over her head she tried to take a breath — and woke with a gasp, sweat beading her face. She rolled over with a groan and looked at the bedside clock. She could have stayed in bed another hour before the alarm went off, but sunlight was already streaming through the window and the dream had been too vivid to allow her to sleep again. As she climbed out of bed and headed for the shower, she knew she had to find out what had really happened twenty years ago, otherwise the ghost of the child was going to hang around haunting her for ever.

If there was any information about the

dead child, it would most likely be at Jessica's house. Gina knew Jessica's address — that information had been in the local paper at the time of the accident. Aunt Jane hadn't been in touch so perhaps she hadn't been to the house yet. It wouldn't do any harm to go and have a look. She made herself some breakfast and then went down to the studio and told Megan where she was going.

Jessica Fox had lived with her mother in a house on the end of a row of six. They were old houses on a quiet residential street, the bricks weathered to a rich, pockmarked red, the slated roofs dotted with moss and lichen. The sort of place that used to be called a 'two up, two down', with a loo at the bottom of the garden. Now most of them had an extension on the back to house a kitchen and bathroom.

In the house next door an old man was watering a mismatched collection of tubs, pots and hanging baskets, watching her cautiously as she opened the garden gate. She smiled brightly at the old man and knocked on the front door of Jessica's house. A quick look through a front window showed furniture still inside. The old man watched but didn't speak. Because it was at the end of the row, the house had a side gate to the back garden. After a quick look round and another smile at the old man, she cautiously tried the gate. It was unlocked, only a black iron latch keeping it closed. The back garden was more of a yard; a small concrete area outside the back door and an even smaller patch of yellowing grass. Another gate at the bottom of the garden led to an alley that ran between the houses. Not very hopefully, she tried the back door. Locked, as she had expected. So were all the windows. Before the old man had time to get suspicious and call the police, she retraced her steps, latching the gate behind her.

'Not in,' she called to the old man as she walked back up the garden path.

'No,' the old man said.

She got back in her car and drove round the block, parking near the entrance to the alley. The gate into Jessica Fox's back garden was bolted at the top and she wasn't tall enough to reach it. Glad she kept herself fit, she hung on to the fence with one hand and pulled herself up enough to release the bolt. As she dropped down, a sudden wash of cold air raised the little hairs on the backs of her arms. Someone was watching. She stood quite still for a moment, letting her gaze drift over the row of houses. The upstairs windows overlooking the back yards were still and dark, with no sign of movement. Her imagination playing tricks again.

She unlatched the gate, walked up the garden path and peered through the glass panel in the back door. The kitchen was neat and tidy, a wine glass and mug still on the draining board. There was very little clutter. She noticed an empty bowl on the floor and a small tin plate that must have held cat food, although there was no sign of the animal anywhere around. She hoped someone was feeding the poor thing. Her eyes dropped to the bottom of the door where a cat flap held pride of place in the middle of the door panel. If the back-door key was still in the lock . . .

She rummaged in her shoulder bag and found a metal nail file, a small pair of scissors, her car keys, and various other items that might push the key out of the lock. She thanked God she was a female with a handbag full of rubbish. A hairgrip did it in the end, one of the old types that had recently come back into fashion. The key dropped to the floor with a satisfying thump and she reached in through the cat flap to pick it up. Stifling any remnants of conscience, she let herself into the house.

There was no bolt on the inside of the back door so she put the key back in the lock and turned it before she ventured any further into the house. She tried to convince herself there was no harm in having a look around. The house was empty and Jessica Fox wasn't coming back. Aunt Jane was the one who would do the scavenging, and then there would be estate agents and prospective buyers trawling through the place. She was just the first of many.

The furnishings were comfortable and trendy; a purple throw over the cream leather settee, a modern painting in greens and oranges, lots of stainless steel and chrome in the kitchen, and candles everywhere. She suspected Jessica had changed a few things after her mother died. The daisies in a yellow bowl on the sideboard had shed their petals and the leaves were brown and shrivelled. There was a small pile of post inside the front door, a sad reminder that Jessica really wasn't coming back, and she felt a sudden stab of guilt. What on earth did she expect to find?

The sideboard drawers in the living-room held the usual household mix. Bills in one drawer; table mats, sticky tape, string and an assortment of ballpoint pens in another. The bottom drawer held the Christmas tree decorations. Jessica had been expecting another Christmas.

Upstairs there were two bedrooms and a bathroom. On the floor in the main bedroom were four cardboard boxes. Clothes in one, shoes in another, two filled with books. Jessica had obviously been sorting out her mother's belongings. The bed had been stripped but a large, unsealed manila envelope lay on the mattress. Gina turned the envelope upside-down and shook it. A half-dozen letters in an elastic band tumbled out on to the bed, together with some photos, a diary and a videotape. A faded label on the front of the cardboard video sleeve said *BIRTHDAY PARTY*. She had a little argument with herself about respecting other people's privacy, then read the letters.

They were from Fox to his wife, spread over several years, and very short, just a few lines in most cases, saying he was fine and missing his wife and daughter. The last letter, dated only a few months ago, gave her a reason for his return. He had found out his wife had cancer. 'Somehow,' he had written, 'I will find a way to see you'. At least it explained why Jessica had suddenly started looking for her father. She had found letters from a man she thought was dead.

Gina glanced in the diary, which was bound in leather and almost square, a bit bigger than the usual handbag variety. The diary was for the previous year with a page for each day of the week, and from what she could see at a quick glance the entries were all appointments. Hospital, dentist, hairdresser, dinner engagements, but nothing about a meeting with Nathan Fox. Gina wondered if he managed to see his wife before she died.

She bundled the letters together and stuffed them back in the envelope, together with the diary. The photos were all old and all of the family. Some had been taken outside a small building that looked like a gatehouse, others had been taken on a beach, sometimes just little Jessica and her mother, sometimes father and daughter. One with the three of them together. Jessica looked about eight years old in the photos. There were no pictures of an Asian child. Gina added the photos to the envelope and, after a moment's thought, dropped in the video.

She couldn't leave through the front door in case the old man was still in his garden and she didn't want to leave the house unlocked, so she locked the back door from the outside and dropped the key in her handbag. She let herself out of the gate into the passage at the back of the house and walked round to where she had left her car. Hopefully, no one had been watching her, although she still felt a prickle of unease, an unwelcome whisper of the psychic talent she refused to acknowledge. On the drive home, she found herself looking in her rear-view mirror more often than usual.

'Did you find the house?' Megan asked as soon as Gina walked into the studio.

Gina kicked off her shoes and opened the little fridge where they kept their stash of beer. 'Yep.' She opened one of the bottles and handed it to Megan. 'But that wasn't all I found.' She tipped the letters and photos on to Megan's desk. 'The letters are from Nathan Fox to his wife. He was still writing to her up until a few months ago.'

'So he is alive?' Megan was looking at the photos. 'They look so happy in these pictures. Why did he go away, do you think? What changed everything?'

'Perhaps he killed a little girl.'

Megan shook her head. 'I don't think so, do you? He would have realized after a while that no one had found the body, and then he would have come back. There was no need for him to stay away for twenty years. Besides, he wanted to come back. You can tell from his letters.'

Gina nodded. 'I think he was afraid of something. If he wasn't afraid for himself, he was afraid for his wife and child.'

'Now they're both dead.' Megan put the

photos and letters back in the envelope. 'Did you find anything else?'

'A diary with nothing in it but appointments, and a videotape of a birthday party. Nothing very interesting except the photos.'

9

That evening Gina spent a few minutes watching the video she had taken from Jessica's house. The video was an old thirty-minute one, the first fifteen minutes footage of a birthday party with a little girl shyly receiving her guests, opening her presents and playing games in the garden. Nathan Fox the doting father, the mother short and plump with the same red hair and freckles as her daughter. The video hissed into static and she turned it off.

She tipped the photos out of the envelope and picked up a clear frontal view of Nathan Fox. He was sitting on the beach, laughing into the camera, while a young Jessica covered his bare legs with sand. Gina took a pad and soft pencil from her office and started sketching. Twenty years ago Nathan Fox had been a good-looking young man. Now his cheeks would be thinner, his hairline receding, but however much he changed his appearance, even if he had extensive plastic surgery, she knew she would still recognize him.

She already had.

She was about to put a plastic carton in the microwave when she noticed Adam Shaw's card pinned to the side of the fridge with a Homer Simpson magnet. She turned Adam's card over in her hand. His home phone number was written on the back. Before she had time to change her mind, she picked up the phone and dialled.

'Hello.'

Talking to him seemed to addle her brain. 'It's me,' she said inanely.

'Hello you. Gina, I presume.'

'I felt I ought to tell you the driver who shoved us in the river came into the studio yesterday.'

There was a long pause. 'I take it you're at home. Stay there. I'll be right over.'

He arrived twenty minutes later with a bag of Chinese food and a bottle of Chardonnay. 'Fridge. Microwave,' he said, handing her the bag and the bottle.

She put plates in the oven to warm and piled the cartons in the microwave. The wine bottle had a screw cap, which was damned sensible, she thought — no need to hunt for a corkscrew. She poured two glasses of wine and then put the bottle in the fridge. Adam looked good. Dressed informally in jeans and a wrestler-back vest, the belt of his jeans low on his hips, he was enough to make any girl's

86

pulse quicken. She had to keep reminding herself how much she hated journalists. He caught her looking and she felt her skin heat. She raised her glass to him. 'Thanks,' she said casually. 'I need this. I've run out.'

Adam picked up the other glass. 'Don't heat the food up yet. Sit down and tell me about the driver. I thought you said you didn't get a good look at him.'

'I didn't think I had at the time. He changes his appearance. This time he had nose plugs and a wig, contacts as well. He didn't look a bit the same as he did when he pushed us off the road, but it was the same man. He wanted to see if I would recognize him, and now he knows I did. What does he want with me, Adam?'

'I don't know. All you did was put a photo of a dead child on a missing persons website and, as far as I know, nothing I'm working on has anything to do with all this, so I have no idea why anyone would be after either of us.'

'But you knew Jessica Fox.'

'I told you, I'm doing a piece on Robert Cauldwell, our local MP, and as Fox was a caretaker at the school Cauldwell went to, I spoke to his daughter, but she couldn't tell me anything. She hadn't seen her father for twenty years. I was sorry to hear about her accident, she was a nice girl.'

'If it was an accident,' Gina said. 'She got run off the road the same as we did.'

Between them they finished all the food and most of the wine. Gina had a feeling she had drunk more than Adam, but she let him pour the last of the wine into her glass.

'Have you brought me right up to date now?' he asked.

She fought with her conscience and lost. 'I went to the house where Jessica Fox lived. Aunt Jane hadn't cleared it out yet and I found some things in an envelope. In one of the bedrooms.'

She waited for a reaction. Got nothing. She told him how she got into the house and what she found. She handed him the envelope and he took it without comment, tipping the contents on to the table. He read the letters carefully. Then he went through each of the photos, one at a time, turning them over to look at the back. There were no names or dates on any of them, none of the silly remarks that people used to put on the backs of their photographs. Aunty Margaret at Brighton. Pam and Den on the pier. Nothing like that.

'All taken with a Polaroid camera. The photo of the child that the police have, that was taken with a Polaroid camera, wasn't it?'

She nodded. 'You think Fox took it?'

'Probably. People tend to stick with the same type of camera. Have you looked at the video?'

'It's just a little girl's birthday party.' She popped the cassette in the machine and left Adam to watch it while she made instant coffee. Coming into the room, she waited while he finished watching the children's party, then handed him the mug of coffee, watching his face screw up in disbelief when he tasted it.

'How can anyone make coffee this bad?' He had left the tape running and the fuzz suddenly cleared from the screen, showing a shot of three young men standing by some gates. 'Hang on. What's this?'

'It's must be some more footage,' she said. 'I turned the video player off as soon as the first part finished. I didn't know there was anything else on the tape.'

Adam leant closer to the television screen. 'Students from the college, by the look of it. They're all wearing the same dark trousers and blazers. Why would Fox want to film some students?'

Gina watched the young men. Two of them smoking. One of them running his hand up and down the gatepost. They moved, and the camera lost them for a second before focusing on a car standing just outside the gates. A few moments later the students could be seen standing beside the car. The tallest of the three walked round the car to the driver's side and bent down to talk to the driver. The camera zoomed in but the picture was too fuzzy to see the face of the driver clearly. The young men moved away, laughing and nudging one another. One of them threw down his cigarette and ground it out with his heel, then all three moved out of vision. The camera swung round and followed the car as it moved away. The screen speckled into static and Gina looked at Adam. 'What was that all about?'

'Fox saw them outside his house and remembered he still had film in his camera. I've done the same thing myself, grabbed the camera and started filming because I've seen something interesting. I think he hoped to get a view of the driver's face.' Adam pressed the reverse button on the machine and stopped it almost immediately. 'Let's try the pause button.' Gina's video machine wasn't state of the art and the tape was old. The image shuddered and shook in pause mode, a black band obscuring most of the picture. Adam moved closer to the screen. 'Can't get a fix on the driver's face — he's turned away from the camera — and there's no way of knowing who those students are.'

Gina got up and grabbed a pad and pencil from her little office. 'I think I recognize one of them. I don't know who he is but I've seen him before. A recent news picture or something.' She ran the video back to the beginning of the new bit of tape and started sketching, running the tape back now and again for another look. Adam watched her draw the face of a man in his forties. The hair thinning a little at the temples, the jaw square and firm, the eyes sharp and intelligent.

'Bloody hell,' Adam said. 'Robert Cauldwell.'

'See?' She liked the way he just accepted what she could do. 'It does all fit together. Fox, the Asian child, the school, Robert Cauldwell, you.' She tore the page from the pad. 'I still don't know where I fit in, but my assistant goes to ante-natal classes with Robert Cauldwell's wife. How scary is that?'

Adam laughed. 'Don't get paranoid.' He took the tape out of the machine and put it back in the envelope. 'This is a small town with one hospital. How many ante-natal classes would there be? I take it your assistant is pregnant?'

'Megan, yes, she's due in a few weeks.' It was all very well for Adam to laugh, but she felt as if she was caught in the middle of a spider's web, the strands tightening round her, and she had no idea why she was there. 'I don't understand what this has to do with me? I don't know Robert Cauldwell, not personally, anyway. And where does Fox fit in? He must fit in somewhere.'

'What makes you think Fox has anything to do with this, or that he's even in this country?'

'I know he's in this country. He was at his daughter's funeral.'

'Any particular reason you kept that bit of information to yourself?' His voice was cool.

'I didn't know the man at the funeral was Fox until I looked at the photographs. How could I? He was wearing a long black coat and bumped into me as he was leaving. I wasn't keeping secrets from you. I just haven't had a chance to tell you.'

He didn't look convinced but he stopped bristling. 'How come the rest of the family didn't recognize Fox at the funeral? He can't have changed that much.'

'He's had some plastic surgery. A nose job and some work on his jaw. Cheek implants. Besides, I think he kept well away from anyone who might recognize him.'

'Then why go at all?'

'Because she was his only daughter and he left her when she was a little girl. He needed to say goodbye.'

'And you can relate to that, can't you, Gina?' Adam said quietly. 'A father leaving his daughter when she was just a child.'

She looked him straight in the eye, daring him to elaborate. 'Yes.'

He looked as if he was about to say something, then changed his mind. 'I need more coffee.' He followed her into the tiny kitchen. 'But I'll make it this time.' He bent down and reached round her for the coffee jar and she felt his breath on the back of her neck. The sudden, sharp stab of desire took her completely by surprise. The kitchen was too small for both of them and he was far too close. She cursed her hormones and moved carefully away. 'I think we need to go to the school and talk to people there.'

'No point.' Completely oblivious to her racing heart, Adam spooned coffee into the mugs and poured on water. 'The school is Fletford College, on the Essex/Suffolk border. The place is very expensive and very elitist. They cherry-pick all their pupils. The headmaster's new, he's only been there three years, and most of the teachers who were there twenty years ago will have left.'

She took a sip of her coffee. 'Fox took a film of those boys. We know one is Robert Cauldwell, but what about the others? If we go to the school we might be able to find out who they are. We were shunted off the road and nearly killed, Jessica was killed, and I've had a murderer inside my shop. I need to know what's going on.'

He held up his hands in surrender. 'I think you're exaggerating just a little but OK. I'll see if I can make an appointment with the headmaster.'

'I'm coming with you. I don't like that man under my window at night.'

Adam took hold of her by the upper arms and for a moment she thought he was going to shake her. 'Gina, I need to do this on my own. I don't know what all this is about, but asking questions could be dangerous. I'll go to the school and see what I can find out. Trust me, I know what I'm doing.'

She smiled at him sweetly. 'Good. Then you should be able to keep us both safe. Let me know when you've made the appointment.'

He finished his coffee and let himself out without looking back.

10

Gina ran faster than usual. The knot of curls on top of her head had come loose and there was a film of sweat on her face. Running usually relaxed her, but today she couldn't get rid of the tight ridge of muscle at the nape of her neck or the headache that niggled behind her eyes. The weather was damp and misty, a thin drizzle doing nothing to cool her down. She wiped a hand across her face and tucked the errant curls back in their elastic band. Running wasn't working today for some reason, but perhaps a hot shower and some breakfast would. She was having trouble getting Adam Shaw out of her head, and out of her head he had to go. On second thoughts, a cold shower might work better.

By the time she got herself back to the flat and downstairs to the studio, she was feeling more relaxed. Megan was already sitting at the computer, busy typing. 'Any news from Gary?'

Megan didn't look up. 'No. The kettle's on for coffee.'

Gina got mugs from the cupboard and put them on the desk, together with milk from the fridge. Megan was wearing baggy draw-string trousers that looked as if they belonged to a clown and her hair was streaked with a strange shade of aubergine.

'Aren't you the slightest bit worried about him?'

This time Megan did look up. 'Why should I be? He never worries about me.'

'True.' Gina put coffee in the mugs and poured on boiling water. She added milk and stirred. 'I phoned Adam Shaw and told him about the man who came into the studio. He came round to the flat and brought Chinese.'

Megan raised an eyebrow. 'And?'

Before Gina had a chance to answer, the phone rang. Glad of the respite and thinking it might be Gary, she picked it up. 'Hello.'

'I've got an interview with the headmaster of Fletford College this afternoon.'

'Good. What time are you picking me up?'

His long drawn-out sigh made her smile. 'Two o'clock should do it. Wear something suitable.'

Gina worked straight through her usual lunch break and then hurried upstairs to get ready. She stood in front of the wardrobe in her bedroom wondering what on earth Adam would consider suitable. What did someone wear to interview people? In the end she settled for the same dark skirt she'd worn for

Jessica's funeral, this time with a pale blue, short-sleeved top she'd bought in a blue cross sale. She went downstairs to say goodbye to Megan. 'Lock the door behind me. If anyone rings the bell, check them out first.'

Adam was driving a Fiesta, which was better in the drizzle, he said, than the sports car, and the sports car was still at a garage being dried out. Gina wondered if he drove the sports car with the top down in the rain. It wouldn't surprise her. It took him so long to put the damn top up, he got soaked anyway.

'Why did you let me come along? You more or less told me to keep out of it.'

'And you more or less told me you wouldn't. At least if you're with me I can keep you out of trouble.'

She didn't bother to reply. She'd managed to look after herself for quite a while, and interviewing teachers didn't exactly sound dangerous.

Fletford College appeared between the trees long before they found the entrance gates. A high brick wall surrounded the school, but here and there the wall had crumbled and been replaced with black iron railings. In the gaps she could glimpse an ugly red-brick building with small windows, rather like a prison. All it needed was razor wire on top of the wall.

A lodge stood just inside the gates and she looked at the little house with interest. This was where Nathan Fox and his family had lived. The gatehouse was prettier than the school; the same red brick, but topped with stone curlicues painted white to match the front door. The windows had been replaced with fake sash PVC. She almost expected Fox to come out of the house to meet them, but the man who appeared at the gate was built like a pit bull, with shoulders twice as wide as his hips. She smiled to herself. No matter how clever Fox's plastic surgeon might be, he wasn't that good.

Adam handed Gina a small voice recorder and introduced her as his assistant. The pit bull looked sceptical, but let them through.

The headmaster was not what she had expected. He was in his late forties, tall and athletic-looking, dressed in a navy blue tracksuit and trainers. His office was plainly furnished with a leather settee against one wall and a metal desk occupying the bay window. The rest of the room was taken up with shelves filled with files and books. Two plain wooden chairs had been placed in front of the desk.

The headmaster shook Adam's hand,

squeezed Gina's, and waved them to the chairs. He positioned himself with his back to the window. 'How can I help you?'

'I hope you don't mind us recording this conversation.' Adam looked expectantly at Gina. She fumbled with the controls of the recorder until a red light started flashing, breathing out a sigh of relief when she saw the tape spool turning. 'Your name is Colin Frith,' Adam said, 'and you've been head here for just over three years? Is that correct?'

Frith nodded. 'You said on the phone you were doing an article on Robert Cauldwell. I wasn't at this school when Cauldwell attended.'

'I know, and I'm sorry to take up your time, Mr Frith. All I need is background material, a look at the school yearbooks, perhaps, and maybe a word with anyone who was teaching when Cauldwell was a pupil.'

'Of course. It would be good to think we nurtured a future prime minister within these walls. Judge Pollard was a pupil here many years ago and his son more recently. Judge Pollard is responsible for our new science wing.' The headmaster stood up. 'Sorry to rush, but I have to take a class on the sports field in five minutes. You can stay here in my office if you like and I'll get my secretary to bring you a staff list and the yearbooks.

Cauldwell was here for five years, I believe. Do you want all the books for that period?'

Adam shook his head. 'Robert Cauldwell's last two years will be fine.'

Five minutes after the headmaster had left the room, a secretary arrived with the yearbooks and a list of staff, together with a note of how long each member of staff had been working at the school. Once she had gone, Adam picked up the staff list, leaving Gina to go through the yearbooks. All the photographs were neatly labelled with the names of the pupils. There were award ceremonies and end-of-term get-togethers, annual balls and sports events. Robert Cauldwell played most sports, was actively involved in the debating society, and was president of the sports and social club.

'I've found Robert Cauldwell.' Gina said. 'And one of the other students in the video film.'

Adam looked over her shoulder. 'I might recognize him if you drew him as he looks now, but let's see if one of the teachers can tell us who he is. What about the third boy?'

'I can't find him.'

Adam looked up from his lists. He was wearing his dark-rimmed spectacles, giving him a studious appearance. 'The third one must be in there somewhere. He was at the school at the same time as Cauldwell.'

'Well, he's not in any of the photos.' She flicked through the pages. 'Hang on, I'll look at the end of the school year. Here they are, receiving their diplomas. All the names are listed. He must have finished with a certificate in something, surely — this place costs more than most people's mortgage.'

'That's why Cauldwell doesn't talk about his childhood. His daddy had loads of money, but Cauldwell lives in a modest four-bedroom house on an estate where he can pretend to be part of the local community. He'll send his children to the state school and hope they're clever enough to get into grammar school. Castlebury is one of the few places in England that still has a selective school system.'

'Here he is,' she said triumphantly. 'Trevor Pollard, right at the back, on the end of the row. Short, fat and spotty. Hardly one of the beautiful people.'

Adam came round the desk and stood beside her. 'Judge Pollard's son. The judge is one of the most influential people in the county. It would have paid Cauldwell to keep in with Trevor Pollard; a high court judge is a handy person to have on your side.'

'The other one is named Martin Edge, according to this, and he definitely hung around with Cauldwell.' She frowned. 'But if you look at the photographs, Trevor Pollard is always in the background. He doesn't look like a friend of the other two — not a real friend. Cauldwell and Martin Edge are always together, like real buddies, but Pollard is usually some distance away, just looking on.'

'A voyeur.'

She looked up in surprise. 'Exactly. He watches, but he doesn't take part.'

Adam put his hand in his pocket and took out a small digital camera. He took a dozen or so photos of the pictures in the year-books, working quickly. Then he closed the books, leaving them neatly on the desk, and dropped the camera in his pocket. Gina turned off the recorder, slipped the cord over her wrist, and stood up.

'Where to now?'

'There are only two teachers here from twenty years ago.' He consulted the list. 'A Miss Mayberry who teaches English and French, and Professor Stott. The professor is no longer teaching, but he has a flat on the premises, and according to the note by his name, he's employed as a part-time consultant.'

Miss Mayberry was in the teachers' common room. She was a small, dumpy person and could have been anywhere between forty and sixty years old. Her skin was soft and pink; her hair dead straight, short and steel grey. She was dressed in a pleated navy skirt and a startlingly white blouse topped with a navy cardigan. She was marking papers at a table when they came into the room, rimless glasses balanced precariously on the end of her nose. She looked up and smiled politely while they both took chairs on the other side of the table.

'Headmaster told me you might be seeking me out.'

Gina switched on the recorder while Adam made the introductions.

'Anything you can tell us about Robert Cauldwell would be useful. If Cauldwell should become prime minister, I want to be the first with an unbiased article on how he made it to Number 10.'

'Goodness, how exciting.' Miss Mayberry blinked behind her spectacles. 'What can I tell you, I wonder? Bobby Cauldwell was a perfect pupil. He was clever, popular, and never in any trouble. We all expected great things from him and we haven't been disappointed. The day he becomes prime minister will be a great day for this country.' She beamed at them and started stacking her papers together. 'You can quote that, if you like.'

Afraid they were about to be dismissed, Adam jumped in quickly. 'How about Cauldwell's friends? Who did he go around with?'

'Martin Edge, mainly. He's a famous cosmetic surgeon now, in Harley Street.' Miss Mayberry frowned and her glasses slid down her nose. She caught them expertly. 'And Trevor Pollard sometimes.'

Adam flicked a quick glance at the tape player to make sure it was still running. 'Was there a problem with Trevor Pollard?'

'It was nothing, really. A lot of fuss over nothing. The local girls were invited to our end-of-term dances. I did tell Headmaster I didn't think that was a good idea. When I attended my girls' convent school we were made to dance with one another.'

Gina thought boys dancing with one another might not be a good idea, either.

Adam Shaw turned on his best smile. 'What was the fuss about, Miss Mayberry?'

The teacher took off her glasses and peered at him worriedly. 'I don't want to say anything that might damage the reputation of the school in your article. It was a long time ago, and there was nothing to suggest anyone had done anything wrong. Just a young girl making up stories. Michael Spooner was the headmaster back then but Mr Spooner's dead now, poor man. He died two years ago.' Miss Mayberry put her glasses back on. 'Where was I? Oh, yes, Trevor Pollard. He was a quiet boy and never really interested in girls, and the other two . . . ' She gave a deprecating little laugh. 'The other two were exemplary pupils, beyond reproach.'

'The other two were Robert Cauldwell and Martin Edge?'

'As I said, it was nothing. Trevor Pollard used to tag along with Bobby Cauldwell and Martin Edge and all three happened to be together that night. The boys admitted being with the girl, but the girl wasn't all she should be, even her father knew that. She already had a reputation. Judge Pollard spoke to the headmaster and everything was cleared up satisfactorily. It was a very minor incident.'

'What sort of incident, Miss Mayberry?'

Miss Mayberry collected her papers together and stood up. 'I have to get to my class. If you write your article, Mr Shaw, please report that I had nothing but good to say about Bobby Cauldwell. He was a lovely young man and the school is very proud of him.'

Gina turned off the recorder as Miss Mayberry scurried out of the room. 'You didn't tell her we were recording.'

'She was so scared of saying anything that might incriminate her or the school, I thought it best not. I'm not going to quote her. Interesting, though, don't you think?'

'She was obviously very anxious not to say anything that might incriminate the next prime minister.' Gina smiled. 'She didn't like spotty Pollard, though, did she?'

Adam got to his feet. 'Let's see if Professor Stott has anything to add.'

11

The professor lived in the old part of the building where he had a couple of rooms in the main house. In front of his door was a little courtyard garden filled with clumps of herbs; lavender, thyme and rosemary vying with sage and marjoram, and all planted higgledy-piggledy between the stone slabs. The rain had stopped and hazy sunshine peeped through the trees. The garden smelled wonderful.

Adam rang a pockmarked brass bell on a door that looked as old as the house. The man who answered looked even older, much older than anyone Gina had ever seen alive. He was bent almost double and walked with a stick, tilting his head to one side to look up at Adam.

'Yes?' Surprisingly, his voice was deep and strong.

'Professor Stott? I'm writing an article on Robert Cauldwell and I believe you were one of his teachers.'

The old man shuffled backwards to make room in the doorway. 'Come in, both of you, it's nice to have company.' He moved quite fast up a small corridor into a big, bright room, the furniture ancient but comfortable looking. A worn leather settee stood against one wall, a wing-backed chair with a sagging bottom was tucked in a corner, and an ancient oak table stacked with books looked as if it was about to collapse any minute. The books were everywhere; Gina had to move several from the settee before she could sit down. Adam moved another book and sat beside her while the old man lowered himself gingerly into the sagging chair. 'What can I tell you? Young Bobby Cauldwell was a pain in the backside, so were his buddies. Nothing but trouble. Probably haven't changed a lot.'

Adam looked at Gina and raised an eyebrow. 'Miss Mayberry seemed to think Cauldwell was a model pupil.'

The professor made a sound that might have been a laugh or a death rattle. 'So you've talked to the old bat, have you? She won't say a bad word about any of her pupils in case it reflects on her teaching. I don't teach any more, so I can say what I like. Besides, they think I'm senile.'

'Miss Mayberry mentioned an incident with one of the girls from the village.'

The old man snorted. 'Mayberry would call it an incident. The boys denied anything happened. Said the girl made it all up. Made the poor little bugger sound like a whore — asking for it, and all that.'

'Miss Mayberry said the judge's son was one of the boys involved.'

Stott chuckled. 'Mightbe, we used to call her. We always thought she was a queer.' The professor bent down to pick up a tin of tobacco, almost falling out of his chair in the process. 'They don't use that word now, do they? Not politically correct. Gay, or something, isn't it? Miss Mightbe was anything but gay. Miserable old bugger, if you ask me.'

Adam tried to get the old man back on track. 'What exactly happened? Was Cauldwell involved?'

'Not according to him. Just some fifteen-year-old girl complaining about a date that went wrong.'

Gina couldn't keep quiet. 'So she was under the legal age of consent. Technically a child.'

The old man cocked his head, looking at Gina as if he was seeing her for the first time. 'Pretty girl, she was. Little thing, with curly hair, like you. Cauldwell and Edge tried to put the blame on Trevor Pollard, and rumour had it Judge Pollard paid the father quite a lot of money not to take it any further. Everyone paid off, everyone happy.'

'Except the girl,' Gina said quietly.

'Are the family still living in the village?' Adam asked.

The old man had carefully rolled a long, thin cigarette. Now he lit the wispy bits of weed hanging out of the end and puffed it alight. Gina knew that smell. Not your usual tobacco, more like the stuff Gary smoked. She looked at the old man with renewed interest.

The professor took another long drag on his cigarette and closed his eyes with pleasure. 'Girl's name is Susie London,' he told Adam. 'She still lives in the village, but she's had enough trouble, that girl. Don't go raking up any more.'

'Thank you, Professor.' Adam took Gina's arm and steered her to the front door. The old man looked sorry to see them go.

'God, how did they get away with it?' Gina asked in disbelief as she got in the car. 'She was only fifteen.'

'Like the professor said, if the father said there was no problem, that would have been it. Let's see if we can find the victim.'

Stott hadn't known Susie London's address, so Adam asked at the post office.

'Susie works here, at least I thought she did,' the woman behind the counter told them. 'I've not set eyes on her for a week. If you catch up with her, tell her I could do with some help.'

Susie London's house, an older style semi-detached council house, looked in need of attention. The front garden was overgrown and littered with rubbish that had blown in from the street. A rusting child's bicycle lay on its side and a half-deflated football poked out from the hedge. There was no answer to Adam's knock. After peering through the front window into a sparsely furnished living-room, he looked at Gina. 'Now what?'

'I don't know.' She felt uneasy. The house looked more than just neglected — abandoned would be a better word. 'Do you think she's gone? Just left her job without a word? Why would she do that?'

'I have no idea, but I doubt she's lying dead inside, slaughtered in her own front room. Stop reading some sinister motive into everything, Gina. We'll go back to the shop and say the house looks deserted. Pass the problem on to someone else.'

She was about to agree when her mobile phone buzzed against her thigh. She had turned off the ring tone when they entered the school and dropped the phone into the pocket of her skirt.

Inspector Reagan kept it brief. 'Where are you?'

She wasn't about to tell him where she was, or what she was doing. 'I'm on my way home. Why, what's up?'

'Can you come to the hospital? Castlebury General. We have someone here who's been severely injured. A young white male. We don't know who he is, but he evidently knows you, and we need to identify him.'

'We have to go to the hospital,' she told Adam. Her hand shook as she turned off the phone. 'I knew there was something wrong when he didn't turn up. He sounded frantic on the phone. I should've gone and looked for him.'

'Who?' Adam opened the door of the car. 'Get in and tell me what you're talking about.'

'I think someone just tried to kill Megan's boyfriend. He called the studio a couple of days ago and said he was in trouble. We haven't seen him since.' It had to be Gary; there was no one else it could be.

There was no room in the car park so Adam drove the car round to the casualty department and pulled up outside. 'You go on in. I'll find somewhere to park and come and find you.'

As she ran through the doors a policewoman caught her by the arm. 'The young man is still being treated, you can't see him yet, and Inspector Reagan wants a word with you first. He's in one of the side rooms. I'll show you the way.'

Gina knew she had to slow down and stop running around like a crazy person but she could feel the adrenaline coursing through her body, making her heart beat at twice its normal rate. Somehow she had to get herself under control. She took a couple of deep breaths before she opened the door and faced Reagan. 'What happened?'

Reagan waved her to a chair and sat down on the empty bed. 'We don't know. The victim's ID is being checked, but there's not much to go on — apart from a piece of paper with your studio telephone number.' Reagan waited a beat but when she didn't speak he carried on. 'The young man was found in a ditch. The doctor thinks he was hit by a car but he looks as if he's been run over by a bus. He left most of his face on the road, which is making it difficult to identify him.'

She sat on the cold plastic chair and tucked her shaking hands between her knees. 'I give my phone number to a lot of people. The injured man may be a client.' Who was she trying to kid?

'Possibly, but he won't want his picture painted now. He had a little cash on him, but no credit cards or other form of identity.

We're checking, but you'll be quicker — and even if we do find his family, they may not recognize him, the state he's in.'

She knew she should phone Megan straight away, but decided to wait until she'd seen Gary and identified him. Much as she hated everything about Gary, she didn't want to have to identify him in a hospital room.

It was another half an hour before a nurse told them they could see the patient. Reagan had left the room several times but Gina just sat. Eventually a nurse led them to the intensive care unit. The creature on the bed hardly looked human. Most of the flesh had been scraped from one side of his face, the deep grazes covered with thin gauze; his eyes were swollen shut and his head shaved in random patches. Sterile dressing covered wounds on his arms and shoulders; elsewhere the tattered skin had been patched with tape. His hands lay on top of the sheet connected to drips. Various tubes snaked from beneath the sheet and disappeared under the bed. She moved closer, catching her breath as the man on the bed moved restlessly. Turning to Reagan she said, 'His name is Andy Crabtree and I've only met him once.'

'Relatives? Mother, father? Who do we contact?'

'I don't know.' She turned back to the bed,

making him whole again in her head, knowing it wouldn't last. 'I met him at the HiLo bar in Ipswich. He said he knew everyone in the wine bar, so he was local, but I have no idea where he lives.'

Reagan put his notebook away. 'Is that it, Gina? You're telling me this was a chance encounter, nothing else? So why did he have your phone number?'

'I gave it to him. I thought he might find some contacts for me, and I never saw him again, not until today.' Which was almost the truth. Lying was getting easier — probably because the truth was getting harder. She couldn't tell Reagan she was still chasing the bones of the child. He would tell her to stop, and she couldn't.

'His name should be enough to go on. Without positive ID it was tricky.' The inspector obviously wasn't happy, but he let Gina go.

Adam was waiting outside the room. 'Was it Megan's boyfriend?'

She shook her head. 'Andy Crabtree from the HiLo bar. He was so young, and so pretty, and now he's just a mess. And Reagan knows I'm not telling him everything.' She walked round in circles in the narrow corridor. 'Andy was injured by a hit-and-run driver in a big car. They know it was a big car because of his injuries. We were at the HiLo, weren't we, snooping around asking questions, and we got shunted off the road. A warning, you said. Was poor Andy another warning, do you think?'

'That would be a bit drastic. Crabtree was just a messenger, and the man with the information didn't turn up, if you remember. This was probably just a coincidence.'

'No, it wasn't. Andy phoned me a few days ago and told me he had some information for me but I wouldn't listen. I told him to stop asking questions. I was trying to save his life, for God's sake, not get him killed.'

'If you told him to stop and he still carried on, then it's his own fault. Besides, he isn't dead yet. What exactly did he tell you on the phone?'

'I can't remember,' she said distractedly. 'I think he said he had some more information and that he'd found out something weird. I didn't want anyone else killed so I thought hanging up on him might keep him safe.'

'But you think he got shoved off the road deliberately?'

'Andy was on foot, so he wouldn't have stood a chance. Whatever that car is, it's a nightmare on wheels.'

'It's a Hummer with a 6-litre, V8 engine.'

She looked at Adam curiously. 'Aren't they army vehicles?'

'This would be the civilian version. Big and beautiful and costs lots of money.'

'But very distinctive, I would think, so why use a car like that?'

'Because it adds to the excitement.'

12

Gina pushed the button to open the car window. She felt claustrophobic. Andy had looked like a young pop idol at the wine bar, all spiky hair and confidence, but not any more. Even if he survived, he would never look the same again. She'd put him back together in her head, but she couldn't make him stay that way.

Adam glanced at her, then turned off the air conditioning and opened his own window. 'Where to?'

She looked at her watch. Where had the day gone? 'Megan will have locked up and gone home.' She wanted Adam to stay but she wouldn't ask.

He pulled up outside the studio and turned to look at her. 'Got time for a drink somewhere?'

'Yes, please,' she answered gratefully. 'I don't want to be alone this evening.'

The evening worked out better than she had expected. Adam suggested food as well as alcohol as neither of them had eaten all day. He picked a small bistro on the edge of town that had a good menu and she chose chicken ravioli with blue cheese sauce, enjoying the taste of something that hadn't come pre-packed. The wine was a Rioja that she hadn't tried before, and by the second glass she was starting to relax. She watched Adam Shaw expertly twist his fork in the bowl of his spoon, then pop the resulting neat spiral of spaghetti in his mouth without getting sauce on his chin.

'How do you eat spaghetti bolognaise without getting it all over you?'

'Several years in Italy.' He picked up his glass of wine. 'Your father was Italian, wasn't he? Gino Minnelli if my information is correct.'

The evening was suddenly in danger of being spoiled. 'I don't want to talk about my father.'

'Why, Gina? Aren't you even a little bit curious? Don't you want to find out what happened to him? He disappeared, didn't he? Just like Fox.'

Damn investigative journalists. He was like a kid poking at something with a stick. She sat for a moment, playing with the food left on her plate. 'My grandmother told me both my parents were dead. She told me they were on a plane that went down in the sea. After she died I found out my mother's name was on the passenger list but not my father's. He never got on the plane.'

She remembered her shock when she saw the names of the dead listed in the old newspaper. If he was alive why hadn't he come to find her? She couldn't tell Adam how scared she was. Scared that if she found her father he wouldn't want to meet her. Scared he might have left because of something she said or did. Something that had made him stop loving her.

'He didn't want to find me, Adam, otherwise he would have done. I lived with my grandmother all my life, right up until the time she died, and then I sold her house and bought the studio, still in the same town. I wasn't that hard to find.'

'Perhaps there was a printing error with the passenger list and your father was on the plane all the time. Newspapers make mistakes.'

'Perhaps.' She shrugged. 'Can we talk about something else?'

'Very well.' He looked at her over the rim of his wine glass. There were dark lines under her eyes. She looked too tired and vulnerable to be badgered. 'What do you want to talk about?'

'You, Adam Shaw. Who are you? I'm sitting here having a meal with you, but I know nothing about you.' She studied him, slitting her eyes. 'You're ex-army.' He looked surprised and she smiled. 'No, I'm not psychic. I Googled you. Why did you leave the forces? You look the type who would be in for life.'

'Invalided out. I was in Iraq with the military police. Trained as a negotiator. This particular day I thought I was trying to keep the peace, but someone else thought I was causing trouble. I got a knife in my gut for asking too many questions.'

She smiled at him. 'You're still asking too many questions. Do you really think Robert Cauldwell is mixed up in all this?'

'I think he must be. He was involved with a young girl at the school, wasn't he? A girl who was only fifteen at the time. Like you said, technically a child. Which suggests Cauldwell likes them young. And Nathan Fox definitely has something to hide otherwise he wouldn't have gone missing.' Adam frowned. 'But then why would he come back?'

Gina didn't have an answer. Perhaps because his wife had cancer — or perhaps he just wanted to see his daughter. 'How did you find out the big black car was a Hummer?'

'Very distinctive tyre prints on the grass verge, and the dents in Jessica's car were high up, probably caused by a bull bar. I have secret spies in the force, but if you'd asked your friend the inspector, he would probably have told you.'

The wine had gone. She was surprised to find the bottle empty, and decided drink was definitely getting to be a problem when you couldn't remember drinking it. Adam suggested another bottle, but she thought it was time to go home.

Outside her flat she let Adam take her keys and climb the stairs in front of her to open her door. She thanked him for the meal but didn't ask him in.

★ ★ ★

For some inexplicable reason she woke up crying in the middle of the night. She had been dreaming about a little girl on a beach. Not the Asian child. This little girl had long dark hair that turned into corkscrew curls in the salty air, and this little girl had a beautiful mother and a handsome Italian father. They were playing with their pretty little daughter, chasing her on the sand, and she was squealing with delight.

She rubbed a hand over her damp face and looked at the clock. It was much too early to get up. Just after her grandmother died, she'd had lots of dreams like this, but not recently. In her dream she could see her mother's face clearly, but as soon as she woke the images drifted away like mist. Trying to hang on to them just made them fade more quickly. She slid back into a fitful sleep, peppered with fragments of dreams she couldn't remember, and then overslept, staggering down to the studio nearly an hour late. Finding the studio locked up and deserted, she looked at her watch. Megan was never late. She let herself in and saw the note propped up on Megan's desk.

I have to meet Gary. Back soon. Sorry.

How could Megan be so stupid? She remembered Gary's panic-stricken voice on the phone. Whatever sort of trouble Gary was in, it wasn't Megan's problem. She looked at her watch again. She didn't know what time Megan had left the studio. It could have been any time in the last hour. Should she interfere? Probably not — her interfering just got people into more trouble — but that didn't stop her worrying.

Half an hour later she tried the phone at Megan's flat, then rang Megan's mobile. There was no answer. The phone at the flat often got cut off because Gary ran up a bill Megan couldn't pay, but Gina was getting a dial tone on the landline and Megan's mobile was operational as well, so why wasn't the girl answering either of them?

She sat at her desk chewing her bottom lip, unable to get on with anything. She dare not call the police. She didn't know what sort of trouble Gary was in; whatever it was it was bound to be something against the law. She didn't want to get Megan into trouble — but it was difficult just to sit and do nothing.

Half an hour later she picked up her bag and locked up the studio. If someone wanted a portrait painted, they'd have to wait.

Megan lived on the old council estate. The estate had been tarted up with the addition of a new shopping area and a community centre. It was part private now, ex-council houses calling themselves 'much sought-after residences'. Megan's flat was on the second floor of an unprepossessing concrete block, up a dark stone staircase. A potted plant stood outside the front door, gamely struggling for light and air, the ends of its leaves turning brown.

The bell didn't work and no one answered her knock.

She tried again, banging on the wood until the door shook. Then she lifted the letterbox flap and peered inside. She couldn't see much but she thought she heard a sound. A tiny sound, muffled, as if someone was afraid of making a noise. She called tentatively through the letterbox. 'Megan? Megan, are you in there?'

'Gina?' Barely more than a whisper.

'What's wrong?' She banged on the door again. God, what had Gary done this time? 'Megan, let me in.' The silence lasted almost longer than she could bear.

'I can't get to the door.' Megan's voice was louder this time. 'You've got a key, Gina, I gave you one.'

So she had, a long time ago. Gina fished frantically in her bag. It had to be there somewhere. She found it on her keyring, the obvious place. She fumbled with the key in the lock, turned it the wrong way, turned it back, eventually got the door open.

Megan was sitting on the floor in the living-room, her back against the settee. Her lip was swollen and cut, blood crusted on her chin; her left eye was almost closed and her arms were wrapped around her stomach. Tears had made tracks in the blood on her cheeks.

Gina dropped to the floor beside her friend. 'Did Gary do this?'

Megan nodded. 'When you started banging, I thought it was him come back. That's why I didn't answer you.'

Gina fished in her bag for her mobile phone and pushed the emergency button.

'Ambulance,' she said, and gave the address. 'Yes, it is an emergency. She's pregnant. She's been beaten up. She's injured and can't move. Will that do?' Silly to get shirty with a switchboard operator. She put her arm round Megan. 'They'll be here in a minute. What can I do? Can I do anything to make you more comfortable?'

Megan shook her head. 'The baby's stopped moving, Gina.'

'I'll get a flannel with cold water for your lip, or some ice, that might be better. It must hurt when you talk, so don't. Just sit quiet and wait for the ambulance.'

She had to do something, anything. She was scared to try to move Megan in case she made matters worse. Why hadn't she taken that first aid course when she had the chance? Gary's slaps had obviously progressed to something much more serious. She found some ice cubes in the fridge, wrapped them in a reasonably clean cloth and slammed them against the counter top to break them up, wishing she could do the same to Gary.

Megan held the dripping cloth against her split lip. 'The man with the big car picked Gary up yesterday,' she mumbled through the cloth. 'Took him to a warehouse by some water somewhere. There were two more men waiting there.'

'But Gary doesn't know anything.'

'I know.' Megan took a breath and screwed up her face in pain. 'But they thought he did, so they beat him up and dumped him outside my door. He let himself in and phoned me at the studio. Said he was hurt and needed help. When I got here he just went mad. I think he wanted to hurt me as much as they hurt him. He was shouting at me, telling me what they did to him, telling me it was my fault.' Another tear tracked down her face.

Gina felt sick. Christ, how had she managed to get Megan involved in all this? 'Where's Gary now?'

Megan rocked, hugging herself. 'Gone. The people who took him, they wanted to know what you took from the house. I told him you only took some old photos and stuff, but that made him even madder. He punched me, knocked me over — kicked me some. When he realized I couldn't get up, he ran out. He slammed the front door. I tried to get to the phone — I probably could've crawled — but I started bleeding, and I've got a pain in my stomach. It's bad, Gina. I think I'm going to have the baby.' She clutched Gina's hand. 'I'm so fucking scared.'

'Shush.' Gina rubbed Megan's shoulder.

'I'll stay with you.' She was as scared as Megan, but she couldn't allow herself to go to pieces. Her grandmother would have told her to be brave, but she got so damned sick of being brave.

13

The paramedics were gentle and efficient. They loaded Megan on to a stretcher and put her in the ambulance. Gina followed behind in her own car, hating to leave Megan alone, even for the few minutes it took to get to the hospital. When she got there, she found the wait intolerable. She actually got around to keying in Adam's mobile number, but what could he do? He didn't even know Megan. She thought of calling Reagan, to get him out looking for Gary, but now was not the time.

A midwife came in to speak to her. 'You're Megan's friend? The one who brought her in? She's going to surgery in a few minutes. Is there anyone else we can call? The baby's father?'

Gina shook her head. 'He did this to her. I suppose you'll have to speak to the police . . . '

'Not without Megan's consent.' She patted Gina on the arm. 'Go and get a coffee. I'll get someone to call you when Megan comes out of surgery.'

Gina wandered down to the coffee machine. It was now way past lunchtime but she wasn't hungry. Restless, she patrolled the hospital corridors. She asked at reception about Andy Crabtree and after she mentioned Inspector Reagan's name the woman was more forthcoming. Crabtree was still critical, but off life support. She tried to convince herself that Andy was nothing to do with her. She had told him to stop asking questions so it was his own fault he had ended up in hospital. She had to believe that.

A midwife eventually came to get her and told her Megan was out of surgery, conscious, and asking for Gina. The midwife offered to take her to the bereavement suite and she was outside the door to the room before the woman's words sank in.

'Bereavement suite? Why the bereavement suite? Did something happen to the baby?'

'I'm so sorry. Everyone did all they could.'

Gina moved away from the door. 'Can you give me a minute?'

'Of course. Go in when you're ready.'

She put her hand on the wall to steady herself. Was she responsible for the death of Megan's baby? More small bones? Leave well alone, her grandmother used to say, let the sleeping dogs lie, but she hadn't listened. Now she had to go into that tragic place and ask her friend's forgiveness.

Megan looked up as Gina came into the room. Spider stitches crawled across her bottom lip and her eye was still puffy, streaked with purple and nearly closed. She tried to smile, but didn't quite make it. The midwife must have made a mistake, Gina thought. Megan had her baby in her arms, rocking it gently.

'Come and look at her. She's beautiful.'

Gina forced herself to walk across the room and stand by Megan's bed. She looked down at the baby. The child was perfect. Long eyelashes resting against velvet-soft cheeks, a tiny hand, a wisp of pale hair, a mouth so like Megan's it broke her heart. She touched the baby's face, felt the coolness of the skin, saw the blue tint creeping into the slightly parted lips.

'I'm so sorry, Megan.'

Sorry was so far from what she felt, the word was meaningless. She had looked at a dead baby's face and nothing would ever be the same again. This was something she couldn't mend.

'In a minute they're going to come and take her away,' Megan said. 'But they took photos, so I'll always know what she looked like. I named her Rosie. It's a pretty name, isn't it?' The long breath had a sob in it. 'Can you find out where she's going? What they'll do with her? I don't want her to just . . . be forgotten.'

'She won't be forgotten, Megan, I promise.'

'I had it all planned, babysitters and everything, so I could come back to work. Nursery school vouchers and all that stuff.'

Gina couldn't think of anything to say.

Megan lifted Rosie's hand, letting the baby's limp fingers curl round her own. 'I wanted you to be special for her, Gina, like a sort of godmother. Someone else to love her.'

The midwife came in and took the baby, lifting the tiny bundle very gently from Megan's arms, pulling the blanket away from the baby's face so Megan could have one last look. 'The surgeon said everything inside you is fine. There's nothing to stop you having another baby when you're ready.'

Megan kissed her daughter's small, dead face. 'I don't want another baby,' she said softly. 'I want this one.'

Gina left the room. She knew she should have stayed. She knew she should have put her arms round her friend and comforted her, but her world had changed in those few moments almost as much as Megan's, and where she was treading now frightened her. She had always been able to keep her distance from the dead — they were strangers — but this time it was personal, and it hurt more than she could have believed possible.

When she went back into the room, Megan had her eyes closed. Propped up on the pillows, she looked very young. She had been battered, both physically and emotionally, but Gina knew Megan would recover the same way she recovered from everything else. It was just another kick in the teeth, and Megan was used to being kicked.

'Gina?' Megan opened her eyes and winced as she moved. 'They had to cut me open but it doesn't hurt as much as I expected. Only if I move suddenly.'

'Then don't move suddenly.' Gina sat on the chair beside the bed. 'Do you want to sleep? Shall I come back tomorrow?'

'Probably a good idea. I'm so tired.' She put out her hand as Gina got to her feet. 'The bones they found, Gina. Find out how that little girl died. Someone must have loved her.'

'I can't. I don't want any more people hurt.'

Megan's eyes were already closing again. 'Please, Gina,' she said.

By the time Gina got back to the studio, it was time to lock up. She had driven home through a rainstorm, driving by instinct, her tears blurring reality like the rain on the windscreen. She took the flowers Gary had given Megan out of their vase and dropped them in the waste bin. Where was Gary? The police should be out looking for him, but she resisted calling Reagan for the moment, worried about stirring up more trouble. God, hadn't she done enough?

She locked the door to the studio and went upstairs. It was still raining outside, thin lines of water running down the window going nowhere in particular, perfectly in keeping with her mood. She wasn't hungry, even though she couldn't remember the last time she had eaten. The wine had all gone, as had the beer. She should really ask Megan before she phoned Reagan, but someone had to be told about Gary.

Reagan already knew all about Gary Marsh. He was on file as a user and possibly a dealer. Reagan said he would make sure Gary was found. They knew most of his regular haunts and it shouldn't take long. He promised not to question Megan yet, but asked if he could send someone over to talk to Gina. She told him no. She didn't want to talk to anyone. She wanted a drink, but going down the road to buy a bottle of wine would take too much effort. She wished she smoked. She didn't even bite her fingernails. Too much control, sometimes.

Half an hour later, when she was looking at a programme on the television — not watching, not listening, just looking — the doorbell rang. Adam Shaw stood outside. When he made to move past her, she put a hand on each side of the door, blocking his way. She really didn't want to talk to anyone.

He moved back into the rain. 'I tried phoning the studio on and off all afternoon. You weren't there.' When she didn't answer he ran a hand over his head, spiking his hair. 'I'm getting wet.'

She moved away from the door and walked back into her living room. Adam followed. 'I was at the hospital with Megan,' she told him. 'Gary beat her up. He kicked her half to death and she lost the baby. Her baby's dead.'

'Got anything to drink?' When she shook her head, he walked past her into the kitchen and filled the kettle. 'How is Megan? How badly beaten up?'

'She'll get better. There's nothing broken. She had a Caesarean and they reckon she'll need about four days in hospital.'

She watched him make coffee. Watched him find mugs, coffee, milk, as if he already knew where everything was. But he remembered things, didn't he? It was his job. He carried the mugs into the living room, waited while she sat, handed her a mug. 'You look dreadful.'

As comments went, it was just what she

needed. He took a flask from his pocket and poured something into her coffee. She didn't ask what it was. She took a sip and the jolt of strong spirit thawed the numbness a little. 'Why are you here?'

His hair was still wet, clumped into spikes where he'd run his fingers through it, his shirt sticking to him. 'I came to share information, like we agreed. I tracked down Susie London. She's been away, a neighbour says, went without telling anyone.'

Gina tried to appear interested. She'd forgotten all about Susie London. 'Strange to just disappear like that and give up her job at the shop.' Gina remembered the tacky council house, the unkempt garden. 'I would have thought she needed the money.'

'Stranger still that she decided to disappear at this particular moment in time. She does have a child, by the way. A boy.'

How did he find out all this information? 'I spoke to Inspector Reagan,' she said, sipping her coffee. The alcohol was beginning to warm her. 'Andy Crabtree is still sedated so he won't be able to talk to anyone for a while yet, but the police have booked it as a traffic accident. Hit and run.' Gina stared into her mug. Alcohol made the instant coffee almost drinkable. 'I think Gary Marsh must have been followed. He was picked up and taken to a warehouse somewhere near some water, that's what he told Megan. Interrogated, tortured — something like that. They let him go when they found out he really didn't know anything and dumped him on Megan's doorstep. He was so angry he beat her up.' She took a breath. 'And kicked her in the stomach.'

'Why would they follow Megan's boyfriend?'

'Because Megan lives with him and she works for me. They've been following me, Adam.'

'Or following this Gary Marsh because of some drugs deal that went wrong, and you just happen to be someone he knows. That sounds a lot more likely.'

'The men who took Gary wanted to know what I found at Jessica's house. He didn't know, so they beat him up.' She finished her coffee. 'If I hadn't gone to that house, Megan would still have her baby.' Adam tried to say something but she waved him into silence. 'I thought I was so damned clever. Just goes to show, doesn't it?'

He got up from his chair and sat beside her on the settee. He didn't try to touch her. 'You remember I told you I got stabbed in the stomach? I thought I was helping someone that day too, but I got that person killed. If I hadn't interfered, they might still be alive. Shit happens, Gina. Gary Marsh would have beaten Megan up at some point. Maybe killed her. And can you imagine what he might have done to the baby if he lost his temper? Someone is responsible for what happened to Megan, but it isn't you.'

She shrugged, unconvinced. She wanted to feel guilty, needed to bear some of the pain Megan must be feeling. If she had been a Catholic she would have gone to confession and asked to be forgiven. She would never be able to forgive herself.

'Why does someone want to know what I took from the house?' she asked Adam. 'The photos and letters don't seem important enough, or the diary. Maybe it's the video, but how could a shot of some college students mean so much?'

'If someone wants the video, or any of the other stuff, they must think it's more important than it is, or know something we don't. Fox may have hidden something else somewhere in the house and they think you took it. By the way, have you eaten?'

She smiled for the first time. 'You're always asking me that. I'm really not hungry. I just want to be on my own for a bit.'

Before he left he checked to make sure she had food in the freezer. 'Don't go to bed on an empty stomach. Have something to eat even if you don't feel like it, and take a couple of aspirin or something. You'll sleep better.'

She waited until she heard his car start up and then sat down to finish her crying.

14

When Gina got to the hospital the next day, Megan had been moved. She had been put in a room with three other women and already had a visitor. A tall woman with ash-blonde hair and a nervous smile was sitting in a chair beside Megan's bed. She was very obviously pregnant. Megan was sitting up in bed looking even more nervous. The swelling was still bad round her eye but her lip looked less painful. An enormous bowl of flowers sat on the bedside table, a card tucked in the blooms, and Megan had a box of chocolates tied with a large bow resting on her lap.

'This is Cindy Cauldwell,' Megan said with false brightness. 'You remember? I did my classes with her.'

Gina didn't speak. She was sure her thoughts must show on her face. This was Robert Cauldwell's wife. Did she know her husband had once raped a fifteen-year-old girl?

'You must think me really callous, coming here like this,' the woman said. She looked down apologetically at her bulging stomach. 'I agonized whether to visit or not, but the other women in the class wanted to send Megan their love.' Cindy looked pleadingly at Gina. 'Sometimes it's really hard to know what to do for the best.'

You drew the short straw, didn't you, you poor thing? Gina thought. The politician's wife. Who better to make a diplomatic visit? 'I'm sorry.' She sat down on the end of the bed. 'I'm being very rude. I'm Megan's friend, we work together.'

'She's my boss.' Megan said. 'She's an artist.'

Cindy smiled a quick, little-girl smile, uncertain still. 'Megan told us all about you at the classes. You work for the police as well, I believe.'

Exactly what had Megan been telling people? 'I do some forensic work for them now and again.'

'She can look at a photograph,' Megan chipped in, 'and make the person in it look older or younger. She helps the police find people who have been missing for years and years.'

'And Megan's very good at PR work,' Gina said, a touch more coolly than she intended.

Cindy Cauldwell got to her feet. 'I must be going. Thank you for seeing me, Megan, I won't go on again about how sorry I am, because you know how I feel — how we all feel.' She bent down and gave Megan an awkward hug. 'Get better soon.'

Gina watched Cindy leave. Megan knew nothing about Cauldwell's connection with Nathan Fox, and Gina wasn't about to enlighten her. 'Flowers and chocolates,' she said. 'You're doing well.'

Megan tried a grin round the stitches in her lip. 'I just got a visit from our MP's wife, and flowers from your boyfriend — how good is that?'

Gina grabbed the card. *Get well soon. Best wishes, Adam Shaw.* She pushed the card back in amongst the flowers. 'He's not my boyfriend.'

'Pity.' Megan tried another smile, half-hearted this time. 'They're sending me home day after tomorrow.'

Gina remembered the flat. Megan couldn't go back there. It was a cold, dark place, and no one would have been in to clean it up. There was probably still blood on the floor. 'You can't go back to the flat. Stay with me for a bit. Until you feel better.'

'Don't be silly, I'll be all right.'

'No, you won't. You'll have to sleep on the futon in the spare room, but I bought it in case someone came to stay, and no one ever has. You'll be my first guest.'

'Just for a couple of days then, thanks.'

Megan hesitated. 'The flat was in Gary's name. I may get kicked out.'

'The council won't make you homeless, Megan. They have to give you somewhere to live. Look, don't worry about it — just get better, OK?'

Promising to come back tomorrow, Gina walked the long corridors to the exit. She decided she would have a word with the housing people. It might be better if Megan was rehoused somewhere else. With Gary still at large, Megan wasn't safe in her flat.

For the next few days she was going to have to manage the studio and the paperwork on her own. She had two portraits to finish. One of a dog, which she hated doing but it brought in the money, and the portrait of the old lady, which she knew she had to get on with. She wondered if the family would tell the old woman it was OK to go ahead and die once they had something to remember her by. It was a relief when the day was over and she could lock up the studio. Tomorrow was Sunday and, apart from another visit to Megan, she had the day to herself.

When she got upstairs she took the videotape out of the envelope and put it in the machine. There was something else she hadn't told Adam. She had noticed something he'd missed. He said the driver of the car had his head turned away all the time, but that was not strictly true — a second before the tape ran out the man turned his head slightly before driving away. When Adam had the picture on pause, Gina had seen the driver in profile for a split second. Now she wound the tape to the same place and pressed pause again. The black line of interference cut across the picture as before, but it was too low down to obscure the man's face. She reached for her sketchpad and outlined his profile. The shape of the man's face wouldn't be exactly the same on both sides, no human face was completely symmetrical, but it would be near enough. Once she had finished the drawing in profile, she tore out the sheet and put it on the table. Working from her drawing, she produced a full-frontal sketch of the man's face.

It was no one she recognized, but she had been expecting that.

She started another sketch and aged the face by twenty years. Age progression was often used to help find a fugitive, or a family member who had been missing for some time. This was routine work. She put the profile and full-face sketches in the envelope with the tape, and the aged version in her handbag. When she got a chance she would show it to Adam. He might know the man in her picture, or at least have seen him somewhere.

She felt restless, unable to read or watch television, and wished Adam would phone or knock on her door. She wasn't going to ring him, not again. Damn the man, she had been fine without him, the same way she had been fine without Simon. Her grandmother had never liked Simon and she wondered what Josephine Cross would have thought of Adam Shaw. Not a lot, probably. The old lady never had a lot of time for men and Gina sometimes wondered if her grandmother's lack of respect for the male of the species had rubbed off on her. She had been brought up in a female household. She knew how to change a plug, plumb in a washing machine and deal with a dodgy boiler. She could pick up a spider in her bare hands and catch a field mouse by the tail.

So why was she prowling the room waiting for the phone to ring?

She turned off her alarm before she went to bed, determined to have a lie-in on the Sunday morning, but she woke at six when a shaft of sunlight fell across her face, and got up at seven when she got bored with lying in bed. Sometime soon the weather would break, but for the moment it was one glorious day after another, and it would be a shame to waste the sunshine.

There were no messages on her answerphone so she checked her email. Nothing from Adam; he was obviously having a busy weekend. Everything else went straight in the bin, except for one odd message with a cryptic email address.

Meet me by the water today at the usual time.

Gina smiled to herself. Someone had messaged the wrong person. She shut down the computer and made herself breakfast, sitting by the open window to eat toast and marmalade. She hoped whoever had left the message on her computer had realized his mistake by now, otherwise he was going to be very disappointed.

But what if the message really was for her?

Adam wouldn't email her, Megan didn't have a computer, and Andy Crabtree was in hospital. That didn't leave anyone she particularly wanted to meet.

She left the remains of her toast and booted up the computer again, going back into her email and checking the message. No, she was being ridiculous. What water? And what was 'the usual time'? The message had nothing to do with her. But she still had a queasy feeling and her heart wouldn't quite settle back to its normal rhythm.

Thinking a run might settle her stomach, she changed into her running gear and headed for the park.

15

The park looked beautiful in the early morning sunshine — formal flowerbeds a mass of summer flowers, squirrels playing tag among the trees, and sprinklers on the cricket pitch sending the scent of wet grass wafting up the hill. Gina stopped for a moment, looking down towards the river. Fox had no reason to contact her, even if he was still alive, and the Hummer man had already met her face to face. But there was water — and this was about her usual time for a run on a Sunday morning.

There were plenty of people in the park, even this early in the morning. A mum pushing a buggy, a man with a dog, boys on bicycles, a couple of teenagers kicking a football around. It would have been difficult to find anywhere less threatening, but she felt her feet slow as she neared the bridge over the water. There was no one around who remotely resembled Nathan Fox and, annoyed with herself for being so stupid, she scowled at the ducks and started running again, keeping to her usual route down the path, then left round the pond and back up to the castle.

She'd forgotten the pond.

What if the person who left the message hadn't meant the river? What if he'd meant the boating pond? That patch of water was far less exposed than the bridge. She slowed again, studying the few people near it. A woman was feeding the ducks, and several fluffy grey cygnets, full size but still in their ugly duckling stage, hustled the smaller birds out of the way in their haste to get to the bread. Gina paused to watch, head bent, hands on knees, getting her breath.

Then she saw him.

Nathan Fox was sitting on a bench by the pond. He wasn't feeding the ducks although now and again one would walk hopefully past his feet. He was alone on his wooden seat, and that wasn't really surprising because Nathan Fox was a dirty old tramp, and there was no chance anyone would want to sit near him. There was also no chance anyone would recognize him — anyone but her.

She remembered the good-looking man she had drawn. The sharp cheekbones, firm chin and aquiline nose, the iron-grey hair streaked with white, the slim build and straight back. The man on the bench looked old. His face was puffy, his nose pushed off-centre, his hair hidden beneath a tatty woollen hat. He was bent over on the seat, his shoulders hunched arthritically. The beard that covered most of the lower part of his face was a dirty grey colour and looked as if it might have things nesting in it.

Gina picked up a piece of bread from the path and made her way round the pond until she was standing in front of the bench. She squatted on the ground and broke off a piece of bread, holding it out for an interested duck.

'Come on,' she said. 'You'll have to take it from me, or you won't get it.' Lowering her voice, she added. 'Good morning, Mr Fox.'

She heard a chuckle behind her. 'You're very good. I was told you were. Sit on the end of the bench where I can see you.'

She got up and sat on the very edge of the seat. He even smelt like a tramp.

'How did you get a picture of the child, Gina?' His voice didn't match his looks.

'They found her bones in a pond. You must know what happened to her. Your daughter had a photo. I want to know the child's name and how she died.' Nathan Fox was silent for so long Gina risked a look at him. He was lighting a dog-end and she wondered if he'd picked it up off the path. 'Did you kill her?' Again there was silence.

She had nearly run out of bread and the

squawking ducks were starting to peck her feet, when he said, 'I don't know how the child died.'

A group of children came rushing down the path towards the pond, the mother shouting to the little ones to stop. Gina put her arm out to halt a toddler before it tipped into the water. The mother was profuse in her thanks. 'I should move if I were you, dear.' She glanced at Fox then back at Gina. 'Carry on with your jog.' The woman went round to the other side of the pond, dishing out bread to her brood, and Gina asked the question that had been festering in her head ever since Jessica's funeral.

'Why did you leave your daughter, Mr Fox?'

'I had no choice,' Fox said, so softly Gina could barely hear. 'I took something that didn't belong to me and it put my family in danger. Don't turn round, Gina, just tell me what you took from my wife's house.'

'You were watching me, weren't you? I knew someone was there. I took some letters and photos, a video, and a diary. That's all. I'm going to put them back.'

Fox said, 'Don't put them back. Keep everything safe until I tell you what to do with it.' Another batch of mothers and kids was heading towards the pond. 'I'll be in touch again soon,' he whispered, and she heard him shuffling away.

She still had so many questions to ask, but she dare not follow him. His disguise was brilliant. The plastic surgery was good, but the beard and old clothes turned him into something else. Nobody looked at a tramp. People might stop to throw money, but their eyes would skitter on by, afraid to look too closely in case they were accused of staring. Put the homeless in the same category as the obese and the handicapped — the invisible people. No one would see Nathan Fox because no one would look at him.

She had cooled down from her run and was glad of the sun on her back as she jogged slowly up the hill. It was only a short run from the castle gates to her studio. She paused at the bottom of the stairs leading up to her flat. Something was wrong.

Nothing she could put her finger on, nothing tangible, just a feeling. She walked round to the front of the house and peered through the window into the studio. Everything looked fine, so why the creepy feeling? Normally, she managed to suppress any strange sensations — one odd talent was enough — but something was sending little shivers up and down her spine. Reluctantly she climbed the stairs and opened her front door.

The flat was a mess.

Her first thought was that an animal must have got in somehow and gone berserk. Then she realized whoever had done the damage had definitely been human. The seat cushions had been thrown about the room and the pictures pulled from the walls. In the kitchen the drawers and cupboards were open; glass, cornflakes, rice and assorted dried pastas crunched underfoot. The computer was still on the desk in the spare room, but the monitor had been smashed. The bedroom was slightly better. The dressing-table drawers had been emptied and the wardrobe door was open, but nothing appeared to have been taken. There was no money in the flat; she always took her purse with her when she ran, her money and credit cards inside. The only thing of value was the computer, and perhaps the few bits of jewellery she had inherited from her grandmother. The jewellery was still in its box on the dressing-table.

Was trashing her flat the same as dumping her in the river? Another warning?

She picked up the telephone, surprised to find her hands reasonably steady, and dialled the police station. She asked to speak to Detective Inspector Reagan and he arrived fifteen minutes later. He had been about to go home, he said, so her place had been on his way. The first thing he did was examine the door to her flat.

'How was this locked when you went out? Did you use the dead-lock or just pull the door shut on the Yale?'

'Just pulled it shut,' she told him guiltily. 'I wasn't gone long.'

He looked around. 'Long enough, obviously. What do you think a deadlock is for? Fun?' He sighed with exasperation. 'Some people don't have them fitted, but you've actually got one on the door and you don't bother to use it.'

'I do of a night,' she said defensively. 'When I go to bed. But this is broad daylight on a Sunday morning.'

'Most burglars don't want you home in bed when they break in. They want a nice empty house.' He moved around the room, not touching anything. 'Anyway, the Yale lock wasn't broken, it was picked, so whoever did this was a professional.'

She felt another little shiver run through her. Tonight the deadbolt would definitely go on.

'Check everything when you clear up, check if there is anything missing, and then notify your insurance company. I'll send someone round to take some details. If you're pretty certain nothing was taken, that's about it. There's not much we can do. Anyway, I'm glad they didn't spraypaint your walls or slash your furniture.'

As soon as he had gone, she had a shower. What with sitting next to a tramp and having her flat turned over, she felt contaminated. She didn't want to put on clothes that might have been touched by a stranger, so she took denim shorts and an unironed top out of the airing cupboard and then started on the job of clearing up. She worked angrily, shoving things back in drawers, determined not to sit down until she had the place back in some sort of order. This was her home.

Halfway through she realized she was crying, which made her feel stupid, so she poured herself a glass of wine. Not a good idea when she hadn't eaten, but better than sitting on the floor sobbing. She finished the wine and pulled herself together enough to get on with the job of clearing up.

It took her nearly two hours to tidy the flat and she was putting the last of her underwear back in the dressing-table drawer when she realized there was something missing. She went back into the living-room to check. The envelope with the stuff she had taken from the house was no longer on top of the video machine. It wasn't anywhere else, either, but the letters and photos had been scattered about on the floor and she found the diary underneath a chair. The video was missing, and so were her drawings of the man in the car and the sketch of Fox.

For a while she had managed to convince herself this was just a run-of-the-mill burglary, nothing special. Lots of people got burgled. Something or someone had disturbed the burglar and he had run off without taking anything. But now she knew the burglar had got exactly what he wanted. What he had come for. The tape.

She needed another glass of wine. Brandy would have been better, but wine was working fine. She poured herself another generous glass, pulled Adam's card off the fridge and sat down on her settee, now complete with cushions.

There was no answer on his home phone and his mobile gave her his messaging service. 'Phone me,' she said. He rang her back ten minutes later and said he was on his way.

She hadn't got the energy to do anything to herself. She was dressed in creased clothing, without makeup, her hair a mass of tangled curls, her eyes red from crying. It was 'take me as you find me' day. 'Mind the bits of glass,' she told him as she let him in. 'I haven't managed to clear it all up.' If he said anything nice she was going to start crying again. He didn't.

'What was taken?'

'The video from Jessica's house. It wasn't exactly hidden. There was no reason to trash the place.'

'Yes, there was. It was another warning, telling you not to mess with things that don't concern you.' Adam was prowling round the flat, looking into rooms, gauging the damage. 'Where were you when they broke in?'

'Out running. Do you want a drink?' She held up the bottle of wine. When he shook his head, she poured herself another glass. 'I met Fox in the park.' Adam's eyes darkened when he was cross, she noticed, like a storm coming. 'I didn't go to the park to meet him. He was just there.'

'By accident?'

'Well, no, probably not by accident. He knows I run every Sunday morning at about the same time. He was waiting for me. He's clever, Adam. He was dressed like a tramp so no one would recognize him, and he knew I took the stuff from the house. He told me to keep it all safe until he gets in touch. But now the tape's been stolen.'

'There was nothing incriminating on the

tape, was there?' Adam paced her small room. 'Nothing important? Unless we missed something.'

'We did miss something.' Gina fetched her handbag and handed him her sketch of the car driver. 'I managed to get a profile of the man off the videotape and did a full-face sketch. I've aged him twenty years, but it's no one I recognize.'

Adam studied her drawing. 'I recognize him. This is Trevor Pollard's father, Judge Pollard.'

'I did a couple of other sketches before I did this one, but they seem to be missing. Whoever took the video took the sketches as well.'

'Which means they know you recognized the judge.'

'But like you said, there was nothing incriminating on the tape. The judge had a perfect right to be at the school. His son was a pupil there.'

'All mysteries have a logical solution. You just have to find it.' His eyes were back to their normal cornflower colour, much too pretty for a man. 'I bet you haven't eaten since breakfast and it's now half past two. Sunday lunch at the pub. My treat.'

She was about to tell him she couldn't go because she was all creased and her hair was a mess, but after all the wine it didn't seem to matter. And she was hungry.

He took her to a pub on the river and treated her to roast beef and Yorkshire pudding with homemade horseradish sauce. They both cleared their plates. Sitting on the deck in the sun with another glass of wine in front of her, Gina felt her eyes closing.

Adam stood up. 'You're nodding off so I think it's time to get you home. Give me the key to Jessica's house. Now we've lost the tape, it's worth another look. There might be something you missed.'

Gina reached into her bag and handed over the key. 'I didn't miss anything.'

16

Gina sat in the car outside the hospital watching the ducks in the stream that ran through the grounds. She had found a parking space straight away for once, but now she was having second thoughts about her decision to invite Megan to stay. She told herself if the baby had lived, Megan would be back in her council flat now, coping all on her own and doing a good job of it — except Gary might come back, and she couldn't live with the thought of Megan being beaten up again. Guilt sucks, she thought.

She took a breath and got out of the car. The sun was shining and the front of the hospital was landscaped prettily with a bridge over the stream, more ducks, and pregnant women leaning on the arms of their partners, happily walking through the early contractions and expecting a healthy, live baby. Megan was on her own, expecting Gina to give her a safe home for a few days. How could that be a problem?

Megan was waiting in the reception area, looking pale and ill, and Gina could only remember Megan with a bump, her face puffy, her ankles swollen, but always cheerful. This sad, fragile teenager was a stranger. 'How do you feel?' she asked worriedly. 'You still look tired.'

Megan put a hand on her stomach. 'Still a bit sore but not too bad. I'll be fine. Perhaps it would be better if I went home to my flat. It was great you asking me to stay with you but I'll be all right on my own.'

'No, you won't. Stay with me just for tonight, otherwise I shall worry about you. You can go home tomorrow if you feel better. You don't have to talk to me, or be nice — in fact you don't have to say a word if you don't want to. You can watch the telly, or go to bed, or whatever. OK?'

Megan nodded, attempting a smile. Sometime in the next few days her baby would be cremated but she had already said goodbye. Now she had to get on with her life. She stayed with Gina for nearly a week, almost silent at the beginning, just sitting watching television all day, but talking again at the end. 'I'm just so tired,' she told Gina. 'I'm scared I'll be like this for ever.'

'They have bereavement counsellors,' Gina suggested. 'Perhaps you should go and talk to someone.'

'I don't want to talk to anyone. I know my baby died; I'm not pretending she didn't or anything. I want to go back to work. I get more tired doing nothing.'

Having Megan back at work would certainly help. Gina had been struggling with a sudden influx of people wanting pictures of their children, children wanting pictures of their parents, and everybody wanting a picture of their pet. Her desk was littered with photographs of grinning dogs and snooty cats, even a lone parrot. For once in her life she welcomed a phone call from Inspector Reagan asking for her help with a 'before' picture for reconstructive surgery.

'Have I got to go to the hospital again?' she asked with a sinking feeling. She was becoming a regular at the hospital; the receptionist greeted her by name.

'No, a home visit, a child in a car accident. A trip to the local shop with Daddy, just around the corner, so no one was wearing a seatbelt. The kid smashed her face on the windscreen and Daddy was killed.'

'When do you want me to see her?'

'Tomorrow would be good. Poor little thing's only three. Kids change so much at that age, and the mother doesn't have any pictures the hospital can work with. Can you manage without a recent photo?'

'Yes,' Gina said.

'I've got to go out tomorrow,' she told

Megan, 'so it would be great if you could mind the studio until I come back.' She didn't want to leave Megan on her own but she couldn't afford to close the studio. 'I don't want you to do any work or anything. Just answer the phone and wait for me to get back.'

★ ★ ★

The child Reagan had sent Gina to see had been a very pretty little girl before the accident. Most of the damage was to one side of her face where recent scar tissue had pulled down the child's eye and twisted her mouth up at the corner.

'We haven't taken any photos at all in the last year,' the mother said. 'We were waiting to get a better camera. One of those megapixel digital ones.' She lifted the toddler on to her lap. 'I don't have any recent photos but I remember exactly what Leanne looked like as she got into the car with her daddy and waved goodbye.'

'I don't need photos,' Gina said. 'I just need to look at your daughter. I'll do a sketch of her without the scarring and you can tell me if you think I've got it right.'

The child's mother was so pleased with the sketches, she kissed Gina goodbye. 'I don't know how you do it,' she said, gazing at the drawings in awe, 'but you have her just right. How did you know she had that little mole on her cheek? The scars have covered it up.'

'Sometimes,' Gina said, 'I don't know how I do it, either.'

She drove back to the studio feeling pleased with herself. She hoped her sketches helped the plastic surgeon get the little girl's face as near perfect as possible, with or without the mole. She was a lovely child, and looking at a real person, however badly scarred, had to be better than looking at a dead body.

When she got back to the studio, Megan greeted her with a smile. 'Adam was here — you only just missed him. He says he'll phone you later.'

Gina kicked off her shoes, ignoring the treacherous quickening of her pulse. 'Why the big smile? He never has that effect on me. What did he want?'

'I made him a cup of tea. He seems really nice. He said I shouldn't go back to my flat in case Gary comes back, but he knows a photographer who's working in Thailand and needs someone to look after his house while he's away. Adam said I could stay at the house for a couple of weeks and be a house-sitter.'

Gina put her hand on the kettle. It was still warm so she topped it up with water and turned it on. 'Sounds all right, I suppose.' Anything was better than Megan going back to her flat.

'The house is only a few streets away, so I can walk to work, and Adam said I can move in tomorrow.' Megan watched while Gina dropped a tea bag in a mug and poured on water. 'There's something else,' she said. 'It's on your bed.'

Gina walked into her bedroom and saw something strange between her two pillow shams. She had no idea what it was. She touched it and jumped back when it moved. The cat opened one startlingly blue eye and gazed balefully at her.

'What the — ' She swung round to find Megan right behind her, looking guilty.

'It's Jessica's cat. Adam went to the house and someone had broken in. The cat was hiding in a cupboard, really scared. The old man next door had been feeding her but he can't take her in because he has a cat already.' She looked at Gina pleadingly. 'She'll have to stay here one night, but only one night. She's a pedigree seal point Siamese and her name's Blossom.'

Gina walked back into her living-room and sat down. 'Blossom?'

'Well, it's really Softypaws Orange Blossom, but that's a bit of a mouthful. Can she stay here tonight? Please? I'll take her with me tomorrow.'

'I suppose, but it's going to have to get off my bed.' Gina didn't think she liked cats very much, but she'd never been allowed a pet so she wasn't sure. 'Did you say Jessica's house had been broken into?'

'Adam said to tell you it looked the same MO as yours, whatever that is.'

'I got burgled as well. Didn't you notice the computer monitor is missing? The insurance company is sending a cheque, but God knows when that will arrive.'

'Why?' Megan looked shocked. 'Not why is the insurance company sending a cheque, but why did you get burgled?'

Gina shrugged. She didn't want to go into any more detail, Megan had enough worries. 'They didn't take anything much. I think they got scared off.'

After they had eaten, Megan fed the cat the remains of the shepherd's pie and went to bed. Adam had found the cat's basket at the house, also litter and a tray, so the cat was settled in the spare room with Megan. Gina had replaced the broken living-room TV with the one from the bedroom, which was still intact. She sat staring at the screen for half an hour and then realized she hadn't a clue what was going on. She was waiting for Adam to call. Angry with herself, she undressed and went to bed. If he called now, she wouldn't answer the phone.

17

Gina woke up the next morning to hammering on the front door. She glanced at her bedside clock, swore, and climbed out of bed. Grabbing her dressing gown, she pulled it on and opened the front door.

Adam raised an eyebrow. 'Did I wake you?'

She tied the belt of her robe. 'No, I always wear this to work.' She moved away from the door and let him inside. She was furious with him. She knew exactly what she looked like when she'd just woken up and it was not a pretty sight. 'I'll get dressed,' she muttered, and disappeared back into the bedroom, closing the door behind her.

Adam walked into the kitchen, smiling to himself. She looked all pink and sleepy, he thought, as if she'd just had sex, although he was quite sure she hadn't. He put the kettle on for coffee and sat down to wait.

Megan was the next one to appear. She came out of the spare room fully dressed, carrying the cat. She was still walking carefully, but she looked a lot better than she had when he had seen her at the hospital. 'I heard you come in. Gina won't be happy if you woke her up.'

Adam grinned. 'Tough. It's moving day for you, girl. I thought I'd come and give you a hand.'

The cat howled, a sound similar to an ambulance siren starting up. Megan put the animal down and Blossom walked into the kitchen, sniffing her empty bowl. By the time the cat had been fed and the coffee made, Gina had reappeared from the bedroom.

'Toast,' she said. 'If you want breakfast, that's all I've got.'

Adam held out a bag. 'I brought doughnuts. Jam, with sugar on.'

'It wasn't even seven o'clock when you woke me,' she told him crossly. 'My alarm doesn't go off till half past.'

Adam raised an eyebrow. 'So?'

'So it was too bloody early to come calling.'

He passed her the bag. 'Have a doughnut. Sugar calms the nerves.'

For some reason he seemed to enjoy taunting her. He was watching her, sugar on his top lip, and for one unguarded moment she wondered what it would be like to lick it off. She took a sip of coffee and burnt her tongue. 'I'll help Megan pack.'

Adam offered to take Megan to the house while Gina opened up the studio. She was going to miss Megan, even though she was looking forward to having the place to herself again.

She found a cardboard box for the cat, who wailed in protest, but eventually everything was loaded into Adam's car. Gina wandered back into the studio, wondering why she felt so desolate. She found it difficult to settle down to work. She was just thinking of popping out for a sandwich when she had an unexpected telephone call.

'My wife tells me you are an artist, Miss Cross,' Robert Cauldwell said, 'and I need a portrait of myself for my office at Portcullis House. Terribly narcissistic, I know, but the done thing, evidently. Perhaps we could arrange a sitting. I'll pay any expenses, of course, on top of your fee, and if the picture is good I can recommend you to my associates.'

Once she had got over the initial shock, she nearly made the excuse that she was too busy, which was more or less true, but she wanted to meet Cauldwell. She had seen him on television and remembered thinking at the time he would probably make a good prime minister, but that was before she found out he had been involved with a fifteen-year-old girl. Even now, she couldn't quite believe he had anything to do with the death of the

Asian child. She needed to meet him so she could make her own judgement.

'When would you like me to call, Mr Cauldwell?'

'Monday morning would be good for me. I don't have to be in the House until the afternoon. Is a morning session long enough for you?'

'For the preliminary sketches, yes.'

They agreed on a time and he hung up.

Adam arrived back at the studio an hour later. 'Megan's fine,' he said. 'She needn't pay any rent, only the fuel bills. I contacted Jack Lowry and he said he'll be glad to have someone in the place for a few weeks to keep it looking occupied.'

'Thanks,' Gina answered. She was working on a sketch of a large black dog, wondering if the owner really wanted that mean look in its eye. The dog was probably a sweetie but for some reason the animal's eyes told her different. 'It was good of you to think of Megan. She's had a rough time.'

'I wanted to put her somewhere safe, somewhere Gary can't find her.' He hesitated for a second. 'Look, Gina, I know you don't really like all this intrigue, so it would probably be better if you kept out of it altogether. If Judge Pollard is involved, it's too dangerous.'

She put down her pencil. 'I can't keep out of it. I promised Megan I'd find out what happened to the little girl, and Robert Cauldwell has asked me to paint his portrait.' She smiled at Adam. 'So, you see, I'm sort of in it right up to my neck. Probably past my neck.'

'Don't get cute with me, Gina,' he said impatiently. 'Jessica Fox died, we were shunted into a river, Andy Crabtree is in hospital, and Gary Marsh has gone missing. It's my job to investigate, not yours, and you're making things worse by interfering. God knows what Cauldwell is up to. Perhaps he's heard what you can do.'

'You mean my witchcraft is common knowledge?' She held up her hand when he frowned. 'I know, don't get cute with you. Is that journalese? OK, OK, but don't try and keep me out of this, Adam. I have to see Cauldwell. He'll think it really strange if I pass up this opportunity. Besides, I can't believe he has anything to do with Fox and the Hummer man. If Cauldwell is going to be the next prime minister, he's got to be squeaky clean.' Wishing she believed that, she asked, 'What happened to Jessica's house? Megan said it was broken into.'

'Yeah, ripped apart, more like. I'm not surprised the cat was frightened. They're still looking for something. They already took the videotape, so it isn't that.'

'I feel really bad about losing the video. It's probably the only video Fox had of his daughter, and I let someone steal it.'

'No point blaming yourself. As far as we know there wasn't anything important on the tape. You were right about the car outside the school, though. It was registered to one Jacob Pollard twenty-two years ago.'

Gina sighed. 'I can't see anyone stealing the tape just because Judge Pollard was sitting in a car outside the school. It doesn't make sense.' She looked down at her drawing. 'I've made this lovely Labrador look like a Rottweiler, so I think I'd better take a break. Probably get something to eat. Do you fancy a coffee?'

'Not yours. If you can lock up for half an hour, we'll go out.'

'What's wrong with my coffee? No, don't answer,' she said quickly, reaching for her keys.

Outside, the air was warm and humid, damp and sticky like a rainforest. The café was only a few doors down from the studio, small and often noisy with students from the university, but it did serve good coffee. Adam sat her at a table and went to the counter. He brought back two cappuccinos and a couple of croissants with butter and marmalade, and they sat in silence until they had finished eating.

Adam put his empty cup back in the saucer. 'That was a good cup of coffee.' He was silent for a moment and then looked at Gina speculatively. 'Any more messages from Nathan Fox? He said he was going to tell you what to do with the stuff from the house.'

'No. No more messages.' She finished her coffee and wiped the froth from her mouth with a serviette. Adam watched her.

'Fox will probably send you an email. Like he did last time.'

She stared at her empty cup for several seconds before she looked up. 'Then I won't have picked it up because my monitor's broken.' She knew he was cross with her but she refused to feel guilty because her monitor had been smashed. 'It's not a problem. I can use the computer in the studio to pick up any email messages.'

'But you haven't, have you? Fox could have sent you half a dozen messages by now, couldn't he?'

'I do work for a living, you know,' she snapped at him. 'With Megan off I've been really busy.'

'I'll come back with you and I'll check it myself.' He didn't wait for her to answer but stood up and headed for the door, throwing some money on the counter on the way out. He strode back to the studio, not bothering to check she was following. He waited while she unlocked the door, and then went straight to the computer on Megan's desk.

'How do I get into your emails?' He was sitting in Megan's chair, his fingers poised over the keyboard, waiting for her answer. When it didn't come, he looked up. 'Did you hear me?'

'Oh, yes,' she said. 'I heard you. There's absolutely nothing wrong with my hearing; I've just got out of the habit of obeying orders. Ever since Simon left I've been a bit slow off the mark when it comes to orders. Requests are OK, as long as the person asks nicely, but orders . . . ' She pursed her lips and shook her head. 'I just don't do them any more.'

Adam leant back in the chair and folded his hands in his lap. 'Sorry. Maybe I was a bit short, but Fox is the only contact we have.'

'I know, but the message, if there is one, is on *my* computer, in *my* studio.' She was trying to keep her voice steady. 'So would you just fuck off, please, and let me check my emails. I think I can manage that all by myself.'

'Gina . . . '

She shook her head, not looking at him. 'Just go, Adam. If I get another message from Fox, I'll let you know.'

Adam stood up, wishing he could turn the clock back a few seconds. Her hair was a mass of damp curls and her legs were brown and slender beneath her short cotton skirt. Very sexy. But her fists were clenched at her sides and he knew she was ready to fly at him if he said another word so, for the time being, disappearing seemed a better option. He let himself out and walked to his car, wincing as the studio door slammed behind him.

There were no new messages, Gina saw with relief, so Adam had been getting himself all worked up about nothing. Maybe she should have thought about checking her email but she wouldn't let anyone dictate to her, particularly a man. If she had been six feet tall and built like Grace Jones, perhaps Adam wouldn't be so quick to boss her about. As there were no messages, she hoped Fox was safe somewhere. His disguise was good, so he should be OK, unless someone was following her when she met him at the pond. She wished she didn't have this prickle at the back of her neck all the time, as if someone was watching her.

She went to the window of the studio and looked out. Several cars were parked outside but they all looked empty. It would be easier if she knew who she was looking for, just who the enemy actually was. The Hummer man wasn't likely to park his big car right outside her studio again. The Hummer was just a killing machine, too conspicuous to be used for surveillance. She moved away from the window, wishing she hadn't sent Adam away quite so quickly. After a minute, she went back to her drawing of the dog.

The weekend passed slowly. On Saturday she took several orders for sketches of children and animals, and one for a large watercolour of a lady in her traffic warden uniform. Some people are very strange, she thought. On Sunday she helped Megan finish unpacking. The house had been lived in by a man and needed a few feminine touches to make it more like home, so she took flowers, and Megan hung a couple of pictures. Blossom liked having the run of a garden, but didn't stray far from the back door.

Gina felt restless. She was meeting Robert Cauldwell the next day and although she didn't really believe she was in any danger, not from a Member of Parliament, something deep inside her kept telling her not to go.

She slept badly and woke with a headache.

18

She stopped outside Cauldwell's house, staring at it curiously. So this was where an up-and-coming politician lived. The houses were large, double-fronted and identical, all set in a little cul-de-sac round a circle of neatly trimmed grass. An attempt at individuality was evident in the landscaped front gardens, complete with tubs and water features.

There was only one car in the drive of Cauldwell's house, a three-year-old Mercedes, so she drove in through the wrought-iron gates and parked behind it, hoping the spider-web design on the gates wasn't symbolic.

Cauldwell opened the front door himself. She watched him look her up and down, and then gave him her best smile. She knew he would be far less charismatic in ten years' time — muscle would have turned to fat and he would be going bald — but standing in the doorway he was more or less what she had expected.

She had seen pictures of him, but in the flesh Cauldwell had a magnetism the media couldn't capture. She could imagine him in the House. If Cauldwell spoke, people would listen. He was of medium height, pleasant-looking, with a dimple in one cheek when he smiled and a smooth, confident manner. Perfect prime minister material. Why then, she wondered, did he remind her of that big, kind-looking dog with the vicious spark in its eyes?

The floors inside the house were polished oak strip dotted with rugs. She could see an open-plan living area with a conservatory tacked on the back, and a large kitchen with double glass doors, all nicely furnished but impersonal, like a show home. Cindy Cauldwell was either a very meticulous housewife or she employed a very good maid.

'Where would you like to set up your equipment?' Cauldwell asked.

'The conservatory would be just fine.' She gave him her best smile. 'Then if I drop paint on the tiles, it won't matter.' She opened the bag she carried and took out her easel and collapsible stool. She asked Cauldwell to sit in a cane chair with a view of the garden behind him. 'I can use the greenery behind you as a background,' she told him.

'Whatever you like, Miss Cross.'

God, did he have to be so polite? On first sight she didn't particularly like the man, but she couldn't fault his manners. She told him it was OK to talk, but to keep as still as possible for the first few minutes. She took several digital photos so she could finish the picture in her studio if necessary. He looked bored already, but that didn't surprise her. She had a feeling he wasn't really interested in having his portrait painted, and was curious to see when he would tell her the real reason he had summoned her to his house.

'You work for the police, I believe, Miss Cross,' he said, after a short silence. Silence always seemed to make her clients nervous and she wondered why some people felt compelled to fill holes in a conversation. At least her dead bodies didn't answer back.

'Call me Gina,' she told him absently. Getting the right look in the eyes was going to be difficult. There was something hidden in the depths, beneath the slate-grey iris, something she couldn't quite fathom. With a few deft strokes she got the outline of his face down on the paper. 'Yes, I work for the police on a freelance basis.'

'As a forensic artist, I believe. Do you do this aging thing, where you make people look older?'

'Age progression? Sometimes. If a person has been missing for some years it can help to have an idea of what they might look like at the present time. Nowadays it's all done on a computer.'

He was silent, just looking at her. After a moment he said, 'But you're special, aren't you, Gina? You don't need a computer.'

She wished she hadn't told him to call her by her first name, it was beginning to annoy her. 'I think you've been misinformed, Mr Cauldwell. I'm an artist, not a psychic, whatever the newspapers may say. I can do skeletal reconstruction and some age progression, that's all.'

Cauldwell lay back in his chair and stretched his legs out in front of him, a picture of relaxed confidence. 'My wife attends the same ante-natal class as your studio assistant, and I believe we have a mutual acquaintance. A young girl who was killed in a car accident recently.'

'Jessica Fox,' Gina said, looking straight at Cauldwell. 'Her father was the caretaker at Fletford College, where you went to school.' She knew she would never get the man's eyes right. Whatever was in there wasn't still for a second. It could never be captured on paper because it was always moving, trying to hide — a tiny spark of evil.

'But you went to her funeral — and to her house, I believe.'

'I had permission to go to her house,' Gina

lied. How the hell did he know that? 'Jessica's aunt gave me a key.'

'I see.' This time the silence was longer. 'Then you intend returning the items you took.'

It was her turn to be shocked into silence. She felt appalled. How did he know she had taken anything from the house? Was he having her followed every minute of the day?

'If you mean the videotape, it was taken by a burglar who trashed my flat.'

'But the burglar didn't take everything, did he, Gina? If you give me the rest of the things you took, I'll return them to Jessica's family for you. That will save you a lot of trouble later on.'

Was he threatening her? 'I prefer to deal with things myself, Mr Cauldwell, but thank you for the offer.'

'You might regret that decision later, but I'm sure you know best.' His smile stopped a long way from his eyes. 'Have you met Jessica's father, Nathan Fox?'

'I was under the impression Nathan Fox was dead,' Gina said carefully. She was going to have to watch every word from now on.

'No, he's not dead. He left the country for a while, but now he's back in England. Nathan Fox is living in a shelter for the homeless in Castlebury, a place for people unable to take care of themselves. He'll look completely different now, twenty years on, but you'd recognize him, wouldn't you, Gina?'

She tried to look suitably confused. 'I can only predict what a person *might* look like in the future, Mr Cauldwell, not what they will look like.'

Cauldwell smiled. 'So if I gave you a photograph of Nathan Fox taken twenty years ago, you could draw him the way he *might* look now, is that correct?'

She took a deep breath. If he'd seen her sketch of Fox, he was involved in the burglary — and he was very clever. He'd used her own words against her. She stood up and folded her stool. 'You don't really want a painting, do you, Mr Cauldwell?'

'On the contrary. I'm looking forward to hanging it on the wall of my office. Why else would I have asked you here?' He smiled, but the dimple didn't show this time. 'Nathan Fox is a dangerous man. He's a thief and a blackmailer. He took something that didn't belong to him, and your help in getting that item back would be worth a lot more than the cost of a painting. In fact, I would say you could almost name your price, Gina.'

'You may be surprised to hear this, Mr Cauldwell, but you couldn't possibly afford my price, so if you'll excuse me, I'll be getting home.'

She tried to hide the quiver in her voice, hoping he couldn't see her knees shaking. The pencils rattled as she put them back in the box. Where was Cindy? Had he sent his wife out so he could have the house to himself? Would anyone hear if she screamed?

Don't go there, she told herself, just walk out and he can't stop you — but she knew very well he could. She packed her stuff away in her bag and started for the door. Don't run, she told herself, just walk. She had almost reached the safety of the hall when he spoke.

'Just one moment, Miss Cross.'

He had one of those voices you obeyed. No wonder his wife did as she was told. She stopped in her tracks, and he came up behind her very quietly, putting his hands on her shoulders, keeping her turned away from him. She knew he must be able to feel her body trembling. He bent down so his mouth was only a few inches from her ear.

'You're playing a dangerous game, Gina. More people are going to get hurt and you'll only have yourself to blame. You're not as clever as you think you are.'

She still didn't run, not even when he turned round and went back into the conservatory, which was probably a good thing because her legs weren't working too well. She made it to her car and threw her stuff in the boot, driving out of the gates so fast she kicked up a shower of shingle.

When she got back, she didn't go straight into the studio, she parked where Megan couldn't see her car and went up to her flat. She needed a while to herself, somewhere to give her time to stop shaking. She found a bottle of Shiraz and poured herself a generous glass, sipping it slowly, which took a great deal of willpower under the circumstances. Cauldwell had been trying to frighten her when he told her she was responsible for people getting hurt, she knew that, but she also knew it was true. The butterfly effect. The more you tried to put things right, the worse they got.

She thought of phoning Inspector Reagan, but what could she tell him? That the local MP had offered her a large sum of money to identify a tramp? That sounded really threatening. But she had to speak to someone. She took a deep breath, picked up the phone, and dialled.

He answered straightaway. 'Shaw.'

Why did he always answer the phone like a bloody sergeant major? She had to take another breath before she could speak. 'It's

Gina.' Silence. 'Look, I need to speak to you. I've been to Robert Cauldwell's house and he told me where Nathan Fox is staying. Maybe we should go and talk to Fox. He's obviously in danger.'

'We?'

Oh, God, why was he being so awkward? 'Adam, I can't do this on my own.'

'Strange. The last thing I remember was being told to fuck off. I was under the impression you wanted to do everything on your own.'

She sighed. 'OK. Sorry. I just don't like being pushed around.'

'By me in particular? Is it a height thing? Perhaps you feel inferior to tall men.'

'I don't feel inferior to anyone.' She was not going to let him provoke her; this was too important. 'Robert Cauldwell wants my help. He said I could name my price.'

'And?'

'I told him he couldn't afford me. What did you think I was going to say?'

'Not some dialogue out of a bad film. It might have been more sensible to go along with him for the time being. If you're the only thing that stands between him and whatever he's looking for, he'll come after you again.' It was his turn to sigh. 'I'll be over in about ten minutes.'

Gina put the phone back in its stand and looked at her watch. Megan could hold the fort a bit longer. She wouldn't be expecting Gina back yet anyway, a first sitting often took a while. Against her better judgement, Gina tidied her hair and put on a bit of lipstick. She didn't feel hungry but she stuck a couple of beers in the fridge.

'You're late,' she told Adam when he arrived twenty minutes after her phone call.

'Traffic.' He looked at her with concern. 'Are you all right?'

Did she look that bad? So much for the lipstick. 'Cauldwell just rattled me a bit. He's not a very nice man. God help the country if he ever becomes prime minister.'

'Actually,' Adam said, 'he'd probably be very good at it. No scruples at all. He'll just get the job done and mow down anything that gets in his way.'

'The 'anything' being me.'

'Exactly, so let me do this on my own, like I wanted to in the first place.'

Gina ignored him. 'According to Cauldwell, Fox is a thief and a blackmailer living in a homeless shelter in the town, but Cauldwell doesn't know what Fox looks like after all this time, and I do. Besides, you can't do anything on your own, because you need me to identify Fox, same as Cauldwell does.'

'Ah — yes. Well, in that case, let's put our heads together and work out a plan. A safe plan.' Adam knew there wasn't a safe plan, but Gina would be safer with him than on her own.

'Beer?' She held up two bottles. Beer on top of wine probably wasn't a good idea, but what the heck. 'We have about half an hour and then I have to get back to work. I don't want to leave Megan on her own too long.'

'Right. Let's go over what we've got. We know where Fox is, because Cauldwell just told you, and we know Cauldwell can't identify Fox, but you can. We know Fox took something from Cauldwell and probably used it to blackmail him, and we know he thinks you're hiding it somewhere. Cauldwell is dangerous, but Fox may be even more dangerous. He might even be the one responsible for the death of the little girl.'

'I don't think so. That's why we have to talk to him. Besides, I liked him better than Robert Cauldwell.'

Adam ran a hand through his hair, making it stand on end. 'Do you know which shelter Cauldwell was talking about?'

'There is only one. The Refuge of St Agnes.'

Adam thought for a minute. 'Suppose I make an appointment to see someone at the shelter about an article, fundraising or something. You come along as my assistant and point out Fox. Then we'll have to play it as it comes.'

'We still don't know who the Hummer man is working for, or what they were looking for in my flat. I haven't seen the car outside again but I have a feeling someone is watching me all the time. Cauldwell knew exactly where I'd been and what I took from the house. I bet he knows you've come here today.'

'Don't worry about it. I parked my car right underneath your window, so anyone watching will think we're having an affair.' He paused, and Gina felt her skin prickle. The silence lasted a little too long.

'Technically, it's only an affair if one of us is married,' she said at last, 'and I'm not.'

Adam laughed. 'What a clever way to find out if I'm married. No, I'm not either. Not any more.'

Gina felt herself getting hot. 'I didn't mean it to sound like that. I'm really not the least bit interested in your marital status.'

She finished her beer and walked into the kitchen to drop the bottle in the bin. He followed her, and his hands didn't feel a bit like Cauldwell's when he rested them on her shoulders. 'You're a liar, Gina Cross.' He turned her round and kissed her, and she let him, then she kissed him back. She was going to regret this tomorrow, but not today. They moved in unison to the bedroom.

'How long have we got?' Adam asked, as he pulled her blouse over her head.

Gina was struggling to undo his belt. 'Depends how long you take.' Neither of them spoke much after that.

It had been so long, Gina wondered fleetingly if she had forgotten what you had to do. She needn't have worried; Adam was true to form and took complete control. Gina had never experienced anything quite like this before. Simon had bragged he was good in bed, but Adam was bloody marvellous. She tried to tell herself it was just because she had been without sex for so long, but that wasn't strictly true. Adam knew exactly which button to push — exactly where, and exactly when. There was a point when she thought she was going to die.

'Sorry,' he murmured, his mouth against her neck. 'That was a bit rushed. Now we can take our time.'

Gina was about to protest. This was the middle of the day and she had work to do, but a few seconds later she wasn't thinking about that — she wasn't thinking at all. She still wasn't thinking a bit later, as they lay naked on her double bed. She felt deliciously used, as floppy as a rag doll, warm and loved. The doubts hadn't yet begun to creep in. Adam sat up and bent to kiss her stomach. His lips lingered and she smiled as she watched the involuntary reaction of his body.

'You have to stop me when I do something like that,' he told her. 'Otherwise, we shall be here all day and Megan will come looking for us.'

Gina sat up. 'My God! Megan! What's the time?'

'Don't worry.' He grinned at her. 'Just tell her we had a leisurely lunch.'

He stood up and stretched, and Gina wanted to launch herself at him again. The jagged line of an old scar ran from his navel to his hipbone, but that was just an added attraction. Gina already knew that scar intimately. She knew what it felt like beneath her fingers, and what it did to him if she ran the tip of her tongue along it.

Make the most of this while it lasts, she told herself.

'I'll arrange an appointment with the people at the shelter,' he said as he left. 'Ring me if you need me.'

Which will probably be two seconds from now, she thought. She took a quick shower and opened another bottle of beer as she dressed. Probably better to be an alcoholic than a nymphomaniac, she decided.

She thought she looked fairly normal as she let herself into the studio, but the slow smile that spread over Megan's face told her otherwise.

'He parked his car right outside the window,' Megan said. 'He's no use as a secret lover. He doesn't know the rules.'

'Who said anything about a lover, secret or otherwise?'

Megan raised an eyebrow. 'Well, you've obviously been shagging someone. Besides, I could hear you.' She laughed at the look on Gina's face. 'Only kidding, but you've given the game away now.'

'I hate you,' Gina said. 'You know me too well.'

'I'm pleased for you. He's nice. How did the sitting with our future prime minister go?'

Gina hesitated. Would putting Megan in the picture make her more, or less, safe? There was no good answer, so Gina told Megan about Cauldwell.

'I know you can keep your mouth shut, Megan,' Gina said. 'But if one word gets out, he'll sue us, or worse, and we still haven't got any proof. Cauldwell can't afford one bad thing against him at the moment; that's why he's so frantic to find Fox.' She paused. 'If Cauldwell is having either of us followed, he probably knows where you've moved to. Better than Gary knowing, though, I suppose.'

'Yeah,' Megan said. 'Thanks. Perhaps I'd better move in with Fox. That'd be safer.' She let out her breath in a little whoosh. 'Fox and hounds,' she said. 'And the fox always loses.'

'Sometimes the fox gets away.'

'But it never wins, does it?'

19

Gina got an unexpected visit from Inspector Reagan the next day. A cold case, he told her. A woman had been murdered fifteen years ago and the son had been the prime suspect, but he managed to leave the country. Now DNA evidence had been found to prove he was the killer. He had only been sixteen at the time of the murder, and would look very different fifteen years on. Reagan knew Gina would give him a better picture than the computer programme, so he'd brought a photo of the boy to the studio.

'Andy Crabtree is conscious and out of danger,' he told her while she was working on the sketch. 'He said he wants to see you.'

Gina felt the burden of guilt lighten slightly. 'I'm really glad. Does he know who hit him?'

'He described the car, a big black four-track with a chrome bull bar on the front. The car was seen in the area by several witnesses. We got a partial reg on it, but the ground was too hard for tyre tracks.'

The Hummer man again. He probably changed his number plates as often as he changed his appearance. She finished her sketch of the wanted man and handed it to Reagan. 'The man you're looking for might have had plastic surgery. If so, I can't tell unless I see him. Catch him and bring him in, and I'll ID him for you.'

'Thanks. We need to know we've got the right man.'

'What do you know about Robert Cauldwell?' she asked casually as Reagan was about to leave. 'He asked me to do a portrait of him for Portcullis House.'

Reagan looked at her curiously. 'Did he now? From what I've heard our local politician is clever, a good liar, and completely ruthless. He's got all the right qualities to make it to Downing Street.'

Nothing she didn't know already, Gina thought, as she saw the inspector out. She had too much work to catch up on to go to see Andy straightaway, but as soon as she'd locked up she grabbed her car keys and took off for the hospital.

'Hi, Gina, who have you come to see this time?' asked the receptionist.

'Andy Crabtree.'

'Oh, right. He's been moved from ICU.'

She followed directions and found the ward. Andy had lost a lot of weight and Gina hardly recognized him. His face was a mess of scar tissue and all she could remember was his youthful swagger and the gold in his hair. Now he was propped up in bed looking small and sick.

Gina sat in the chair beside his bed. 'Hi, Andy.'

He managed a smile for her. 'I'm glad you came. I've lost a few pounds — and a few weeks somewhere — but I'm still alive.'

'Thank goodness for that. I was feeling really guilty for not listening to you when you phoned.'

Andy reached for her hand and smiled apologetically when the IV wouldn't let him. 'No, it's me that should feel guilty. I lied to you. A man gave me money to get you to meet him at the HiLo. I didn't want to phone you in case you asked a lot of questions I couldn't answer, so I got Gary Marsh to give you a message and I split the money with him.'

'What did the man look like?'

'Big bloke, shaved head, earring, looked like a bouncer.'

'You told me you'd been asking questions and found out something weird.'

'Somebody told me the bouncer guy is some sort of hit man. I couldn't work out why someone like that would want to meet a nice lady like you.' He smiled painfully. 'So I asked around but no one seemed to know anything, or if they did they wouldn't tell me.'

Gina sighed. Asking all those questions had put Andy in hospital. 'Did you see the car that hit you?'

Andy shook his head and winced. 'No chance. It came up on the path and got me from behind. Police said it was just one of those things, being in the wrong place at the wrong time. Guy must have been drunk or zoned out.'

She squeezed his hand. 'Take care of yourself, Andy.'

She backed out of her parking space and drove slowly round the car park until she was back where she started. A car pulled out behind her and she waited just outside the exit, letting it go ahead of her. Paranoia, or just being careful? She no longer knew. She wanted to phone Adam and hated herself for that as well. Her grandmother had repeatedly told her it's a weak woman that needs a man. It took four chapters of a book, three glasses of wine and two aspirin before she finally fell asleep.

Adam phoned her at eight o'clock the next morning. 'We've got an appointment at the shelter at 4.30 today. Can you make it?'

Brief and to the point, as usual. 'I think so. Yes.'

'Good. I'll pick you up. Look efficient but not too smart. I'm freelance, remember. I can't afford a posh assistant.'

Sex had obviously been a spur-of-the-moment thing. Not important. Fine, if that was the way he wanted it. Then why, she asked herself, was she feeling so annoyed?

He parked outside the studio at a quarter to four and hooted. She waved out of the shop window to tell him to shut up. She was wearing her trusty black skirt with a blue blouse, and sandals with low heels. Too smart was not going to be a problem. As she buckled her seatbelt, he dropped a notebook and pencil on her lap. 'You take notes, I'll carry the camera. If I can get a photo or two of Fox it might come in handy.'

When they stopped outside the shelter, he put a hand on her knee. 'Just keep with me and don't go wandering off on your own. I need you in one piece.'

Was there anything significant in the word 'need'? She doubted it. She picked up her pad and pencil and followed him inside.

The staff were helpful and charming and everyone wanted to be a film star. An old man posed in front of the camera, showing rotting teeth in a big smile; a teenager pulled his hoody over his head and gave them the finger; and one of the helpers brought them both a cup of tea. The rooms had too many beds and not enough blankets, the floors were stained with God knew what, and the air was heavy with hopelessness; but the kitchen was spotless, the rooms clean and bright, and the volunteer staff the stuff angels were made of.

Gina took notes and Adam took photos. There was no sign of Nathan Fox.

'Would you like to see the garden?' one of the women asked. 'We only opened this place last year, so we've done really well, considering.'

The garden was a small courtyard filled with an assortment of chairs and small tables. A young man sat on a bench, his hand shaking as he tried to light a cigarette. He eyed Gina and Adam warily. Another man sat bolt upright on a white plastic garden chair, his chin on his chest, sound asleep and snoring noisily. A couple of ancient-looking men sat at a table playing cards. Neither of them looked up but Gina recognized Fox immediately.

Now what? There was no way they were going to get Fox on his own, not out here. She couldn't read the expression on his face behind all that growth of beard. He must be wondering what on earth she was doing at the shelter, probably thinking she was trying to get him killed. She turned her back on him and wrote in her pad, tearing out half the page and folding it to the size of a ten-pence piece, then she wrote on the next page and walked over to Adam, who was telling the woman how much he admired a dusty rose bush in a tub. Gina handed him her notebook.

'Is that the sort of text you want to go with your pictures?'

DISTRACT HER, she had written.

Adam looked up, and Gina gave an almost imperceptible nod of her head towards the two men. He handed the notebook back to her. 'Yes, that's about right. We're nearly finished here, I think.' He turned to the woman. 'Can we have a last shot of you here in the garden? How about with the two old gentlemen in the background. I'm sure they won't mind.'

While Adam posed the woman, Gina dropped the folded paper on the table. Fox whisked it out of sight while the other man was still staring at his hand of cards. They left with promises that the photos would appear in the local paper, and that there would be a forthcoming donation from a charity organization.

'I'll make sure all that actually happens,' Adam said as they drove away. 'Those women are saints.' He glanced at Gina. 'I thought you wanted to talk to the man. What did you do? Give him a note?'

She nodded. 'I just said 'he knows where you are'. I didn't have time to write anything else, and I didn't want to mention any names, or draw attention to him.'

'So much for asking Fox any questions.' He pulled up outside the studio. 'Listen, about the other day . . . '

'Forget it,' Gina said lightly while her pulse rate climbed alarmingly. She got out of the car. 'I don't believe in post mortems.'

'No,' he said. 'No, you're quite right.' He turned in his seat and looked straight into her eyes. She watched a slow smile spread across his face. 'Till next time, then.' He was still grinning as he drove away.

Till next time? What the hell did that mean? Did he think he was just going to pop round for a quickie whenever he felt like it? If so, he could think again. Why on earth had she let it happen in the first place? She really ought to have learnt her lesson by now. She ran up the outside stairs into her flat, kicked off her shoes and grabbed a beer out of the fridge. The trouble was, she realized, sex is a bit like smoking — you can go without for years but one lapse starts the craving off all over again.

She looked at her watch. Megan would

have locked up and gone home, so no point in going down to the studio. She walked restlessly round the flat, the beer bottle in her hand. What if Adam had asked to come upstairs, would she have let him? Of course she would! She didn't have any control over her damn body.

Mission accomplished, though. She had got a message to Fox and now it was up to him. Blackmailing Robert Cauldwell would be a very dangerous game. Twenty years ago Cauldwell had been young and inexperienced, now he was a powerful man who wouldn't let anything get in the way of his path to Downing Street. Certainly not someone like Nathan Fox.

Gina slept badly that night. She dreamed of Simon. He made her crawl on the floor and pick up thousands of tiny beads, one by one. By six o'clock she knew she wouldn't sleep again, so she changed into shorts and a tank top and went for a run.

The mist was back on the river and her hair had corkscrewed into a tangled mess by the time she got back to the flat. It took some time to shower, sort her hair out and grab a bowl of cereal, but it was still only eight o'clock when she opened up the studio. Megan wasn't due in until 8.30, so Gina got on with a sketch she was finishing and answered several telephone calls, then she began to get worried. Her watch told her it was five minutes to nine and Megan wouldn't take a day off without calling in, however bad she was feeling.

Gina picked up the phone and dialled Megan's new home number. There was no answer. When she tried Megan's mobile there was no answer to that, either.

Déjà vu.

This time Gina didn't wait. She closed up the studio and drove round to Megan's house. Had Megan been more depressed than she let on? Surely not to the extent where she was suicidal. Or had Gary found her and left her so badly injured she couldn't answer the phone?

Gina didn't have a key to the new house. She tried shouting through the letterbox and looking through the downstairs window, but the curtains were pulled shut and she couldn't see anything. The front door was white PVC with a gold-coloured handle. When Gina tried the handle she found the door was unlocked. She walked straight into the front room, calling Megan's name, before making her way through to the kitchen and then upstairs. The house was empty.

She came back downstairs and stood in the

middle of the living-room, not knowing what to do next. She jumped when something rubbed against her legs, quite forgetting Blossom would be around. The cat gave a little mew and started to lick its foot, and it was then that Gina noticed the cat's footprints on the cream rug. She bent down. Were the brown stains blood? She stroked the cat, gently lifting her paw, and saw a raw wound on the pad as if a claw had been ripped out. 'You poor thing,' she said. The injury looked clean so there wasn't much she could do to help.

If Megan had gone to pick up some medication from the local vet, she would have phoned to explain, and she would have locked the front door behind her. Now Gina had stopped to look around, she was beginning to notice things. The rug was not only bloody but also folded over at one corner. A table lamp was on its side, and there was a splatter of blood on the wall, too high for the cat. There must be lots of explanations, she told herself, feeling her chest tighten. The cat might have got its claw caught in the rug and panicked, knocking over the lamp and splattering the blood on the wall. That was one explanation, anyway.

She tried Megan's mobile again, hearing

the phone playing some stupid pop tune instead of a proper ringing tone, and then realized the sound was coming from upstairs. If the phone was fully charged, why hadn't Megan taken it with her?

Blossom was screeching, limping in and out of the kitchen, staring pointedly at the empty food bowl. As Gina filled the cat's dish and topped up the water bowl, she noticed a bunch of keys on the work surface. Something wasn't right. Even if Megan had just popped out, she would have locked the door and taken her keys. It was very tempting to phone Adam, but Gina remembered his confident grin as he'd driven away. Besides, there was probably nothing to worry about. She could hardly call Reagan and report Megan missing, not when the girl was only an hour late for work. It would be best to go back to the studio first, just in case they had missed one another and Megan was safely at work.

★ ★ ★

Megan wasn't at work, but the message light was flashing on the telephone. Gina grabbed the phone and punched the message button. The voice was muffled but the meaning was perfectly clear. 'We *both have something that doesn't belong to us. Perhaps we can swap.'*

Cauldwell had told her she wasn't as clever as she thought she was. Now he was proving his point.

20

The evening before Blossom lost her claw, Megan had locked up the studio at 5.30 and walked home. She hadn't expected Gina back before locking-up time and as she walked the short distance to the house she was thinking it was about time Gina got herself a new boyfriend. Adam was nice, but it would take more than nice to get Gina involved. Gina was looking for perfect.

Megan really liked Adam. He had listened to her Essex accent, which is not the prettiest in the world, and looked at her piercings and tattoos, and still trusted her with a house that belonged to his friend. She loved him for that.

Blossom met her just inside the front door with an ear-splitting screech of welcome and, once again, she silently thanked Adam. The demands of the Siamese had forced her out of her depression far quicker than any counselling. She scratched the cat's ears and went into the tiny kitchen to find food for both of them. The house might be small but it was better than her council flat. The furniture was typical male, sparse but comfortable.

Whether the house was any safer was another thing. She still blamed herself for what had happened. She should have left Gary ages ago, and if she hadn't been so damn big and ungainly when he attacked her, she would probably have managed to dodge his kicks.

Sometime during the night Megan woke to a noise that ended before she was properly awake, the sound just a memory in her head, an echo of something already gone. She sat up, reaching for the soft body of Blossom, usually beside her. The cat was no longer there.

Again, a slight sound. Definitely somewhere in the house.

Megan kept her bedroom door open during the night so Blossom could get to her litter tray, but this was the first time the cat had left the bed in the middle of the night. Perhaps it was the cat she could hear downstairs. Worrying that Blossom might be ill, she got out of bed and reached for her dressing gown. Still not completely healed, her body protested when she moved suddenly.

The next sound was a banshee wail. Megan was halfway down the stairs when she heard the cat hiss and spit at something, then Blossom gave a screech of anger or pain that rose in volume to a howl. It sounded like a one-sided catfight. The silence that followed frightened Megan more than the noise. She ran the rest of the way down the stairs and was in the living-room, about to turn on the light, when a hand closed over her nose and mouth. She struggled for breath as her arm was twisted up behind her back. When she was pushed hard against the wall, her first thought was Gary — until the light went on.

The person holding her was someone she had never seen before.

She opened her mouth to scream and he punched her in the stomach. It was only a light punch, but the pain was so intense she thought she was going to faint. Her knees buckled and she grabbed the coffee table for support, knocking over the lamp. She stared at the man in pain and confusion. He was big, with a shaved head and a ring through his left ear. A deep scratch, still bleeding, ran from just under his eye to his chin, and his shirt was torn on the shoulder.

'This can be easy, or very, very hard. It's up to you.'

Megan looked for Blossom. 'Where's my cat?'

'Dead, I hope.' The man ran a hand across his face, wincing. 'Fucking thing attacked me. Nearly had my eye out.'

Megan clutched her dressing gown round

her, hoping Blossom was hiding somewhere. The pain in her stomach was easing. 'Can I get dressed?'

He shook his head. 'It's a nice night. You'll be warm enough.'

Megan was used to violence, but the violence she knew usually stemmed from anger. This was something else. The man looked at her with a cold detachment that was much more frightening.

She was naked beneath the terry-towelling robe, but he showed no interest as he stuck a piece of tape over her mouth and tied her hands together. She wished she could fight, but she was still too weak from her operation, and she knew if he punched her in the stomach again she might die.

The man checked outside to make sure there was no one about and then led her to his car. At last she was getting a look at the notorious Hummer. It was parked by the kerb, a big black brute, the engine still running. The street was deserted, with hardly any house lights on, everyone tucked up in bed. If this was the Hummer man, Gina had been right about him changing his appearance. Without the hairpiece and the thick black eyebrows he looked completely different. He bundled Megan on to the back seat of the car and shut the door, then he got in the front, put the child locks on and pulled away from the kerb. For a big car the engine was surprisingly quiet.

Was he taking her to the same place they had taken Gary? Were they going to torture her or beat her up? She hadn't any idea what they wanted. If they wanted information, she didn't have any, but she'd make something up, anything to stop them hurting her. She remembered what Gary had looked like.

She was lying face down on the back seat, the seatbelt holding her down, the smell of leather almost overpowering. With her hands tied behind her it was impossible to reach the belt release and when she eventually managed to turn over and then sit up, they were already pulling into an area of old buildings that looked like derelict warehouses. There were no lights on anywhere but she could see a reflection of hazy moonlight on the surface of water. It sucked and gurgled noisily and smelt of the sea.

Megan tried to work out how long they'd been driving. Not more than half an hour, probably less. She hadn't checked her bedside clock before she went downstairs, and she wasn't wearing a watch. It could be near midnight or near dawn. The buildings were too small and run down to be one of the major docks, so she was probably at one of the waterside villages just outside the town. She didn't recognize the immediate landscape or the lights on the other side of the water. She could be anywhere.

The Hummer man unclipped the seatbelt and pulled her out of the car. It was a long way to the ground and she tripped over her dressing gown and almost fell. He tightened his grip. 'Keep on your fucking feet, bitch. You're too heavy to carry.'

He dragged her towards one of the buildings, pushed open the door, and turned on the light. A single bulb hung from a corrugated iron roof, not enough to illuminate the corners of the large room. Old oil cans, rotting cardboard boxes and folded tarpaulins littered the floor. The door was hanging off its hinges and escape would have been easy, but he tied her to a chair. First her ankles, one to each of the front chair legs, then he untied her hands and retied them at her sides, the rope passing under the seat of the chair.

She wanted to fight him, to punch, kick and scream, but it would have done no good, just got her another punch in the stomach. She tried to get more comfortable by shifting her bottom on the chair, but with her hands secured the way they were it was impossible to move at all. The tape over her mouth was making her feel sick. What if her nose got blocked? She almost panicked at the thought, but a look at the man's face told her he didn't care whether she panicked or not, so she swallowed saliva and sat still.

He was about to leave but he turned back to look at her. 'If I come back and find you've been messing with the ropes, I'll have to kill you.' He turned the light off as he went out.

Megan felt sick again. If she threw up she'd die, the same thing if her nose got blocked. The tape over her mouth bothered Megan more than being tied up. She had to keep reminding herself to breathe through her nose. Her arms were fully extended so she couldn't get them any further under the seat, the knot tantalizingly just out of reach, even though she could feel the frayed ends with the tips of her fingers. She thought of rocking the chair. If she could tip herself over she might be able to get the rope out from under the legs, but if she rocked backwards too far she would crack the back of her head on the stone floor, leaving her unconscious or brain damaged. Knowing her luck, probably both.

It was beginning to get light, which was good, because Megan had heard little noises coming from the dark corners, the sound of things moving under the tarpaulins. Most likely rats. She remembered a film where rats had crawled all over a man who was tied up, and then started taking bites out of him.

The Hummer had gone; she'd heard it drive away. There were no other sounds, apart from the odd slap of water against the posts of the dock and the rustling in the dark corners of the room. Megan wiggled her feet to keep the circulation going, wishing she could move her arms, and glad she'd got up in the night to go to the loo. At least her bladder wasn't full. The main problem was trying not to think about what was going to happen next, and why they wanted her here. She didn't know anything. Was she just going to be left to die of hunger or thirst?

Her mouth was getting dry and swallowing was difficult. She tried to cough and found she couldn't. Panic made her heart race and the feel of the blood pounding in her veins panicked her even more. She suddenly felt hot, and sweat started to run down her face and between her breasts. She squirmed in the chair and nearly tipped it over, sure she was either going to faint or be sick. As the room started to fade around her, she dropped her head forward between her knees, feeling bile rise in her throat. In spite of the tape over her mouth, she managed to swallow, determined she wasn't going to choke on her own vomit. She had seen someone do that and it was a disgusting way to go. After a few seconds she felt better.

With her head down she could see the knotted rope under the chair. She bent further forward and found she could slide the rope down the legs of the chair and touch the floor with her hands. If she could get the rope out from under the front legs of the chair she could free herself. She sat up again. If she rocked the chair backwards she might knock herself out, but what if she fell sideways on to something softer than the concrete floor, like the folded tarpaulins on the other side of the room? She found she could move a few inches at a time if she gripped the sides of the seat with her hands and shuffled the chair along with her feet. Each movement hurt her stomach, but just doing something was making her feel better. If the man came back and found she'd moved, she was in trouble, but she wasn't going to think about that.

Falling sideways on to the tarpaulin took more courage than she had expected. What if she broke something, like her neck or her arm? She wedged the chair against the edge of the folded tarpaulin and leant sideways. The chair tipped over easily, but trapped her wrist under the edge it, making her cry out. She quickly rocked on to her back, but in that position she couldn't reach far enough to get her hands down to her feet. It was like trying to do sit-ups with your feet in the air.

Crying with pain and frustration, she rolled on to her front, her forehead pressed against the smelly tarpaulin, her bottom in the air, but that didn't work either. Back on her side, the other one this time, she found she could get the rope down to her feet. Thanking God the Hummer man hadn't given her time to put on shoes, she worked the rope over the legs of the chair and then her bare feet. With the rope no longer holding her down, she arched her back and slipped her feet free.

Her hands were still loosely joined together, but in front of her, so she managed to untie the rope and release them. The first thing she did was rip the tape from her mouth. Sitting on the floor, she pulled the remaining bits of rope from her ankles and stood up shakily. At first she felt so faint from the pain in her wrist and stomach she almost blacked out. She sat down again and put her head back between her knees. She needed to leave the place quickly, but if she fainted she wouldn't be going anywhere.

It was almost daylight outside, a thin mist lying on top of the water, the sun a dim curve of yellow light low on the horizon. A seagull swooped down and picked up something from the rotting boards of the dock, squawking as it flew away. Megan had no idea where she was. The sea mist was cold and she pulled the robe more closely round herself, knotting the tie belt at her waist. Behind her, a jumble of outbuildings huddled beside a wooden dock, completely derelict, doors hanging off, windows broken, roofs caved in. The road, such as it was, appeared to end at the buildings. Back the other way the road curved round a bend between mist-obscured fields with not a house in sight.

Once Megan started walking, she realized her bare feet weren't going to stand up to the gritty, unmade road. Besides, if the Hummer man came back, there was nowhere to hide — she couldn't cross the water to the houses on the other side or risk being caught in the middle of a field. Before she had time to think of a plan, she heard a car coming up the road towards her. As the road went nowhere, it had to be the Hummer man. She ran behind the nearest building and hid from sight.

21

Gina dialled Adam's number and his messaging service picked up. Why was he never around when she wanted him? She left a message. 'Someone's taken Megan. Where are you?'

What on earth did she expect him to do? Ride up on a white horse and save Megan from the baddies? Gina didn't even know who the baddies were. Robert Cauldwell might be responsible, but he hadn't kidnapped Megan himself. Someone else had taken Megan, and Gina had no idea what she was supposed to do to get her back. If she didn't have what they wanted, how was she supposed to do a swap? She didn't have the videotape and Cauldwell knew that, so what did he want?

Ten minutes later her phone rang. 'Gina? What the hell's going on? I've only just picked up your message.'

'You didn't answer your phone.'

'I was at the library,' Adam told her. 'I didn't have the phone switched on. Did you say somebody's kidnapped Megan?' He paused. 'Are you crying?'

Gina ran a hand angrily over her face. 'Just get here, will you?'

'I'll be with you in ten minutes.'

She hung up and went to see what was left to drink in the fridge. God, what a sad creature she was, crying down the phone. She opened the last bottle of Stella, not bothering with a glass, and the ice-cold liquid made her catch her breath. She hated feeling helpless, she wanted to go rushing out and find Megan, but she didn't know where to start. She finished her beer but didn't go looking for more. She wasn't going to drink herself stupid waiting for Adam to turn up, she was going to need a clear head. She was listening to the phone message again when he came charging in.

'You took your time,' she said.

Adam Shaw took a deep breath. If she'd seen the way he'd driven to get here, he thought, she might have been more impressed. He was lucky not to have been stopped by the police.

It took her several minutes to tell him everything that had happened. 'Robert Cauldwell didn't leave the message, but it didn't sound like the Hummer man either. The voice was fuzzy.'

Adam listened to the message and put the phone back in its cradle with a frown. 'It could be anyone. A cloth over the mouthpiece, probably. It may be a cliché, but it works.'

'I didn't know what to do next, that's why I phoned you. Megan hasn't been missing long enough for the police to take an interest and the message didn't sound like a threat, did it? There won't be any proof, there never is. Robert Cauldwell told me I was too clever for my own good. Now he's going to punish me by hurting Megan.'

'They won't hurt Megan. They need her to get to you.'

'You didn't see what they did to Andy Crabtree.'

Adam heard her voice catch. He grabbed her by the shoulders and turned her to face him. 'Stop it, Gina. Nothing bad is going to happen to Megan.'

She shrugged away from him. 'Perhaps I should do what he wants and give him the things I took from the house — the letters, the photos, everything — but they're not mine to give, are they? Jessica's father told me to keep everything safe for him. I don't know what to do. I have to get Megan back.'

'We'll get Megan back. We'll go and find her.' He watched her take a steadying breath. 'Can you remember anything Megan said about the place they held Gary? If they've got a safe hidey-hole, they'll probably use it again. A warehouse, she said, didn't she? Somewhere by water. It has to be somewhere not too far away, and with not many people around, so what does that leave?'

'About ten waterside villages within a fifteen-mile radius.'

'All with docks?'

She frowned. 'Why a dock? Gary didn't mention a dock.'

'That just means he didn't know he was at a dockside, but I bet he was. Most warehouses by water have some sort of a dock so boats can move stuff in and out. This one was obviously very quiet.'

'Not in use, then. An old dockyard in a quiet spot, so probably a village rather than a town.'

He smiled at her. 'We make a good team. Got anything to drink?'

She went on a wine hunt upstairs in her flat and came back with half a bottle of red. 'Are you driving? Because I've already had a beer.'

He poured her a generous glass and half a glass for himself. 'I'll drive. I haven't had any alcohol yet today — you caught me before lunch.'

'Sorry. So that leaves Addlestone and Fenston. Fenston's near the school, and the judge's house — I Googled him — so let's go there first.'

Adam leant forward and took Gina's hands in his. They were cold. For the first time he noticed her eyes were full of golden flecks, like the fire in a piece of amber. They looked coolly back into his. 'Please, Gina,' he begged her, 'let me do this on my own. I don't want to have to worry about you while I'm looking for Megan.'

'Then don't.' She had brought a jacket down from the flat and now she slipped her arms in the sleeves and picked up her bag. 'Are you ready?'

Fenston didn't have a dockyard, not any more. Where the wooden dock had been was a row of designer flats boasting the Barratt flag. A sign said they were all sold. Addlestone was more interesting. At the end of the village a wooden sign said 'Dock — one mile', but the road got progressively worse, eventually disappearing altogether. There were several old warehouse buildings by the water, all falling apart.

'Stop the car,' Gina said. 'She might be here somewhere.'

Adam didn't hold out much hope but he stopped the car as instructed. He put his hand on Gina's arm as she was about to get out. 'Look, I think we should park the car off the road and go on foot. If she is here, someone might be guarding her.' He parked the car behind some bushes and they started to search the buildings. They were all empty and in such a bad state of repair there was nowhere to imprison anyone. 'All the doors are missing or falling off. You couldn't keep anyone in any of these buildings — they'd just walk out.'

'Not if they were tied up.' Gina picked up a piece of rope near a pile of tarpaulins and held it out to him. 'This is new.' The small piece of bright rope still had kinks in it where it had been knotted.

'There might have been an animal tied up in here,' Adam said. 'We don't know it was Megan.'

'If it had been an animal, there would be droppings.'

'So now what? Even if she was here, she's not here now.'

'Look, there are marks on the floor as if something was moved.' Gina had the vision of a body being dragged across the room. 'I told you. Someone was here.'

Adam bent down to look at the floor. 'Brush marks,' he said. 'Someone's been sweeping up, making sure there are no footprints in the dirt.' He looked around with renewed interest. 'So, you're right. Someone was here. Recently, by the look of it.'

She twisted the rope in her hands. 'Where would they take her? Have they killed her, do you think?'

'They won't kill her, I keep telling you that. Think about it, Gina. As far as we know they haven't killed anyone yet except Jessica Fox, and she was an accident, she ran into a tree.'

Gina let him take her arm and lead her back to the car. There was nothing else they could do. Megan was gone. He started the engine and was just pulling away from the buildings when something ran in front of the car. Adam slammed his foot on the brake, glad he'd only had half a glass of wine.

Megan put her hands flat on the bonnet of the car and stared at them, white faced, through the windscreen. Her hair was a mess, her pink towelling dressing gown torn and studded with burrs, her bare feet bleeding, but she was so glad to see them she couldn't stop grinning.

'Quick, we have to go,' she told Adam anxiously as he helped her into the back of the car. 'He's been driving around looking for me, that's why I couldn't go any further. There's fields on each side of the road from here on; nowhere I could hide.'

'Who?' Gina asked, leaning over the back

of the seat as Adam pulled away. 'Who's looking for you, Megan? Who took you?'

'The Hummer man. He was furious when he found I'd gone. I could hear him swearing and banging about. He's not been back for a while. Probably gone to report.'

'We knew you were tied up,' Adam said. 'We found a bit of rope. How did you get away?'

Megan pulled a face. 'Don't ask. I'll tell you later. I would've hitched a lift if I could've, but nobody comes along this road so I started to walk. Those little stones don't half hurt. When I heard your car I hid, in case it was him coming back.' She took a breath. 'Then I thought you were going to drive off without me.'

'I nearly ran you over.' Adam looked in his rear-view mirror. The road behind them was deserted, no one following. 'We'll take you straight to hospital and get you checked over.'

'I'll be all right. My mouth is a bit sore where I pulled the tape off, and the Hummer man punched me in the stomach, so that hurts a bit. Couple of times I did think I might die, but I don't need the hospital.' She looked at Gina, almost afraid to ask. 'Did you find Blossom?'

'She'd hurt her foot, pulled out a claw, I

think, but otherwise she seemed OK. I fed her when I went round to your house. That's why we came looking for you. The cat hadn't been fed and you'd left your keys in the kitchen.'

Megan grinned. 'I think Blossom left her claw in the Hummer man's face. She didn't half go for him.'

'It's a wonder he didn't kill her.'

Megan shook her head. 'She's too fast for him.'

In spite of further protests, Adam insisted on taking Megan to the hospital. Permanent residency was a definite option, Gina decided, as she sat down to wait while Megan was examined. The waiting-room was beginning to feel like home.

The hospital had been told Megan got up in the night and tripped in the dark, hitting her stomach on a low table, so they decided to keep her in overnight for observation. Gina promised to feed Blossom and check the cat's injured foot, wondering how Megan managed to cope with all the things life threw at her. Sometimes bad luck came in lumps, and one person seemed to get the lot.

'Will they come after Megan again?' she asked Adam as they left the hospital.

'I very much doubt it. The plan didn't

work, so no point in trying it again, but I'll get someone to put a deadlock on the front door and a couple of bolts on the back. She's as safe there as anywhere.'

'I suppose,' Gina said doubtfully, 'but if Megan doesn't want to go back to the house, she can stay with me again for a bit.'

Adam turned his head to look at her. 'Megan and her cat?'

When Gina unlocked the door to the studio she saw her message light was flashing again. 'I bet it's him,' she said to Adam. 'He probably doesn't know Megan escaped.'

Adam picked up the phone and punched the button. 'It's a message from Inspector Reagan. He wants you to call him back.'

'I'll call him in the morning,' Gina said tiredly. 'I can't cope with anything else today. Poor Megan's going to have to spend another night in hospital all because of Robert Cauldwell.'

'We don't know for sure Cauldwell had anything to do with this. It was more likely Judge Pollard's idea. The judge is like a lobotomized ferret, daft as well as dangerous. I can't imagine Robert Cauldwell agreeing to anything as stupid as kidnapping Megan.'

'Cauldwell must have done something pretty bad if Fox was able to blackmail him.

They were paedophiles, weren't they? All three of them.'

'Still are, I expect. I don't think it's something you grow out of.' Adam was silent for a moment. 'You have to tell the police someone kidnapped Megan. You can't just forget about it.'

'I have to talk to Megan first. The police gave her a rough time after Gary beat her up. Like, why did she stay with him, and didn't she care about the baby? I can't put her through all that again. Not yet.' Gina pulled a face as her stomach rumbled audibly. 'Did I eat today?'

'Probably not since breakfast.' Adam looked at his watch. 'It's six o'clock, time to lock up the shop. Do you want to eat out or in?'

'Take-away pizza and red wine if you don't mind doing the shopping.'

'I'll pick up some wine from home. Go upstairs and set the table.'

'Yes, sir,' she said as he let himself out, but this time she smiled.

He brought back pepperoni pizza, coleslaw and Chianti. He said he'd left his car and taken a taxi so he could drink, and he'd get a taxi home, but Gina had other ideas. Tonight she needed a warm body beside her when she went to sleep. She knew things were going to get complicated but for once she didn't care. A lot later, when she was stroking the arm he had casually draped across her stomach, she wondered if she should get a cat. It would be a lot less trouble.

22

When Gina phoned the police station the next morning, Reagan didn't give her a chance to speak.

'How come you're somehow involved with every dead body we pick up?'

'Sorry?' She looked at Adam and raised her shoulders in a shrug. 'I don't know what you're talking about.'

'The body of an old man, left outside the St Agnes shelter in town. Been beaten up. The ladies who run the shelter said he stays there sometimes, so we asked a few questions and found out you were there recently with a photographer.'

'Who's the old man?'

'No idea, just some old chap with a beard. No ID on him. We've taken pictures, so someone will eventually identify him, but it's going to take time. It would help if we knew what he looked like before he hit the streets.'

'I'll come in as soon as I can.' She put the phone down. 'They've found a body outside the St Agnes refuge.'

Adam looked up. He was sitting at her table drinking orange juice, his hair still wet from the shower. 'Fox?'

'I don't know. I'm not jumping to conclusions this time.'

'Did Reagan tell you what happened?' Adam asked.

Gina shook her head. 'Not really. He said they found a body of an old man who'd been beaten up. If it is Fox, he left the refuge because I told him it wasn't safe to stay there. God, Adam, I feel like a serial killer.'

Adam got up from the table and put his arm round her shoulders, pulling her against him. He felt her body tense but she didn't pull away, so he hung on to her until he felt her start to relax. 'I'll come with you. I don't want you looking at any more dead bodies on your own.'

She smiled a little sadly. 'It's my job, Adam.'

The visit to the mortuary meant the studio had to be locked up again but, right at this moment, that was the least of Gina's worries. She was dreading the thought of having to identify Nathan Fox.

Reagan was waiting for them. He looked at Adam with about the same amount of interest he'd give a very small insect, then he turned to Gina. 'Why were you at the St Agnes refuge?'

Adam answered for her. 'Gina was taking

notes for me. I'm doing a feature on the homeless in the town and it's difficult to take pictures and write notes at the same time.'

Reagan kept his eyes on Gina. 'My, my, a new boyfriend and a new job. Reporter's assistant, that's different.'

She didn't blink. 'As you know, Inspector, I've always been very versatile.'

He stared back at her, his expression telling her nothing. 'Just coincidence, then, this body turning up just after your visit?'

'What else could it be? I don't know many homeless old men, not personally, anyway. I might have seen him at the shelter but I won't know until I look at him.'

'Let's go and look then.' He turned to Adam, acknowledging his presence for the first time. 'We won't need you, Mr Shaw. You can wait for Miss Cross here.'

Gina thought Adam's tongue must be sore, he'd had to bite it so many times.

'I might have taken a photo of the victim when we were at the shelter,' he told Reagan. 'It might help with identification.'

Reagan shrugged. They followed him to the room where the bodies were kept. No metal tables with drains or instruments of torture, just a room that looked like a big office. The mortuary assistant studied a list, pulled out a drawer, unzipped a bag and exposed a face.

Gina stared at the man for a long moment. 'I've never seen him before,' she said. 'Do you want a drawing?'

Reagan nodded. 'Show me what he looked like twenty years ago.'

Gina hesitated. Reluctantly she took out her sketch pad and drew the face of an ordinary-looking, middle-aged man. She handed the sketch to Reagan. 'That's what he looked like in his fifties. He must've been about seventy when he died.'

Reagan looked disappointed. 'To be honest, I thought it might be Nathan Fox. We checked up on Fox, and we think he's been sleeping rough somewhere, that's why his daughter couldn't find him. He was abroad for twenty years, then back here with no fixed address.'

Gina was trying not to look at Adam. She had seen his start of surprise when she'd said she didn't recognize the body. 'Was the old man beaten very badly?'

'Funnily enough, no. Certainly not enough to kill anyone under normal circumstances, but an old man living rough, undernourished, with his liver shot to hell? In that case, probably yes. Pity it wasn't Fox. We could've stopped looking for him.'

'Yes,' Gina said. 'What a pity.'

Adam didn't speak to her until they were back in her car. 'There must be a reason why you lied but I can't think of one at the moment.'

'I didn't lie.' She put the car into gear and pulled away from the kerb. 'Where do you live? It would be a good idea if I knew where I was going.'

'Castle Keep apartments, by the river. What do you mean, you didn't lie? You drew a picture of some middle-aged man, nothing like Fox, and told Reagan it was no one you knew. Why didn't you tell him it was Fox at the mortuary?'

'Because it wasn't Fox. It was no one I'd ever seen before.'

Adam turned in his seat to look at her. 'It looked like Fox to me. The same old man we saw at the shelter, the old man you said was Fox.'

'The man at the shelter was Fox. The dead man wasn't. I think Fox deliberately adopted the look of someone already at the shelter. It wouldn't be that difficult — all you need is a dirty grey beard and some old clothes. There were three or four old men at that place who were practically interchangeable.'

'In that case Fox most likely swapped clothes with the dead man before he was killed. The old boy wouldn't argue about it, would he? Fox's clothes were good quality second-hand, probably Oxfam. He'd dirtied them up, but they were still better than most, and Fox wore a red woolly hat, didn't he? Old man, plus beard, plus red woolly hat, equals Fox. As soon as the substitute stepped outside, the heavies targeted him. They were probably going to bundle him into a car and take him somewhere quiet where they could beat the truth out of him, but he died of fright, literally, and they left him where he was. As far as they were concerned, the job was over.'

Gina pulled up in front of the riverside apartments. 'We still have no proof Cauldwell or the judge had anything to do with this. Anyone could have beaten up the old man.'

Adam opened the car door. 'What for? He certainly wouldn't have had anything worth mugging him for. They were after this thing Fox stole from Cauldwell and his cronies.' He got out and stood by the open car door. 'Do you want to come in? See where I live?'

No, Gina didn't want to see where he lived. She preferred her own territory, where she felt safe, where she could kick him out if need be. She looked up at the block of apartments, a converted mill overlooking the river, where a two-bed penthouse flat would cost half a million.

'Your job obviously pays well.'

'I rent' — he paused for a second — 'from

a friend. Don't let the look of the place scare you off.'

Gina stepped out of the car as he'd known she would. 'I'll come in for a minute and let you show off, if that's what you want.' She had to admit the apartment was beautiful. It was on the top floor of the building with views over the rooftops towards the castle, the river glinting at the bottom of the hill. Castlebury looked surprisingly green from this vantage point. She walked around, looking in each room. There was a large, open-plan living/dining/kitchen area with massive steel beams holding up a high ceiling. Through a small square hallway she found one bedroom with an en-suite wet room, and a smaller room set up as an office with the obligatory futon against the wall. Sheets and a blanket were piled on the futon. There was also an opulent bathroom tiled in grey slate. The furniture was more feminine than she would have expected; a thick cream rug on the wooden floor, lots of wine-red velvet cushions on the cream leather settee, and candles in the mock hearth.

'Nice,' she said.

He made real coffee in some high-tech coffee machine and handed Gina a carton of cream. Taking a sip of the coffee, she could understand why he didn't like her instant.

'I just rent,' he said. 'Like your friend Megan, I keep the place warm for the owner while she's away.' He caught the raised eyebrow and could have kicked himself. 'My mother owns the place.'

Yeah, right. Gina sipped her coffee, trying to look uninterested. Would he make something like that up? Surely he could think of something more original. Not that she needed an explanation; she didn't care who he lived with. He could have a different woman round every night if he felt like it.

She excused herself to go to the bathroom and, as expected, the frosted glass wall cabinet held more than just male toiletries. She picked up a long packet of little pills, each marked with the day of the week. Next to the pills, a bottle of designer shower gel and some scented massage oil, not Adam at all. Not very mumsy either. She shrugged to herself; men always had baggage.

He smiled as she came back into the living-room and she flushed with embarrassment. He knew exactly why she'd gone to the bathroom. Now he'd think she cared who he went to bed with when, in reality, she couldn't give a monkey's. So why *did* you go to the bathroom, a little voice whispered, but Gina wasn't listening.

She had a sitting at the studio before lunch

so she made her excuses and left, knowing he was standing at the window, high up in the building, watching her drive away.

When she got back to the studio, Madeline Turner, a woman in her fifties, was waiting outside. Gina apologized for being late, trying to get her mind back into work mode. At the moment Adam Shaw seemed a lot more dangerous than Robert Cauldwell.

'The picture is for my husband's sixtieth birthday,' Mrs Turner told Gina. 'Could you . . . er . . . flatter me a little, do you think?'

Gina started on the preliminary sketch but her mind was still a million miles away. She remembered thinking the woman must have been a real beauty once, but now there were lines round her mouth and eyes, and her short greying hair wasn't cut in the most flattering of styles. By the time Gina stopped thinking about Adam and came back to earth, it was too late. 'I'm sorry,' she told Madeline Turner, handing her the rough sketch. 'I think I've gone a bit overboard on the flattery side.'

The woman caught her breath and put her hand to her face. 'Oh my goodness! I looked exactly like that in my twenties.'

Gina had drawn a young woman with long hair that pooled on her shoulders in waves. She was wearing a low-cut dress with a starshaped brooch pinned to the neckline.

'I was going to bring a photo in to show you,' the woman said, 'but I thought you'd think me a vain fool, wanting to look young again. My husband must have given you the photo. He bought me that brooch the day he asked me to marry him.' There were tears in Madeline Turner's eyes. 'He'll just love this.'

You must learn to concentrate, Gina told herself. Stick to the facts and not let your imagination run riot. She was an artist, not some crazy psychic.

After Mrs Turner left, Gina phoned the hospital to say she would pick Megan up as soon as she was ready to leave, only to be told the girl had got a ride home in an ambulance. Gina looked at her watch and decided to lock up early. She grabbed a couple of beers from the fridge and walked round to Megan's house, picking up sandwiches on the way in case Megan hadn't been fed at the hospital. Megan answered the door in her dressing gown, the cat in her arms. Apart from some heavy strapping on her wrist she looked pretty good.

'Another two days off work,' she said apologetically, 'but you didn't have to come round. Adam got a man to put new locks on the doors. I'm not scared of being on my own.'

'If you change your mind you know I've got a spare futon. I brought beer and sarnies. Chicken for you and seafood for me.'

Megan led the way into the living-room. 'The police came to the hospital wanting to know what happened to me. They think Gary hit me again. They're looking for him but they won't find him. He's good at hiding.' Megan threw Blossom the last bit of chicken. 'I really wanted his baby, Gina. I thought he'd have to love his own baby. I thought he'd want to take care of it, want us to be a family. Doesn't follow, though, does it?'

'Gary's never been able to love anyone except himself. Don't set your sights so low next time. You can do a lot better than Gary.'

'Someone like Adam, you mean? Yeah, great, if you don't want him I'll have him. I like older men, and he'd look after me, buy me flowers and things.'

Gina felt a little prickle of something she refused to recognize. 'I think he's already seeing someone. I went to his flat — just to drop him off,' she added hastily, 'but he's got women things in his bathroom cabinet. Flowery shower gel and contraceptive pills.'

'You looked in his bathroom cabinet?' Megan sounded horrified.

'Yeah, I must have a curious nature.' She

wasn't going to feel guilty for snooping round Adam's flat. He snooped for a living.

'That was really sick, poking around in his bathroom cabinet, and it doesn't prove anything. I've still got Gary's toothbrush and razor, I even moved house with his junk, but that doesn't mean I'm still shagging him.'

Gina shrugged. 'Not important, anyway. I'm just glad you're feeling better.'

'I suppose whatever you get you just have to make the best of it.' Megan managed a smile. 'You know how some people always get in the wrong queue at the supermarket? Well, I must've got in the wrong queue when they were dishing out lives, cos I got a really shitty one.' She stroked Blossom. 'Still, I've got a nice house now, and a cat, so it's not too bad, really.'

23

Gary Marsh walked into the studio at ten o'clock the next morning.

Gina had made herself get out of bed an hour early and managed a three-mile run. She felt out of condition, her heart pumping on the uphill bits, her legs aching on the downhill slopes. The weather was still warm, even though a thin mist blanketed the sun, and her clothes were sticking to her by the time she got back to her flat. She showered and changed, pleased she still had time for some breakfast. She was feeling pretty good by the time she opened up the studio.

Gary arrived while she was finishing a pen and ink sketch of a family of Siamese cats. He pushed open the door and stood just inside, leaning against the door jamb for support. He looked ill, she thought. He'd lost weight and the skin on his face had shrunk back against the bones. His clothes hung on him and he was wearing a fleece jacket, although the temperature must have been in the seventies.

Gina had imagined she would feel hatred the next time she saw Gary, perhaps fear after what he had done to Megan, but all she could feel was pity. 'Do you want to sit down?'

He laughed shakily, pushing himself away from the door and letting it swing shut behind him. 'I thought you'd want to kill me.'

'It looks like you're already doing that to yourself. You were always telling Megan pushers don't use, not the hard stuff. You finish up scoring with your profit.'

'Makes you brain dead, though. Nice to be brain dead sometimes.' He managed a trace of the old grin as he let the jacket slide to the floor. He held out his arms, palms up, in a gesture of surrender. 'Want to see my ankles? I ran out of veins on my arms a long time ago.'

Gina sighed. 'You know Megan lost the baby?'

He nodded, sinking into a chair. He was just bones, bones in grubby clothes. Even his piercings looked tarnished. 'I didn't mean to hurt her.'

'Where have I heard that before? You nearly kicked her to death, Gary. I don't want you anywhere near either of us. You should go right now, before I call the police.'

'I haven't got anywhere to go to.'

She shrugged. 'Your choice.' Pity was OK, but sympathy was different. He wasn't going to get sympathy. 'What do you want?'

'Money,' he said simply. 'I'm not pretty

enough to earn much on the street.' He went to get up, stood for a minute, and then sat down again. He put his head in his hands and she saw his shoulders shaking. She looked at him dispassionately. Megan had cried for her dead baby; Gary was crying for himself.

Gina went to the till and took out five ten-pound notes. 'I know this won't last long because you'll spend it on drugs, but it's all you're going to get, so shoot it in your foot, your arm, or the top of your head, I really don't care. You killed your baby daughter and you nearly killed Megan. I can give you money, Gary, but if it's forgiveness you're after, I'm right out of that.'

He snatched the notes out of her hand. 'Someone locked me up for two fucking days. I was sick as shit. They wanted to know what you took from some woman's house and where you'd hidden it. How the fuck would I know what you stole? You're just as much to blame as I am.' He stood up and put his jacket back on, tucking the money in his pocket. 'And if I find out who got me beat me up, I'll fucking kill him.'

'Unless he kills you first. Robert Cauldwell is a very dangerous man. Go back to the flat, Gary. Megan doesn't live there any more. There's still blood on the floor.'

She closed the door after him, feeling she

ought to decontaminate the place. All she had was fly spray, but she gave the studio a quick squirt anyway. With Gary back on the scene, she worried about Megan. Gary might look weak and broken, but if he needed money badly enough he would go to any lengths to get it. She should have called the police, but Gary wouldn't survive in prison, and Gina knew she wouldn't sleep again if she put him there.

Saturday passed in a blur of work. It was always the busiest day of the week, and without Megan there to help it was a nightmare. Gina found herself trying to work, answer the phone and deal with clients all by herself.

The post was late, which always annoyed her. Instead of being able to deal with it as soon as she opened up for the day, she had to stop in the middle of whatever she was doing to go through a pile of letters. Junk mail went straight in the bin unopened, and any bills she threw on Megan's desk, which left just three personal-looking ones she put aside for later. One in particular, a cream, handwritten envelope, intrigued her, but she didn't have time to look at it during the day.

She wasn't able to close the studio until well after six o'clock, but before she went upstairs she checked her emails in case Fox had left a message. Still nothing. She closed the computer down with a sigh of relief, telling herself she must do something about getting a new monitor for upstairs, although, most of the time, she found the absence of a working computer in the flat pleasantly relaxing. Once she had changed into a halter-top and jeans and had a meal in front of her, she opened her personal letters.

One was from a woman thanking Gina for a picture she'd done of a Yorkshire terrier, another was from a man asking if she would draw him in the nude — she didn't think so — and the last, in the heavy cream envelope, was an invitation to the forthcoming mayor's banquet at the town hall. Embossed in gold, the invitation was addressed to Miss Gina Cross and signed by the mayor.

Gina had intended having at least one meal without any alcohol that weekend, but now she opened her last bottle of red and poured herself a glass, making a mental note she needed to stock up. Why on earth would the mayor invite her to his banquet? It must be a mistake, and of course she wouldn't go. The mere thought brought her out in a sweat. The mayoral dinner was a glittering affair, with people willing to kill for an invitation. Gina almost laughed at the thought of being invited to something like that. She had a flowery cotton frock she wore to weddings and one pair of sandals with heels but, as far as posh frocks go, that was about it. Pity it wasn't fancy dress.

Somebody was playing games with her. Ignore it, she told herself, but she dropped the invitation in her handbag. It would be a talking point, at least, something to make Megan laugh.

Gina slept badly, dreaming of Adam chasing a scantily clad blonde female round his flat. Luckily, she woke up before he caught the girl, but once she was awake she couldn't get back to sleep again. Why did she always wake early on a Sunday? She rolled out of bed and walked, naked, to the shower. On the way she caught sight of herself in the full-length mirror on the wardrobe door. What she saw wasn't bad, but not perfect either. If she could have changed anything it would have been the length of her legs. Whatever she did to herself she would always be short. She supposed everything was in proportion, but she got really fed up with having to look up to everyone.

She had a quick shower and put on her running gear. There was time for the five-mile route skirting the woods on the edge of town, then along the riverbank and back up through the park. A lovely run, and no sign of Fox this time, but right past Adam's waterside apartment.

She needed a drink of water by the time she got to the river, so she hitched herself up on the wall and shielded her eyes to look up at Adam's window. The blinds were raised, so he must be up, and it might be fun to tell him about the invitation. Perhaps she should give it to him — he was bound to have the right clothes in his wardrobe. Before she could change her mind, she ran up the path to the entrance. There was a security call system but just as she was about to press the buzzer a woman in designer running gear opened the door from the inside. Gina thanked the woman for holding the door and went inside. The concierge desk was unmanned so she took the lift straight up to Adam's floor. Am I doing this just to check on him, she asked herself, and what if he has someone with him?

Then she'd know for sure, rather than speculating.

The woman who answered the door to Adam's flat was tall and slim, wearing a silk kimono draped over an angular body. 'I'm looking for Adam Shaw,' Gina said, feeling foolish.

'Oh, please come in.' The woman moved aside to let Gina into the hallway. 'He's just gone for the Sunday papers. He'll be back in a minute. I'm Alison Shaw, Adam's mother.'

Adam's mother was still a good-looking woman, although Gina knew she must be at least fifty. Her silvery blonde hair was tied back in a ponytail and her eyes were a clear sky-blue like her son's. The scented oil was very appropriate, Gina decided, and the pills were no doubt HRT. She felt ashamed for looking.

Alison Shaw invited Gina inside, waited until she was seated on the settee, then sat down opposite. She studied Gina with interest. 'Have you known Adam long?'

'Not long. We're more ... business associates.' Gina moved uncomfortably on the settee, feeling her legs sticking to the leather.

'You're a photographer?'

Gina shook her head, feeling more uncomfortable by the minute. 'No, I'm an artist. I have a studio in town.'

When Adam walked in the door, she saw the surprise in his eyes, and suddenly remembered how she must look. With sweaty patches on her cotton top and dirty trainers on her feet, she was very much in contrast to his elegant mother and designer apartment. She'd probably already made a damp mark on the leather. While Alison Shaw excused herself to bathe and dress, Gina explained why she had called round. 'Do you think the invitation is genuine, or is someone playing games with me?'

'It looks genuine. Cauldwell's bound to have an invitation to the dinner so he could easily get you on the guest list. The question is, why would he want to?' Adam handed the card back to her. 'You're not going.' It wasn't a question.

'I was thinking about it,' she said perversely. 'Cauldwell won't try anything at a public function, not in a room full of people. Besides, how many people get an invitation to the mayor's ball? I keep thinking of all that free food and drink. It would be a shame to miss it.'

'Now you're just being stupid. Besides, what would you wear? You don't seem to have anything except jeans and running gear.'

Which was very true, but she didn't need him to point out her lack of designer clothes, or her stupidity. Keeping a tight hold on her temper, she stood up. 'Believe it or not, I have a dress or two. Say goodbye to your mother for me.' Her sweaty thighs had stuck to the seat and came free with a sucking sound. She looked worriedly down at the cream leather, but there were no obvious marks. She ran back to her flat and had a long, cool shower, but the embarrassment just wouldn't wash away.

Adam turned up late in the afternoon, when the heat had gone out of the day. By then Gina had changed into shorts and a baggy T-shirt, her hair tied in the nape of her neck. She had checked her wardrobe to make quite sure, but Adam was right, there was nothing remotely resembling a posh frock. Even her underwear was more functional than sexy. She remembered wearing pretty things once, see-through lace bras and skimpy briefs, but Simon had changed all that, telling her she looked like a tart and, judging by her underwear drawer, she must have believed him.

Adam came bearing gifts — six cans of beer. A peace offering, he said. 'I was rude, wasn't I? I'm sorry, but going to that dinner thing really would be stupid.' He put four cans in her fridge and opened the other two. Neither of them bothered with a glass.

'You're right,' she said. 'I don't have anything to wear.' She paused for a moment. 'So, if I go, I'll have to buy something new.'

Adam looked at her for a moment and then said casually, 'Susie London's back.'

Gina licked beer froth from her upper lip. 'We have to go and see her. Find out what really happened at the school. It might explain a few things.'

'I doubt if she has any more to say than she did twenty years ago. Judge Pollard took care of everything then and he'd do the same today. I told you, he still wields a great deal of power and if he can't handle things himself he always knows someone who can.'

'We have to find a connection between Cauldwell and the bones of the child, Adam, otherwise we have nothing. I bet Susie London could tell us a lot about the three boys at the school. If what that teacher said is true, they gang raped her, and when you think about it, they've all got the sort of job where a scandal would ruin them. Cauldwell, the next prime minister, Martin Edge, cosmetic surgeon to the stars, and the other one — I don't know what he does for a living — is Judge Pollard's son.'

'Trevor Pollard is a defence lawyer. One of the best. He stops criminals going to prison.'

'I can't believe Susie London going away was just a coincidence. Something scared her and we have to go and see her before she takes off again.' Gina got another couple of cans of beer out of the fridge and handed one to Adam. 'But I don't want to get her beaten up or killed.'

'If someone wanted to kill Susie London they'd have done it years ago. Besides, she's no threat to anyone. If nobody believed her twenty years ago, they're not going to believe her now. No, I think someone is just trying to mop up the remains of something that happened a long time ago. Something that's come back to haunt them.'

'Like the death of a child.'

Adam shook his head. 'I don't know. The child doesn't seem to fit in anywhere. I looked in all the old newspapers for that time, both local and national, and no child was reported missing. You'd think someone would have missed her.'

Gina walked to the open window. The street below was quiet. A hot Sunday evening with people lazing in their gardens or strolling in the park, not the slightest bit interested in the death of a little girl twenty years ago. Adam came and stood behind her, draping his arm casually across her shoulder, waiting for her to pull away. She didn't. Instead she leant her head back against his chest. 'We have to talk to Susie London,' she said.

24

It was eleven o'clock in the morning, warm, but not too hot, a thin breeze doing its best to freshen the air. The next-door garden had a broken TV in it, Gina noticed, a projectile from an upstairs window by the look of it. An empty Tesco bag flew down the street and took off like a balloon, skimming the tops of the trees. Somewhere a dog barked monotonously. The front garden of Susie London's house had been tidied up. The bike had gone and an Avon catalogue sat on the doorstep, but there was no sign of life.

'If we keep driving up and down someone is bound to notice us,' Adam said. 'We have to stop and park outside.'

Gina nodded, making sure her hat was on tight. She'd found a black sunhat at the back of a cupboard, a leftover from her days with Simon, and tucked her hair up inside the crown. She wore her black skirt and a long-sleeved blouse. Not exactly a disguise, but it would make it harder for someone to recognize her again. She thought she probably looked like a missionary, but it didn't really matter as long as she didn't look like herself. Adam was dressed in a dark suit, wearing new glasses with heavy black rims.

'I like you with glasses,' she told him as she was about to get out of the car. 'You look . . .'

'What?'

'Less scary. More like a librarian or a bank manager.'

He growled at her. 'That's why I don't often wear them.'

They walked up the path and Adam pushed the white plastic button beside the front door. 'Perhaps she's out.'

Gina walked to the front window and looked inside. Then she peered round the side of the house. 'There's a back gate.' She was good with back gates.

'Don't,' he said. 'It looks as if we're about to burgle the place. Follow me round the back as if we know what we're doing.'

The back door to the house was locked, the kitchen empty, and no cat flap this time. A black plastic dustbin was filled to overflowing, its lid askew, flies buzzing noisily round the top. A child's vest drooped listlessly from a washing line strung between the fences, looking as if it had been there some time. The garden was so overgrown it was impossible to see where the lawn ended and the flowerbeds began. Some of the weeds were taller than Gina.

'You don't think . . . ' she said worriedly.

'No, I don't think she's inside lying in a pool of blood. I think she's out.'

Adam had to drive right to the end of the road before he could turn around. As they came back past the house a woman was pushing open the front gate with her hip, a carrier bag in her arms. Adam put his foot on the brake and pulled into the kerb.

Susie London looked older than her thirty-five years. She was wearing a cotton halter-top dress and had flip-flops on her feet. Her hair was still naturally curly, but now a bottle-enhanced auburn. She turned to look at Gina and Adam as they got out of the car.

'Bugger off, I'm busy.'

Adam smiled that drop-dead gorgeous smile of his. 'If I say Robert Cauldwell, will you talk to us for a moment?'

Gina saw the woman stiffen, a tiny movement, but enough if you were looking for it. She put her bag down on the step and put her key in the front door. 'For fuck's sake, come inside. This street's like a friggin' peep show.'

Adam picked up the bag and they followed Susie London inside. She pushed the front door closed behind them, walked into her livingroom, and dropped into a chair. 'It never fucking stops, does it? Christ, I only came back to pack some clothes. You can tell him I got his letter and I'll be on my way again tomorrow.'

'What letter?' Gina asked.

The woman pulled an envelope from behind the cheap carriage clock on the mantelpiece and handed it to Gina. 'If he wants the money back it's too late. I spent most of it already.'

One line was typed on a single sheet of folded A4 paper.

The past is best forgotten. It is time for you to move on.

Gina handed the paper to Adam. 'You think Robert Cauldwell wants you to leave Castlebury?'

'With a cheque for twenty grand I'm not arguing.'

Gina looked round the bare room. 'Where's your son?'

'I left him with friends up north. How d'you know I've got a son? What do you want?'

Adam put the letter back in the envelope and tucked it back behind the clock. 'We just want to ask you some questions. I'm a journalist researching Robert Cauldwell and

I want to find out what happened twenty years ago.'

'I can't talk to you. Not to the newspapers. Wouldn't do any good, anyway. No one believed me then, no one's going to believe me now. Nothing's changed. Besides, if I talk to anyone they'll get rid of me like shit off a shoe.'

'I promise I won't use anything you tell me until Robert Cauldwell is standing in the dock, but we have to collect as much evidence against him as possible so we can put him there.'

'Cauldwell was a bastard, a bastard who liked young girls. Him, and the other two creeps.'

'Martin Edge and Trevor Pollard,' Adam said. 'Yes, we know.'

The woman took a packet of cigarettes out of her bag. She lit one, then waved them to the settee. 'If I tell you what happened, you still can't print it. You'd be locked up for . . . you know . . . telling lies.'

'Libel. Don't worry, these days a newspaper won't print anything without some sort of proof.' Adam hoped she believed him. 'I don't know how much you remember, but anything would help.'

'I've been trying to forget for the past twenty years, and I still remember every fucking detail.' Susie London laughed. 'Good choice of words, eh?' She shook her head, then shrugged. 'OK. You get me in any trouble and I'll just deny everything.' She took a drag on her cigarette. 'D'you want a beer? Talking makes me dry.'

Gina nodded before Adam had a chance to say no. She took the beer Susie handed her and pulled the tab, drinking straight from the can. She hadn't been offered a glass.

'He asked me out, Martin Edge. He wasn't bad looking. Tall, with dark hair and a real fancy accent. I knew what he wanted but I thought I could handle him. I only got worried when the other two came along as well.'

Susie stubbed out her cigarette and took a gulp of beer, wiping her mouth on the back of her hand. 'When three of them turned up I was thinking, who asks a girl for a date and then brings along his mates? Anyway, it started off OK. They bought vodka and bottles of orange squash and I'd not had vodka before, but I remember it didn't really taste of anything, all I could taste was the orange. Martin brought me a box of chocolates, expensive ones, and said I had to let him look at my tits because he'd given me chocolates. Didn't seem like much at the time — I'd let boys see them before. Local boys, though, not anyone from the rich boys school like Martin.' She looked down at herself. 'They were OK then. 'Course, once I'd undone my dress, that was it. I remember Martin telling me if I screamed he'd kill me, and I believed him. He'd kill me now if he knew I was talking to you.'

She stared at nothing for a moment, her eyes blank.

'Christ, it hurt. I still remember that. I'd never let anyone go all the way before so I suppose I was a virgin. God, that's a joke. Anyway, I screamed and Martin put his hand over my mouth. He must have covered my nose as well 'cos I couldn't breathe. I was thrashing about, trying to get some breath, and Trevor was laughing. He laughed like a girl, sort of a giggle, and then Martin hit me. First a slap, then he used the back of his hand and split my lip. I was scared to make a sound after that. I didn't think they could hurt me more, but then it was Bobby Cauldwell's turn.' She shuddered. 'I need another beer.'

'Me too,' Gina said shakily. She looked at Adam, hoping he would say they'd heard enough, but he just nodded when Susie handed him a second can of beer.

'Go on if you can.'

Susie looked at him, then at the recorder. 'I told you I still remember it all.'

'You got to Robert Cauldwell.'

'Mmm. This is the bit I try real hard to forget. Never works, though. Bobby got them to turn me over because he prefers the tradesman's entrance, then one of them stuffed a hanky in my mouth and held my legs. It must have been Martin.' She finished her beer and threw the can in the grate. 'Trevor Pollard never touched me, he just watched, but he had a camera and filmed the lot. He's probably still jerking himself off to it. Anyway, by the time Bobby Cauldwell had finished with me, I was in a pretty bad way and more or less crawled home. Dad told me to have a bath and go to bed. He said he'd go to the school in the morning.'

Adam turned off the recorder. 'But he didn't?'

'No, he got a better offer. Trevor's father came round and they had a long talk. Mr Pollard offered my dad a lot of money to keep quiet, and I wasn't hurt, was I? Not really hurt. As far as my dad was concerned I'd just had a bit of rough sex. Mum got a lot of that when she was alive.'

'I'm sorry,' Gina said. 'I'm really sorry we made you go through it all again.'

'It didn't do me any harm. I've been through it in my head hundreds of times, and at least you believed me. I know why Bobby sent me the money — he's been in the paper a lot, the next PM and all that. He's still scared I might talk. But the money came in handy. I went up north. I've got friends in Middlesbrough and I'm going back next week for good.'

'Can you leave a number in case we need to reach you?'

Susie wrote on a scrap of paper and handed it to Adam. 'You won't get him,' she said. 'He's too clever.'

'Yes we will,' Gina said firmly. She followed Adam out of the front gate, feeling physically drained. She collapsed into the car seat beside him, putting up her hand to pull off her hat.

'Keep it on for a moment,' Adam said.

When she looked out of the car window Gina noticed a face peering through a lace curtain, a crack in the slats of a Venetian blind, a partially open front door. People with nothing better to do than watch. A free surveillance system. Gina rested her head on the back of the seat and closed her eyes, trying to shut out the images still lurking in her head.

'I can't believe how calmly Susie talked about all that stuff they did to her. It's as if she still believes it's her fault.'

'That's because everyone told her it was. If

people tell you something often enough, you start believing it.'

Gina sighed. 'Do you think she'll be OK?'

'In Middlesbrough, maybe. She's been in Castlebury too long. Cauldwell was right about that, it's time she moved on.'

'She probably had nowhere to go before now. You can't just dump yourself on someone else, not with a child, and it's scary starting over again somewhere new.'

He glanced at her. 'Where did you live before you bought the studio? With your grandmother?'

'Yes, still in Castlebury, though, I didn't move far. I'd lived with Gran almost since I was born and I thought she was going to be around for ever, then suddenly I was all on my own.'

'No other family?' He almost added 'apart from your father' but changed his mind.

Gina shook her head 'No. Gran was an only child, so was my mother, so the line stops with me.'

He dropped a gear to go uphill. 'Unless you have children, or use your real name.'

'Cross is my real name. It was my grandmother's name. I changed mine from Minnelli to Cross as soon as I was old enough — and I'm not going to have any children.'

'Any particular reason?'

'I don't like them.' She thought of Rosie, the tiny hands and feet, the soft pale hair, and realized that wasn't strictly true any more. 'Not much, anyway.' She risked a sideways glance at Adam, saw he was smiling, and frowned. 'Not everyone has to like children.'

'No, of course not.' He was still smiling.

25

The next morning Gina told Megan about her invitation. 'I got an invitation to the mayor's banquet.' She put the kettle on for coffee, refusing to acknowledge the exaggerated look of amazement on Megan's face.

'The mayor's banquet? Why? Who would send you an invitation to that?'

'I have no idea.' Gina spooned granules into mugs. 'The invitation looks genuine. It's signed by the mayor.'

'Do you think it's a trap?' Megan looked worried for a minute, then she shook her head. 'No, it's a big, posh dinner with lots of people. Rich people. You've got to go.' She took the mug of coffee from Gina, her eyes suddenly bright with excitement. 'You'll have to dress up, shoes with heels and things. Can I shop with you? When you buy your ballgown, can I come with you?'

'It's not a ball, and I'm not Cinderella, Megan.' Gina looked at the calendar on the studio wall. The banquet was next Saturday so her invitation must have been a last-minute decision. I wonder why? she thought. If it was a trap it seemed far too complicated, and Megan obviously couldn't see any danger in the invitation, but she had less than a week. If she was going she needed all the help she could get. 'If I did go, what sort of thing should I wear?' she asked Megan. 'Long or short? See, I really have no idea.'

'Can I come up and look in your wardrobe? See what you've already got?'

'I don't have anything. No one believes me, but I really don't.'

'Good.' Megan rubbed her hands together. 'That means we have to get everything new. When can we go and shop?'

'Check my appointments,' Gina said resignedly. 'We'll have to shut the studio if you're coming with me.'

Adam phoned Gina that evening to tell her he had put together all the evidence they had against the three men. 'It makes for interesting reading,' he said. 'I've got the stuff you gave me, your meetings with Cauldwell and with Fox, the recordings from the teachers at the school, and the one we did yesterday with Susie London. Also your sketches of Fox and the child, and the one you did of Judge Pollard. It's just a pity we lost the video. That would have backed up your sketch.'

'There must be something else,' Gina said. 'Something that drops the three of them right in the whatsit, like another video, or photos or something.'

'Well, wherever it is, no decent newspaper will touch anything I write without solid evidence, and solid evidence we definitely don't have.'

Gina sighed. 'I think I'd better make an appointment to see Inspector Reagan and dump it all on him. Even if he can't do anything, he knows me well enough to know I haven't made it all up. At least he'll be aware of what's going on and why bodies keep turning up whenever I'm around.'

'Good idea,' Adam said. 'It can't do any harm, and Reagan already knows most of it. He knows a Hummer was involved with Jessica Fox and Andy Crabtree, he's got tyre tracks and eye witnesses, and he's already got people looking for Fox and Gary Marsh.'

'OK. If I can get a meeting organized for tomorrow, I'll let you know.'

'Give me a ring when you've got something arranged,' he said, and hung up.

Another order. That was why he annoyed her so much. He always told, never asked. Well, he wasn't in the army now, and neither was she, so he was going to have to behave like a normal human being and learn how to say please and thank you. That decision taken, Gina cuddled up on her settee with a book and a glass of red wine. Life on your own was pretty good sometimes.

* * *

She managed to set up an appointment for the next day, but Reagan was not pleased to see them.

'What's going on, Gina?' he asked, when they both walked into his office. 'Why bring the photographer?'

'Journalist,' Adam told him. 'If you're still looking for Nathan Fox I might be able to help. I've been putting together a story on Robert Cauldwell, our local MP, and Fox's name keeps cropping up.'

Reagan just looked at him. 'It would keep cropping up. Fox was at Fletford College at the same time as Cauldwell. Fox was the caretaker. So?'

'So — we have reason to believe Cauldwell was involved in something rather nasty. Maybe something to do with the bones you found in the pond. We know Cauldwell and two other boys were involved with the gang rape of a teenager when they were students. One of the boys was Judge Pollard's son.'

Reagan was silent for several seconds. He looked at Gina, then back at Adam. 'You'd better both sit down and tell me what you know — or what you think you know.'

It took an hour of questions and answers before Reagan had the whole story. Twice someone came into his room and was told to go away. He listened to both of them much more attentively than they had expected.

'You should have reported the car accident as soon as it happened,' he told Adam. 'Withholding information vital to an inquiry is an offence. And we might have found something at the warehouse if we'd known about Megan's abduction. One of Gary Marsh's drug-dealing friends with a grudge, I shouldn't wonder.'

'It wasn't to do with Marsh. Someone had already taken Gary to the warehouse and beaten him up, that's why he took it out on Megan.' Adam tossed his notebook on to the table. 'Read that. It's pretty obvious the whole thing was organized by either Cauldwell or the judge. I just can't prove it.'

'I'll tell you straight off, you're treading on dangerous ground, very dangerous ground, and I'll tell you something else — there is absolutely no way my department can touch any of this without solid, written-in-stone proof, so I should keep quiet if I were you. We're talking about a man who could shut this whole station down in the blink of an eye.'

'Cauldwell?'

'No, not Cauldwell.' Reagan's red face creased in a smile. 'Cauldwell doesn't have as much clout as he thinks he has — not yet, anyway. No, I'm talking about Judge Pollard. Judge Dread, we call him. If — and it's a big if — if I only believe half of what you've told me, you two are in serious trouble. The judge may be old, but he's still a very dangerous man and he dines not only at Number 10 but also at Buckingham Palace. Now that's what you call clout.'

'So what do we do?' Gina asked.

'Nothing.' Reagan held up his hand to silence her when she tried to interrupt. 'I mean it, Gina, you do nothing, and that goes for both of you. We have more information than you think and we're following it up, but you two are to leave it alone.' He turned to Adam. 'Give up on your story for the moment. If you go poking your nose in where it's not wanted, you'll put yourself in danger and mess up our investigation. We've had enough bodies in Castlebury and I don't want to be pulling one of you out of a pond.'

'What happened to the child?' Gina asked. 'Do you know?'

'Not yet, but I couldn't tell you even if I did know.'

'You can't stop me investigating Cauldwell,' Adam said, the military authority in his voice quite impressive, Gina thought, when it was aimed at someone else. 'I was after that man long before your bones turned up. Is it possible the judge was running some sort of paedophile ring out of the school?'

'No, too risky. But I'm sure he knew where to find girls, and possibly boys, who wouldn't be missed. Youngsters who were afraid of being deported because something worse was waiting for them back home.'

Gina looked at him in amazement. 'What could be worse?'

'There are worse things,' Adam said quietly. 'Believe me, I've seen worse things.'

Reagan got to his feet. 'Keep out of it, Shaw. You'll get nothing on those men. It all happened too long ago and they've covered their tracks too well.'

'How about the Hummer man?' Gina asked.

Reagan smiled. 'The man with the big black car? Oh, we'll get him. It may take a while but we'll get him. He had his hands on Jessica Fox's bag, we've got prints, so he probably grabbed it before he set the body on fire and then threw the bag in the ditch. He was looking for something. He didn't take the photo of the child because he didn't know it was important, so he's not infallible, he makes mistakes.'

Gina felt slightly better as she walked back to the car with Adam. It seemed the police were on the same track. 'Did you notice Reagan said the body was set on fire? I asked him right at the beginning if someone had thrown petrol over Jessica Fox.'

'People don't burn very easily,' Adam said. 'You'd have trouble setting light to a body, and then it burns slowly, sometimes for four or five hours.'

Gina shuddered. 'Like a candle.'

Adam changed the subject. 'You didn't tell the inspector about your mysterious invitation.'

'It was none of his business.'

'Give me the invitation, Gina. Let me go instead.'

'Don't be silly. Why would I do that? Besides, it's my invitation, in my name. They wouldn't let you in.'

He stopped beside the car and turned to face her. 'You're only going because I told you not to, and you know damned well it may be dangerous. There's a reason you got that invitation, some hidden agenda you don't know about. Anything could happen, and I won't be there to watch out for you.'

'Nobody asked you to.' She got into the car and buckled her seat-belt. 'I'm not a child, Adam, and I won't be told what I can and can't do. I can look after myself. I managed very well before I met you.'

'Oh, for God's sake, Gina! You can't take these men on by yourself. Look at you, there's nothing of you. You're an artist, not a commando, so stop being ridiculous and listen to reason for once in your life. If you're not a child, then stop behaving like one.'

She wanted to get out of his car and walk away, but that would have been childish. She felt tears of frustration behind her eyes and blinked hard. It was a wonder he hadn't reminded her she was just a woman; she was sure he was thinking it. She gritted her teeth and waited for him to drop her off outside the studio. He didn't say a word the rest of the way but she thanked him politely as she got out of his car. He might have mumbled a reply but, then again, he might not.

26

Shopping was not something Gina enjoyed; it was something she did as little as possible out of necessity. She was a standard size ten, so in most shops she could buy what she needed off the hanger. Go in, get what you want, leave.

Shopping with Megan was something quite different. You had to start with a plan of action — and a beer. While you were sitting drinking the beer you worked out your itinerary, which entailed a list of what was required, a route plan of possible shops, and a budget.

'Why can't we just go to Debenhams and buy a dress? Any dress in a size ten that isn't pink will do.'

'Ah,' Megan said, making a note, 'you don't like pink. What other colours don't you like?'

'How do I know? Orange? Puce? Look, I just need a dress I can wear to a dinner. Black will be fine. Black suits everyone.'

'No, it doesn't, and you need more than just a dress. You need decent underwear, shoes, perfume, and maybe jewellery.'

'I'm not spending more than fifty quid.'

Megan just laughed. 'Don't be silly, Gina.'

Megan's plan meant they started with the underwear, but Gina refused to buy a thong. 'I'm always afraid I might have to have it surgically removed.' The bra would fit, she said, so there was no need to try it on. Her boobs hadn't changed in size since she was sixteen. There was, however, some altercation about the rest of the outfit. The little black dress, Megan said, was out, and the shoes had to have heels.

'You're already short,' Megan told Gina, as if she needed reminding. 'If you wear a black dress and flat shoes, no one will see you. If it's dark, you'll get trampled underfoot.'

As Adam had already made disparaging remarks about her height, Gina thought climbing on to a pair of heels for one night might not be a bad idea.

Megan found the dress in a little boutique in one of the back streets. It was made of chiffon petals in various autumn shades stitched to a little shift of brown silk, and she found shoes to match in the same shop: stiletto-heeled, copper-coloured sandals. She clapped her hands in delight. 'You look like one of those fairies you find in woods, you know, a nymphy thingy, and your legs look twice as long in those heels.'

Gina looked at the price tag on the dress and let out a sigh. 'There's no way I can afford this.' Which was a pity, she thought, because it actually made her look sexy, something she had never thought possible.

'Gina,' Megan said seriously, 'if you have to take out a second mortgage, it will still be worth it. You look amazing.'

Gina studied herself in the full-length mirror. The dress matched the colour of her eyes and with her hair a loose tumble of dark-chocolate curls, she did look a bit like a nymphy thingy. Not sure if she had enough in her bank account, she paid by credit card.

'That's what credit cards are for,' Megan said happily. 'To make you look beautiful. I've tried, but no one will let me have one.'

Which meant Gina had to buy the red silk top Megan had been drooling over. 'A present for helping me choose. I could never have done it on my own.'

'Or without your credit card.' Megan said. 'But thank you so much.' She pressed the red silk against her face. 'It was fun.'

Gina wouldn't have agreed it was fun exactly, but it hadn't been as bad as she had expected. Perhaps the secret was to make a day of it and go with a friend; she had never done that before. When she was a child her grandmother had chosen her clothes, suitable attire for a little girl. At college she gradually learned to enjoy choosing her own outfits, experimenting with fabrics and colours, instinctively knowing what suited her, but Simon had changed all that. A nice girl who wanted to become a wife and mother didn't wear a short skirt and high-heeled shoes. He took control of her wardrobe, dressing her in flower prints from Laura Ashley and flat shoes from Clarks, turning her into his image of the perfect housewife. Now Gina chose her clothes for comfort, and if anything had a designer label it was purely by accident.

By Saturday morning she was decidedly nervous. There had been no further messages from Nathan Fox, or from Adam, and she was wondering if she could really go on her own, knowing Robert Cauldwell was going to be there and possibly Judge Pollard. But it was just a dinner, she told herself, and how dangerous could that be?

Megan made her lock up the studio early. 'You need more than half an hour to get ready.' Gina couldn't imagine why. How long did it take to shower and put on a dress? With her warm skin tones, she needed very little make-up, and the jewellery came from her grandmother's jewellery box. Even so, she spent longer than necessary in the shower and then boosted her confidence with a glass of red wine. Halfway through trying to fix her hair she had another glass. She had expected Adam to phone, thinking he might offer to drive her to the town hall, or at least wish her luck. When it was obvious he wasn't going to, she phoned for a taxi.

She had tied her hair on top of her head with little wispy bits hanging down round her ears — Megan's idea — and a gold butterfly clasp holding it all in place. Amber drop earrings and an amber pendant on a gold chain completed the picture. Megan had chosen the perfume for her, floral notes with woody overtones, which seemed appropriate for a wood nymph. She stood in front of the mirror looking at herself. She would have twirled but the shoes wouldn't allow it. To use Megan's words, she didn't look half bad. She picked up a small beaded purse on a gold chain, a leftover from her days before Simon, and dropped in a lipstick and comb. A zip compartment kept her money safe. The taxi was right on time.

Outside the town hall a doorman helped her out of the taxi and someone else took the pashmina she had decided to wear instead of her denim jacket. Her invitation was duly scrutinized and handed back to her. She thanked God for the flunkies holding silver trays of wine just inside the door. Was it bad manners to take two glasses at once?

Damn Adam. She wished she had someone to hold her hand and tell her what to do next. She felt stupid, dressed like a bloody leprechaun with bits of hair dangling round her face. The heels didn't help, either. At least, with the number of people milling about, getting lost in the shuffle would be relatively easy, but as she moved deeper into the melee she felt decidedly claustrophobic, panic not far from the surface. Pull yourself together girl, she told herself. Be brave.

Castlebury town hall had recently had a face lift and refurbishment, courtesy of some lottery money, and Gina had been looking forward to seeing inside the building. The council offices were on the ground floor either side of a rather magnificent main staircase, the upstairs reserved for the mayoral offices and revamped function rooms. The banqueting suite was gilded and chandeliered, dark red drapes with tasselled cords hiding the old windows. The floor was newly carpeted in burgundy, the thick pile catching at her heels.

She drained her glass of wine and looked around for another. She should have taken two when she had the chance. Most of the older women were wearing long dresses, covering up as much as possible, while the younger ones were definitely overexposed, but no one else was wearing a dress quite like hers.

Was that good or bad? she wondered.

The noise in the room dropped a decibel a few moments later, when Robert Cauldwell appeared in the doorway accompanied by an old man with a stick. Gina guessed the tall, skinny old man dressed all in black was Judge Pollard. He reminded her of Freddy from the horror films and she amused herself for a moment stripping him down to his bones, a skeleton in a dinner suit.

Through an archway she could see the dining-room; round tables set with damask tablecloths, crystal and silver glinting in the light from the chandeliers. Panic surfaced again as she remembered why she never went to any of the college balls. It was not knowing who would sit next to her at dinner and the idea that she might have to make polite conversation with someone she didn't know.

Her encounter with Robert Cauldwell took her completely by surprise. Someone pushing past in a hurry to get somewhere, his apology out before he saw who it was he had bumped into. She wasn't expecting his look of shocked amazement.

'What are you doing here, Miss Cross?'

He obviously wasn't expecting to see her

— but if Cauldwell hadn't sent her the invitation, who had?

'I asked a question, Miss Cross?' He was talking to her as if she had crawled in under the wire. She reached into her bag and produced the gilt-edged invitation. He took it as if he didn't believe it was real, but Gina had to admire the way he pulled himself together. 'I'm sorry. Of course everything is in order, I was just surprised to see you.'

At that moment Gina caught a glimpse of someone on the other side of the room, someone she thought she recognized, but Cauldwell was blocking her view. Even on heels she was still shorter than most of the other guests. Who had she seen? She cursed her inability to remember faces.

Robert Cauldwell told her he hoped she had a nice evening and she watched him walk away, running back to report to Judge Dread, no doubt. There were a few people in the room she did recognize, either from a news item on the local TV station or from pictures in various newspapers, but no one who triggered that flash of interest she had felt earlier.

During dinner, with everyone sitting down, Gina had a chance to study the other guests. The class system wasn't dead, she decided, it had just moved on. Now the elite were no longer the white-collar workers; they were the farmers, shopkeepers and franchise owners. She heard a man who ran a car dealership discussing his golf handicap with an elderly lady who owned a chain of betting shops.

'Bread roll on the left, wine on the right,' Gina muttered to herself, hoping they kept the courses in the same order as the cutlery.

The conversation round the table was predictably boring. A discussion on the banning of the local hunt by the men, interspersed with comments about new boutiques and restaurants from the over-dressed women. Gina kept quiet, nodding and smiling in what she hoped were the right places, nursing her glass of wine. Several times she had to put her hand over the glass to stop it being topped up by an over-enthusiastic waiter. She couldn't risk getting drunk. The food was good, all the better because it was free, and Gina wondered what the other guests had paid for their tickets.

After the meal was over and everyone had moved back to the lounge area, Gina started a slow circuit of the room, knowing she would recognize the person she had seen earlier if she came face to face with him, but she couldn't see much in the crowded room, even with her heels.

Another drink might be in order, now she wasn't going to slip under the dinner table and disgrace herself. She fought her way to the bar and just as she was about to give up ever getting served, a glass of lager appeared in front of her.

'You look as if you need that.'

Gina turned to look at the man beside her, not as surprised as she ought to have been. 'Thank you, Adam.'

'We turn up in the strangest places, don't we, us journalists?'

'Press pass?'

'Yup. Gets me in most places, but I didn't get the free drinks, or the free dinner.'

'My heart bleeds for you. Why didn't you phone and tell me you were coming?'

'Masculine pride. My stubbornness sometimes annoys even me.'

'Well, you not only missed the dinner and the drinks, you missed meeting Robert Cauldwell.' She tottered on her heels and Adam caught her arm to steady her. 'It's these damn shoes.' And the wine, and the beer, she thought.

He looked down at her feet and then ran his eyes slowly back up to her face. 'You look quite stunning, Gina Cross, and I like having you up here on those heels where I can see you. Did anyone ever tell you your eyes are an amazing colour, more gold than brown?'

'It's the light in here,' she said, embarrassed. Why had no one ever taught her how to handle a compliment? 'Cauldwell didn't send me the invitation — he nearly had a fit when he saw me — so someone else must have sent it, maybe Fox, but God knows why.'

'I'll have a look round,' Adam said, 'see if I recognize anyone. And I'll have a word with Cauldwell if I can find him. He might give something away if he thinks he's going to get a decent write-up in a national daily. Up to now he's always refused me an interview because he knows the sort of stuff I write about politicians.'

'Nasty, hurtful, biting sort of stuff?'

Adam just nodded, already on his way.

27

Gina had either to find a seat or take off her shoes, neither of which seemed feasible at that moment. She was still looking for somewhere to sit when one of the waiters approached her.

'Mr Cauldwell would like to see you, Miss Cross. He's in the small conference room.'

Gina's first instinct was to say no, which was exactly what she should have done, but curiosity won. What did Cauldwell want to see her about? Not his portrait, that was for sure.

The waiter led her to a corridor with double doors on each side, each room having a name relating to the town's history. She saw Boudicea and Claudius before the waiter stopped at a pair of doors with a small copper plaque telling her this was the Iceni room. Something fluttered in her stomach, but she squared her shoulders, pushed open one of the double doors, and walked into the room.

Cauldwell and the judge sat at an oval table, a tray of coffee in front of them. Behind them another man stood impassively. Gina recognized him instantly: Trevor Pollard, the man she had seen earlier when she was talking to Robert Cauldwell. He was a short, fat man with two crescents of dark hair framing a bald head, his skin pockmarked with acne scars, his eyes deep-set and shrewd. There was no sign of Martin Edge, but Gina remembered reading that the cosmetic surgeon had recently flown out to California to consult with an ageing actress. At the back of the room strange, dour gentlemen peered down at her from gilded picture frames while smoke curled lazily overhead, disturbed by the opening of the door. The room was thick with the pungent aroma of expensive coffee and even more expensive cigars.

'Please sit down, Miss Cross.' Cauldwell poured coffee into a tiny cup and pushed it across the table towards Gina. She sipped the scalding liquid, needing the jolt of caffeine. 'This is Judge Pollard,' Cauldwell told her.

The judge nodded. 'I sent the invitation, in case you were wondering. I've been wanting to meet you, Miss Cross.'

Now that was interesting, Gina thought. The judge had invited her without telling Cauldwell. A little display of power, no doubt, so everyone knew who the boss man really was.

'Thank you,' she said. 'I enjoyed the meal.' She noticed the bright gleam of intelligence behind the rheumy eyes, eyes that never left her face. She waited, remembering the old sales trick of waiting for the other person to speak first. Never volunteer information if you don't have to.

The judge smiled at her, his teeth long and yellow. 'You took some items from a house that didn't belong to you,' the old man said, emphysema causing him to take a breath after every other word.

Gina put her cup back in its saucer without a rattle and looked the judge straight in the eye. 'Such as?'

The old man put his hands flat on the table and leaned towards her. 'Nathan Fox stole a camera from my son and the camera contained a video film. Fox used the film to blackmail my son and his school friends. I explained what would happen to him if he ever tried anything like that again, and he disappeared, but when he found out his wife was dying of cancer, he came back to England.' The old man paused for breath, wheezing. 'Fox says he left something with his wife, probably a copy of the film, which would have been with the things you took from the house.'

'I had a videotape,' Gina said, 'but my flat was trashed and the tape stolen. I'm sure you know it was just a film of a birthday party.'

She looked at the judge contemptuously, adrenalin kicking in. 'I have nothing that belongs to you, Mr Pollard, and if I did,' she added defiantly, 'I wouldn't give it to you. I think all of you were somehow responsible for the death of that little girl, and in the end you'll get found out.' She stood up, breathless herself now, and near to tears. 'I hope you're going to let me go, because if not I shall start screaming.'

Trevor Pollard reached the door before she did and stood with his hand on the handle. 'With all the noise going on downstairs, Miss Cross, do you really think anyone would hear you?' He opened the door and held it wide. 'Enjoy the rest of the evening.' As she moved past him he added quietly, 'It's not over yet, Gina, so remember to watch your back.'

Gina found a ladies' room and sat on the loo until she stopped shaking, then she went downstairs and made her way to the bar. Adam was nowhere to be seen, so she ordered a large brandy and drank it rather quickly. When Adam still didn't appear she picked up her wrap from the cloakroom and walked out into the street. She was halfway home, in bare feet, her shoes dangling from her hand, when Adam drove up beside her.

'Where the hell did you get to?'

His voice was rougher than he intended,

but when he couldn't find her, or Robert Cauldwell, he'd felt something akin to panic. Not a feeling he liked. And it was her fault, damn it. He'd spent ages looking for her because she hadn't bothered to tell him where she was going.

'I got summoned,' she said. 'Robert Cauldwell, Judge Pollard and his son, all cosy with coffee and threats in a little room upstairs. The only one missing was Martin Edge, and he's abroad.' She tried to carry on walking, but he caught her arm.

'Threats? What do you mean, threats? Did they hurt you?'

Gina shook her head and wished she hadn't, as the headache that had been hovering arrived in full force. 'No. Just suggested they might if I didn't give them what I don't have.' She frowned up at him. 'Did that make sense?'

'Not really.' She looked as if she'd been crying and he studied her with concern, forgetting just how angry he had been when he eventually found her wandering along the road. 'Are you sure you're not hurt?'

She couldn't shake her head again; it would have exploded. 'Do you have any aspirin?'

Adam guided her to his car and bundled her inside. 'I'll get you home. When you've had a coffee or two you might make more sense.'

It took two coffees, black and strong, and two aspirin before she became more or less coherent. 'I'm sorry. You weren't at the bar, so I had a brandy, then you still weren't there, so I thought I'd go home.'

'Why didn't you get a taxi?'

'Because I wanted to walk. Those men scared me and I don't like being scared. I told them I wouldn't give them anything even if I had it, but the judge's son told me to watch my back.'

'What is it they want?'

'A film, I think, but not the birthday party one, some other one I don't have.' She looked at Adam. 'Can I go to bed now? You can stay if you want.'

When he lay on the bed beside her, his intention was just to stay with her until she went to sleep, but she moved close, slid her arms round him, and his good intentions suddenly seemed rather pointless.

★ ★ ★

In the morning, after a breakfast of orange juice, cereal, toast and coffee prepared by Adam, Gina felt able to go into more detail about what had happened at the town hall.

'Why do they think I have something I don't?'

'Perhaps you do. What did you do with the stuff you took from the house?'

Gina fetched the envelope and tipped the contents out on to the table. 'Apart from the video, it's all still there. According to the judge, Fox told them he left something incriminating with his wife, but when they searched the house there was nothing there. They were looking for a video and found one at my flat, but it was the wrong video.' She stirred the letters and photos on the table with her hand. 'Perhaps there's something else, something we've missed.' She picked up the diary. 'Maybe this is all code. You know, like they have in books. The dates and times all have a hidden meaning. Solve the code and find the treasure.'

Adam took the little book from her and flicked through the pages. 'I don't think so. We're just missing something. I reckon the camera belonged to Trevor Pollard. We know he took pictures of Susie London, but this was something else, something even worse, and when Fox saw what was on the film he decided to use it to blackmail the three boys.'

'I think you're right about the camera belonging to Trevor Pollard,' Gina agreed, 'but I don't think Fox stole the camera, I think he borrowed it.' She helped herself to more juice. 'Think about it, Adam. When Trevor Pollard found the camera was missing, Fox would be the first suspect, particularly if he had a master key to all the rooms, but what if he just borrowed the camera and intended to put it back before anyone found out? He wouldn't have been able to afford a cine-camera of his own twenty years ago and he wanted to film his daughter's birthday party.'

'So he bought a blank cassette to use but found there was one already in the camera.' Adam stood up and stretched. 'Fox should have taken the film to the police, but he knew the police had been bought off once before. He could have kept quiet, but he decided to use the film to make some money.'

'Which was very stupid, as it turns out.'

'Maybe, but he was working as a lowly caretaker at a school where the pupils got more pocket money than he got in wages, and he had a family to support.' Adam leant over the back of Gina's chair and picked up a photo of little Jessica paddling in the sea. 'Who do you think took the original photo of the dead child?' When Gina didn't answer, he said, 'Polaroid cameras were popular for porn as far back as the 1970s. Andy Warhol used one to take pictures of genitalia — anyone he could find who would drop their pants. The Polaroid camera was the first to have an integral film, so you got your picture straight away. No need to take the film anywhere to have it developed, which made it perfect for paedophiles and the porn trade.'

'You think Fox was a paedophile? That doesn't make sense. He couldn't very well blackmail the other three if he was one himself.'

'I know. God, I wish I had that film,' Adam said regretfully. 'This story would be mind-blowing if it ever came out. Judge Pollard is like the Pope, he's respected all over the world, Cauldwell is all set to be the next prime minister, and Edge fixes celebrities' boobs. A hands-on job, I would imagine. Trevor Pollard may be just a nasty little pervert, but he's Judge Pollard's son. Just think about it. It would make all the other political scandals about as thrilling as Charles and Camilla's wedding.'

Gina looked at his face and saw the excitement there. 'A child died, Adam. Whatever this is all about, a little girl died.' She watched him across the breakfast table, looking for the slightest sign of guilt.

He shifted in his seat. 'Like you said, the child is dead. You can't bring her back.'

'But she was a little girl who was most

likely abused by boys twice her age. You don't really care about the child, do you? You just want your story.' When he didn't answer, she muttered, 'You didn't have to sleep with me last night. I would have been fine on my own.'

'You didn't exactly fight me off.' He picked up the plates, walked through to the kitchen and dumped them in the sink. 'If I remember rightly, you were all for it.'

'That's unfair. I was drunk and I was scared.'

'Then you should keep the hell out of it and stop judging other people by your standards.' When she didn't speak, he grabbed his coat and opened the door. 'Perhaps you should get more sleep. It might put you in a better mood.' She heard the squeal of his tyres as he drove away.

* * *

By the end of the week she was beginning to feel more relaxed. If Fox was sensible he had left the country, gone somewhere he couldn't be found and taken his evidence with him. Cauldwell was about to become a father and was up for a cabinet post, the judge was still wielding a power far too great for a frail old man, but he couldn't live for ever, and Gary seemed to have disappeared off the face of the earth. She was trying not to think about Adam because he obviously wasn't thinking about her.

Funny how things worked out. Just when everything seemed to have quietened down, someone turned up the volume again.

Gina got a call on her mobile phone the following Friday evening, an hour after she had locked up the studio and just as she was about to microwave her dinner.

'Gina?' Reagan asked. Who else did he expect to answer her phone?

'Yes.' Ever hopeful, she pushed the microwave button and watched her dinner start to turn.

'Can you get hold of Megan Pritchard? We need her here.'

Gina frowned at the phone. 'Megan? What for?'

'No time to explain.' His voice faded and Gina could hear someone talking in the background. 'Just get her here as fast as you can. Lincoln Street. We've got a situation.'

The microwave beeped three times. Gina looked longingly at her dinner on the other side of the glass. 'What sort of a situation?'

'A hostage situation. Gary Marsh has a knife at someone's throat.'

28

Half an hour earlier Robert Cauldwell had just finished giving a talk to the Castlebury Ladies' Guild and as he left the meeting with Adrian Troon, his secretary and advisor, he was feeling quite pleased with himself. 'Went well, didn't it?'

'Yes, sir. You had the ladies eating out of your hand. They all promised to vote for you at the next election.'

'Blast, it's started raining.'

'Shall I go ahead and get the car?'

'No, we can cut down beside the National Bank to the car park.'

The two men crossed the road, hurrying to get to the car park out of the rain. Just as they entered the alley beside the bank, Cauldwell felt a sharp pain in his gut, followed by an urgent need to find a toilet. He'd been getting that a lot lately, something the doctor said was caused by nervous tension. While he was talking to the ladies' guild, adrenalin had been keeping his digestive system dormant, now the pressure was off he needed to find a toilet quickly.

'I need a loo,' he told Adrian. 'There's one

just round the corner.'

He knew the public toilet in Lincoln Street wasn't a particularly salubrious place, but he knew he couldn't hold on until he got home. He ducked into the doorway, leaving Adrian outside. 'Won't be a tick,' he said.

The inside was worse than he had expected: a small, stinking rectangle, with graffiti covering the walls like designer wallpaper, crude and explicit with lots of pictures. As Cauldwell was about to enter one of the two stalls, he noticed a small, skinny young man standing by one of the sinks. He looked as if he was rolling a joint, but that wasn't at the top of Cauldwell's worry list. When he came out and went to the sink to wash his hands, the man was still there.

'I know you. You're that politician, Cordell or something.' The man waved a thin roll-up at him. 'You got a light?'

'I don't smoke.'

The hand dryer wasn't working and Cauldwell fished in his pocket for a handkerchief. The man was right behind him. As he went to turn round, Cauldwell felt something touch the side of his neck, a tiny stab of pain.

'I've got a knife in your neck, mister politician man, so keep quiet or I'll cut your throat.'

'What do you want?' Cauldwell didn't wear jewellery, his watch was stainless steel, his mobile phone didn't take pictures, and his wallet contained less than £50. He felt something trickle down his neck. The fucking moron had made him bleed. 'You're in real trouble now. I've got a colleague outside.'

'He's still outside. Put your hands on the basin and stand still.'

At that moment Adrian Troon got tired of waiting. He opened the door to the men's toilet and stuck his head round the corner. For a moment he wondered what he'd walked in on. Robert Cauldwell was standing in front of the washbasin, his hands braced on the rim, a young man standing close behind him. Adrian must have made an involuntary sound, because they both turned their heads, and it was only then that Adrian saw the knife.

'Get the police,' Cauldwell shouted. He put up his hand to grab the knife and the blade sliced across his palm, the pain startling in its intensity. He looked at the blood dripping from the tips of his fingers. 'Get the police,' he said again, more quietly this time.

Adrian Troon wasn't a coward and later he wondered if he could have rushed the man and taken the knife, but the blade was back at Cauldwell's neck, very close to his carotid artery. The youth looked jittery, the knife shaking in his hand, and Troon couldn't risk being responsible for Cauldwell's murder.

'I'll get help,' he said.

'I'm going to kill him,' the young man screamed at Troon's retreating back. 'He killed my baby!'

'What the fuck are you talking about?' Cauldwell pressed his already bloodstained handkerchief to the cut on his hand.

'I wouldn't kill it, would I? Not my own baby.' He sniffed, wiping an arm across his face. 'You got me beat up. Dumped me outside her door and left me.'

'Don't be stupid, I didn't beat you up or dump you anywhere.' Cauldwell had just realized the man holding a knife to his neck must be Gary Marsh and he was in a lot more trouble than he had first thought.

'It was your people beat me up,' Marsh sniffed. 'I was hurt bad.'

Before Cauldwell could answer, his mobile phone rang.

Marsh looked around wildly. 'What's that?'

'My mobile phone. People will be looking for me.'

'Give it to me.' Marsh took the clamshell phone Cauldwell handed him, opened it and held it to his ear, the knife still pressed against Cauldwell's neck. 'What?'

Cauldwell half listened to the exchange while gauging the distance to the door. He felt ridiculous. He was a big man, strong and healthy, while Gary Marsh was skinny and weak. Cauldwell might have tried something if Marsh had been holding a gun, but somehow the knife seemed more personal, more dangerous, and his hand still hurt like hell. The knife was bloody sharp, he knew that.

'I'll tell you what I want in a minute,' Marsh was saying into the phone. 'When I've worked it out.' He dropped the phone into the washbasin.

'You don't know what you want, do you?' Cauldwell said contemptuously. 'You're way out of your league, you brainless idiot. You might as well give up now, before you do any more damage.' He held up his hand. 'This is GBH. You'll get years for this.'

'Shut up! Shut up or I'll cut your fucking throat!'

Marsh was breathing through his nose, noisy puffs of air going in and out, his hand shaking so violently he was having trouble holding the knife. He started waving the weapon around, making little whimpering sounds. Cauldwell waited until the knife was well away from his neck and made a lunge for the door but Marsh was very quick, his reactions heightened by adrenaline and whatever drug he'd taken earlier. He got between Cauldwell and the door, the knife held high, stiff-armed in front of him. Robert Cauldwell couldn't stop in time, and as his momentum carried him forward, he felt the knife go in. There was very little pain, just a blow to his chest, high up under his collarbone. He fell against a cubicle door, staggered inside, and sat down on the toilet seat. As Marsh came towards him he slammed the door, intending to lock it, but there was no lock. He'd picked the wrong cubicle.

Marsh kicked the door open, ramming it against Cauldwell's knees. 'You're going to die. That's what you're going to do. You're going to fucking die.'

Cauldwell put his injured right hand to his shoulder. He couldn't move his left arm and the wound in his shoulder was starting to hurt now. He rolled up his handkerchief and pressed it against the wound. 'If I bleed to death, you're going down for murder. Think about it, Marsh, the rest of your life in prison. No drugs. No nothing.' Cauldwell felt blood running down his chest, the handkerchief already soaked through. 'I need a doctor.'

Gary Marsh wanted to cry. Why did everything always turn out wrong? The phone was ringing incessantly, making his head hurt. He picked up the phone and opened it. 'I've hurt him,' he said. 'Made him bleed. If he tries to get away again I'm going to finish him off.' He shut the phone but it started ringing again almost immediately. He had to stop the noise, it was making his head throb, so he dropped the phone down the toilet in the empty stall.

29

Lincoln Street narrowed down at the top end where it came out into the main road. Traffic was allowed to enter, but not exit. A single police car was parked across the road, preventing anyone driving in, while another car straddled the road further down, lights flashing. Two more cars were standing against the kerb opposite the public toilet. A thin drizzle fell on the half-dozen or so uniformed policemen gathered round the cars and they all looked wet and miserable.

Four men stood outside the toilet entrance. Plain clothes police? Gina didn't know. She looked around for Reagan and saw him sitting sideways on the front seat of one of the cars, his feet on the road, talking into a phone. He saw them approaching, put the phone back in the holder on the dash, and got to his feet.

'Megan?' He took her hand, patted it, and nodded to Gina. 'Sorry to drag you down here on such a filthy evening, but we need you on the spot, just in case.'

Megan looked scared. She looked at Gina,

back at Reagan. 'Where is he? Gary, where is he?'

Reagan sighed, looked embarrassed, waved at the toilets. 'In there.'

Gina looked at the toilet block, at the men grouped outside, one of them talking on a mobile phone, another making notes. There seemed no sense of urgency. There were two entrances to the toilets, one for women, one for men, the women's side sealed with tape. The toilets were old; they had been there as long as Gina could remember, the old buildings above turned into offices, the windows dark. Gina looked at her watch. Six-thirty in the evening. Most of the town offices would be closed, so would the shops, and although it was early evening the street was gloomy and narrow, made even more claustrophobic by the cars blocking the way and the dismal, grey sky.

Reagan reached over and opened the back door of the police car. 'Get inside, both of you, out of the rain. We've got a negotiator talking to Marsh. Hopefully he'll talk the boy down and make him realize how stupid he's being, but Megan might be needed. She probably knows more about Marsh than we do.'

'Can I talk to him now?' Megan asked.

'Not yet. We need more time. We have to

take it slowly, or it gets out of hand, and if the press get to hear of this we'll have a national emergency.'

Gina felt her stomach roll. No dinner. Almost afraid to ask, she said, 'Who's he got in there?'

Reagan just looked at her. He took out a handkerchief and mopped his red face. 'We can't let this go any further or we'll have helicopters and God knows what else down here. If we take our time and keep talking to the boy we can end it without any bloodshed. An armed task force won't help, it would just make matters worse.'

'Armed task force?' Gina said incredulously. She stared at Reagan. 'Who the hell has Gary got in there?'

The big policeman sighed. 'Robert Cauldwell.'

Megan let out a little puff of air. 'Wow, why would Gary do that? Why Robert Cauldwell?' She looked over at the toilet block. 'Funny though, eh? Robert Cauldwell stuck in a toilet with Gary. Best place for both of them, really. They're both bits of shit.'

Gina felt a smile coming but didn't think Reagan would approve. 'Is there another way in, a back door or window? Anything?'

Reagan shook his head. 'No. The council want to pull the whole lot down but the buildings above are listed and have to stay, so it's always too expensive. The toilets are just a hangout for kids on drugs and the local community of perverts.'

Gina knew Reagan was a homophobe, but the toilet block seemed just the place for Cauldwell. He definitely came under the heading of pervert. 'What on earth was Cauldwell doing in a place like that?' she asked.

'Got caught short on his way back to the car park. Me, I'd have pissed in a corner. Anyway, Cauldwell had evidently been talking to some ladies' group in the public library and cut down here to get back to the car park, got caught short, and nipped in there for a quick one. Left his mate outside, thank goodness. The man wondered why his boss was taking so long, went inside, and found Gary Marsh with a knife at Cauldwell's throat. Marsh kept screaming Cauldwell had killed his baby.' Reagan looked at Gina. 'I didn't know the junior minister was a baby killer as well as everything else. I thought Marsh was responsible.'

Gina didn't think this was the time to go into long explanations. 'What happens now?' she asked.

'We wait. We have three choices: overpower Marsh, use a sniper, or use a negotiator. One big problem, though: there's no way to overpower Marsh, the negotiator can't get any sense out of him cos he's high as a bloody spaceship, and we don't have a sniper.' Reagan sighed again. 'I've been told we have to take this slowly, so we could be here all night.'

'Good job Cauldwell's locked in the loo, then,' Megan remarked. 'If he gets caught short again, he won't have a problem.'

Gina had been watching someone talking to the policeman standing by the car blocking the road. She frowned as the man walked towards them. Reagan cursed and got out of the car. 'I said no one in here. How did you get through?'

'Said I was a friend of the family, said I had important information for Inspector Reagan, and said I knew Gina Cross and Megan Pritchard.' Adam beamed at them. 'All of it true.'

'Bet you didn't show your press pass,' Reagan growled. 'They've got strict instructions not to let that lot in. The last thing I want is a poxy reporter on the scene.'

'I'm not here as a reporter, Inspector. I know Gary Marsh has somebody in there and I can get them out.'

'Like hell you can. How did you find out Marsh is in there?' Reagan looked back up the street at his detective constable. 'That man should learn to keep his mouth shut.'

'It wasn't him, I heard it on the police radio band. You should get a safer communications system. As I said, I can get inside, talk to Marsh, and get him to come out.'

'And what makes you think you can do that?'

Gina got out of the car. 'He was a policeman, too,' she said. 'Army.'

'I was a negotiator,' Adam told Reagan. 'My job was to try and negotiate with terrorists and, compared to them, Gary Marsh is a bunny rabbit.'

Reagan sat back down on the car seat. 'You don't know who he's got in there, do you? I didn't put that out on the radio.'

Megan leant out of the rear window of the car. 'Robert Cauldwell,' she told Adam. 'Gary's taken Robert Cauldwell hostage.'

Adam looked at Reagan. 'Knife or gun?'

'Knife.'

Adam was quiet for a moment and Gina thought of the scar on his stomach. Was he negotiating in Iraq when that happened? Tonight he was wearing jeans and a denim jacket, his hair stuck together in little wet spikes, his feet still in sandals. She didn't want him to get hurt again.

'A knife is a tad easier,' Adam said at last.

'Marsh could shoot a gun from any distance but with a knife he'll have to get close. He's only a skinny little thing. I'm taller than him and my arms are longer.' He looked at Reagan. 'And I was trained to be extremely fast.'

'He'll kill Cauldwell before he goes for you. He's nuts. Besides, you're not going in there, Shaw. My team is talking to Marsh and they'll talk him out of doing anything stupid.'

Adam shook his head. 'No, they won't. He's a cokehead and he shoots up. He won't listen to reason because he can't, and if he's stuck in there without a fix for any length of time, we're in real trouble.' He looked at Megan. 'What's he on?'

She slithered out of the car. 'Skag, I expect. You know, smack.'

'Will he have some with him?'

She shook her head. 'That's what he was in there for, I bet, hoping someone would sell him something, and he has to go in places like that to inject himself. Most of his veins are used up, so sometimes he uses his . . . you know, his thingy.'

Reagan was doing a lot of sighing. 'You mean he shoots the stuff into his dick?'

Adam turned to Reagan. 'We can't leave him in there with Cauldwell, he's too unpredictable. Let me go over and see how your man's getting on and find out if Marsh will talk to me. You haven't got anything to lose.'

Reagan led the way over to the toilet block. The two women stayed by the car.

'Why would Gary do a thing like that?' Megan asked. 'He doesn't even know Robert Cauldwell.'

Gina remembered telling Gary who she thought had been responsible for his beating, but she could see no virtue in confession so she leant against the car, getting wet as penance. Her leather bomber jacket protected her top half, but her jeans were soaked. Megan was wearing a bright yellow waterproof jacket she'd borrowed from one of the policemen, which made her look like a lollypop lady, but it was keeping her dry. Gina watched Adam talking to the negotiator, then the men moved into a huddle, discussing something. There was more talking on the phone and she saw Adam shaking his head, then both men started back towards the car. Gina looked at Adam's face and a sudden shiver brought goosebumps out on her arms.

'She can't do it,' Adam said, as they got nearer. 'It's too dangerous. I won't let her do it.' Adam slammed his fist against the side of the car. 'Damn it, I thought he'd go for it.'

'What does Gary want?' Gina asked.

'He wants you, Gina,' Adam told her angrily. 'He wants you.'

30

'What does he want me to do?' Gina's eyes were on Adam.

'You're not doing it, Gina, no way. The idiot has a knife — and he's coming down off whatever he was on, so he's as unpredictable as hell.'

'Just tell me what he wants me to do.'

'I've already organized it,' Reagan told Adam. 'The stuff should be here in a few minutes.' He looked at Gina. 'We promised him a fix if he lets Cauldwell go, but he wants you to take it to him.'

'I can do that.' She looked from one man to the other. 'For goodness' sake, I can throw it through the door or something, then while he's injecting himself one of you can grab him. What's he actually done? Is Cauldwell injured? Dead?' She turned her attention to Reagan. 'Do any of you know anything?'

Reagan squeezed a point just above the bridge of his nose with two fingers. 'We were talking to Marsh, then the phone went dead. It's either run out of battery or Marsh doesn't want to talk to us any more. He did say Cauldwell's bleeding badly.'

'So you need me to do this.'

Megan put her hand on Reagan's arm. 'Why can't I go? Gary knows me.'

'He won't talk to you, Megan. He specifically asked for Gina, but we can't let her go in there on her own, it's too risky. We thought we had plenty of time. Cauldwell's mobile is fully charged and on contract, and we were just going to keep on talking, that's what negotiating is all about, but now the phone's gone dead. We tried shouting through the door, but he won't answer.'

'Let me talk to Gary,' Gina said. 'He can't hurt me if I stay outside, and someone has to do something. I don't care if Cauldwell dies, but Gary isn't a murderer, he's just a poor, sick kid.' She looked at Adam. 'If he won't talk to you or Megan or the negotiator, it'll have to be me.'

Adam caught hold of her arm. 'Listen to me, Gina, you're not going anywhere near Marsh. He's dangerous.'

She shrugged her arm away. 'I don't take orders.' She meant to say it lightly, but it came out as a flat statement of fact.

Reagan stared at the sky, looking for inspiration, rainwater dripping off the end of his nose. 'We could send a couple of armed police in there, but that won't help matters, will it? How about you try just talking to him,

Gina? Don't go inside, just talk to him from the doorway. If you shout loudly enough, he should be able to hear you.'

'She's not going inside.'

Reagan patted Adam on the back. 'No, she's not going inside, that's what I just said, but we have to keep talking to Marsh. Show him our good intentions. We have to give him what he wants if we possibly can. It's not as if he wants a million dollars or a plane ticket to Hawaii, and the longer we leave him the more dangerous he's going to get.'

A police officer came up to Reagan and handed him a plastic bag.

'Everything you asked for, sir. Clean needle and everything. Better than he'd get on the street.'

Reagan took the bag. 'Tell him what you've got, and then just throw it in, Gina. Don't let him get anywhere near you.'

Gina stared at the toilet door. It was open about four inches, not enough to see inside. Suddenly, everyone was quiet. The negotiator moved back and the assistant stopped writing on his pad, but she could hear traffic moving in the High Street and the rain still fell. She walked towards the door and pushed it open a bit more. It was dark inside, a partition shielding the urinals from the street. She couldn't see Gary Marsh and guessed he was behind the partition. The smell was really bad: blood, sweat and fear, mixed with the stink of urine.

She cleared her throat and shouted through the door. 'Gary? Gary, it's Gina. I've got the stuff you want, but you have to let Robert Cauldwell go. Is he badly injured? You don't want him to die, do you?'

There was a long silence. 'Hold the stuff out so I can see it.' Gary sounded jittery, his voice high and scared.

She looked back at Reagan. He was standing a few feet away, next to Adam, and she could feel their combined anxiety, see their fear. She took a step forward, holding the bag out in front of her, one hand still holding the door open. She wasn't expecting the hand that clamped on her wrist, pulling her inside.

Gary had been behind the door.

With a little squeak of fright, she let go of the door and heard it swing shut behind her. Gary wrapped an arm round her, holding her against him, pinning her arms to her sides. He was surprisingly strong and she was too shocked to fight him. Everything had happened too quickly. She heard Adam shout a stream of expletives, words she'd never heard him use before, some she didn't even know. Then the door swung open again and she saw Adam standing in the opening.

'Do her any harm, Marsh, and you're dead.'

It was only then that she realized the blade of the knife was resting against her throat.

'You come in here, I'll kill her. I mean it.'

Adam stood very still. She could see Reagan a little way behind him, the two policemen further back. For several seconds they were a tableau, framed in the open doorway.

'You can't manage two hostages, Marsh. Think about it. You can only keep the knife on one of them at a time. Let Gina go.'

Gary shook his head violently. Gina felt spittle land on her cheek and start to run down her face. 'Not yet. Got to make sure the stuff's OK.'

He pulled Gina backwards behind the partition. She could no longer see Adam and felt sheer terror trying to empty her stomach. She was afraid to swallow with the knife so close to her throat. She had to get a hold on herself, she had volunteered for this and Gary wouldn't hurt her.

Adam walked slowly round the partition. 'Let her go.'

Gary shook his head again. 'After I use the stuff. That was the deal.'

Adam pushed open the cubicle door.

Cauldwell was slumped on the seat, his face grey, barely conscious. 'He's lost a lot of blood. He needs an ambulance.'

'Not yet.' Marsh was trying to pull up his sleeve with his teeth. 'I can't do it myself. She'll have to do it.' He held up the hand holding the bag, it was shaking badly. 'Find a vein,' he told Gina. 'The needle has to go in sideways, otherwise it'll go right through.' He thrust the bag into her hand. 'Get the stuff out the bag, let me look at it.'

The syringe was already half filled with something, the needle capped. She pulled off the plastic cap, looking at Gary. 'Now what?'

'Push the plunger until a drop of liquid comes out,' Adam said calmly. 'Let me do it,' he said to Marsh. 'I've done it before.'

'No, she can do it.' Gary pushed Gina against the partition, leaning against her, still holding the knife to her throat, the blade flat against her neck just under her chin. Gary's whole body was shaking now and Gina had to hold his arm still while she pushed up his sleeve and searched for a vein. She wondered why Adam hadn't made a move. There was no way this could be resolved safely once Gary had his fix, they would have nothing to bargain with. She considered sticking Gary somewhere painful with the syringe, but the blade of the knife was a constant reminder not to do anything stupid. She could already feel a thin trickle of blood where Gary had nicked her skin.

She looked at Adam, and thought she saw an almost imperceptible shake of his head. She looked down at Gary's arm. The skin was flat and pale, pocked with needle marks.

'I can't do it,' she said. 'You haven't got any veins in your arm.'

Adam unbuckled his belt and pulled it through the loops on his jeans. Without saying a word, he took Gary's arm and put the belt round it above the elbow, putting the end through the buckle. He pulled it tight, waited, pulled again, then he took the syringe out of Gina's hand and pushed it into a threadlike blue vein.

'Just enough for one shot, Marsh, that's all you get, but that should be enough.'

Gary undid the belt one-handed, passed it back to Adam. He was breathing fast, waiting for relief. Gina felt the knife slide away from her throat and saw the look of puzzlement on Gary's face. Adam took the knife out of Gary's useless hand and caught him as he collapsed. There was a shocked look of understanding in Gary's eyes just before Adam lowered his limp body to the concrete floor. He'd been had.

'What have you done?' Gina asked in alarm. 'Have you given him an overdose?'

Adam shook his head. 'Not exactly what Gary had in mind, though. That was just a particularly strong sedative. A knockout shot.' He called to the ambulancemen outside to come in and get Cauldwell. 'Pity we can't leave that bastard to die.'

Gina found she was shaking almost as much as Gary Marsh had been. She felt cold, and very tired. As she came out into the rain Megan hugged her, big tears filling the girl's eyes. 'I thought you were going to die.'

Gina looked for Adam and saw him talking to the negotiators. Asking for a job, probably, she thought. He had really enjoyed himself in there.

She watched the ambulance pull away, taking Robert Cauldwell to hospital where he would have a private room and receive the best treatment money could buy. Gary had partly regained consciousness and was being loaded into a police car, his hands strapped behind him. He was still shaking, tremors racking his thin body. He looked across at Gina and she saw the hopelessness in his eyes. Robert Cauldwell would no doubt live, but Gary Marsh was already as good as dead.

Megan was still crying, great sobs that made her shoulders go up and down, and

Gina wished she was better at giving comfort. Some people seemed to know instinctively what to do. Gina remembered her grandmother telling her big girls don't cry, but they do, harder and longer than little girls usually. She put her arm awkwardly round Megan's waist and led her back to the car. 'Come on, I'll take you home.'

Megan fished in her pocket for a tissue. 'Will they lock Gary up?'

'I don't know. He's not worth crying over, though.'

'I know.' She pushed a strand of damp hair out of her eyes. 'Did I tell you we went to school together?'

'Yes, you did. He's still not worth crying over.'

Reagan caught up with them. 'Gina, I'm so sorry, that wasn't meant to happen.' He gave her shoulder a fatherly squeeze.

'My fault. I got too close. What will they do to Gary?'

'I've no idea. It will depend on the court. A spell in prison, perhaps, then rehab, none of which will do any good.' He turned her to face him. 'How do you feel?'

'Fine.' She'd stopped shaking. 'I just want to drop Megan off and go home.'

'You shouldn't be driving.' He called to one of his officers. 'Take Miss Pritchard and Miss

Cross home. I'll arrange for your car to be dropped off later,' he told Gina.

Adam appeared beside them. 'I'll take the girls home in Gina's car. My car's parked at the leisure centre, it'll be fine until tomorrow.' Adam's fingers brushed Gina's throat, almost a caress. 'He nicked you with the knife.'

She stepped back. 'I know,' she said. 'It's nothing.'

Reagan turned back towards them. 'I didn't know he hurt you. Do you need a doctor?'

Gina scowled at Adam. 'It's nothing a plaster won't fix.' Tiredness was enveloping her like a blanket. 'I just need to get home.'

Adam took the keys she handed him and helped her into the front seat, while Megan got in the back. Adam had to move the seat back to accommodate his long legs before he could get in the car and follow the ambulance out on to the main road.

Gina watched the ambulance weave through the traffic until it disappeared from view, the siren wailing. 'He's going to be all right, isn't he?'

'Cauldwell? Probably. It was a deep stab wound but we got to him in time.'

'Why didn't we leave him to die?'

'Because it wouldn't have solved anything and Gary would have been done for murder.'

Adam dropped Megan off outside her

house and waited until she was safely inside, then he drove the block to Gina's flat. He got out with her.

'I'm not going to ask you in, Adam, I'm too tired.'

'I have no intention of coming in,' he answered with a smile. 'I just want to see you safely inside.' He followed her up the stairs and waited until she had unlocked the door. 'Get some sleep, Gina.'

'That's what you said last time I saw you.'

He bent and kissed her on the forehead. 'This time I'm saying it nicely.'

31

Gina woke early on Saturday morning. She had already told Megan to take the day off and she knew she couldn't cope alone with the Saturday morning crowd, so she put a closed sign on the door downstairs and went back up to her flat. She felt restless, but too tired to run. Hungry, but couldn't be bothered to eat. When the phone rang at nine o'clock, it made her jump.

'This is Beatrice Finnegan,' a voice told her. 'From the *Castlebury Times*. I'd really like to talk to you about your part in the situation yesterday evening. I believe you saved Robert Cauldwell's life.'

Gina stared at the phone in dismay. Is that what she'd done? 'No,' she said. 'That wasn't what happened.'

'May I come and interview you, Miss Cross? I've been told you work for the police. A psychic artist or something?'

'No, you've got that wrong as well. I'm a forensic artist. The two words are spelt differently. If you want a story, Miss Finnegan, you'll have to speak to the police.'

She slammed the phone back in its holder.

Damn! How had the paper got hold of her name? The last thing she wanted was to be plastered all over the local paper as a psychic. No one would want to have their picture painted in case she read their minds or put a hex on them.

She let the phone ring for the rest of the day.

In the evening, she walked round to Megan's and they sent out for pizza and watched television. Sprawled on the settee with Blossom on her lap, Megan looked comfortably at home. She'd put back on the weight she'd lost and it suited her. Megan was never meant to be thin. Gina sat in the armchair, her feet tucked up under her, thinking about Robert Cauldwell.

'He's going to get away with everything, that's what really bugs me.' She pulled the tab on another beer. 'That reporter woman said I saved his life, but I would've pushed the bastard's head down the toilet and held it there if I'd had the chance.'

Megan shook her head. 'No, you saved Gary's life. If Cauldwell had died, Gary would've gone to prison for ever. I can't believe he held a knife to your throat.'

'I don't think he would have hurt me. I would have been a lot more worried if it had been Cauldwell with a knife at my throat.'

'Yeah. Even holding a knife to your throat, Gary's still a better person than Robert Cauldwell. I wish Gary didn't have to go to prison. He never means to hurt anyone.'

'But he does, Megan. He needs to be locked up for a while, just to get himself straight, and after what he did to you I will never be able to forgive him.'

The doorbell made them both jump.

Megan put the cat down. 'Who's that?'

Gina shook her head. 'It's late for a visitor. Put the chain on the door before you open it.' It couldn't be Gary, thank God. He was locked up.

Megan had unzipped her jeans for comfort; now she hastily zipped them up again as she made her way to the front door. Gina heard the chain go on the door, and then muffled conversation.

The man who walked into the room a minute later had a duffel bag slung over one shoulder and a metal case under his arm. Gina inspected him from her armchair. Sun-bleached hair, a little too long for her taste, matched with grey-green eyes and the build of an athlete. Gina guessed he was probably in his mid to late twenties.

'This is Jack,' Megan said. 'Jack Lowry, my landlord.'

'Sorry to barge in on you ladies.' He dropped his metal case on the floor and unhitched the duffel bag. 'I'm back in England for a couple of days, but I can easily find a hotel.'

'Shit, no.' Megan was trying to remember if she had undone her blouse as well as her jeans. 'No, it's your house, and there's two bedrooms.' She blushed. 'That's if you don't mind sharing your house with me. I can stay with Gina if you'd rather.'

'Beer?' Gina handed him a can. So this was the photographer Adam had been talking about. He had worked with Adam for some years and was now one of the top ten news photographers in the country. He must have been just a kid when he started.

He took the beer and sat down next to Megan. Blossom immediately started rubbing round his legs.

'I hope you don't mind about the cat,' Megan said worriedly. 'She doesn't strop the furniture or anything.'

Jack scratched Blossom behind the ear and she fell at his feet, flat on her back, looking up at him adoringly. 'Not a bit. Every house should have a cat.'

Gina watched, amused. The two of them looked like a couple of kids on a blind date. She stood up.

'I have to go, Megan. Nice to have met you, Jack.'

Ignoring Megan's look of panic, she let herself out and walked slowly home. It would be nice for Megan to have some male company for a couple of days. Jack Lowry was younger than she had expected, and better looking. She smiled to herself, wondering if he liked older women, but when she went to bed and eventually to sleep, she dreamed of a dragon with Cauldwell's face, and a knight with the tattoo of a snake on his arm.

★ ★ ★

Adam arrived on her doorstep early on Sunday morning. 'You didn't answer your phone all day yesterday. Where were you?'

Gina moved aside to let him in. Blocking the doorway never seemed to work. 'Believe it or not, Adam, I do have a life, and I go out sometimes. Not often, I must admit, but sometimes.' She had only been up a short time and her hair was still wet from the shower. She was wearing nothing but a long T-shirt and fluffy slippers.

'So where were you?'

Gina bit back the obvious retort. 'The local paper got hold of my name so I didn't answer the phone in case it was them calling again, thanking me for saving Cauldwell's life. In the evening, I went round to Megan's and Jack Lowry turned up.' She looked up at the ceiling. 'Have I left anything out? I don't think so.'

'Jack's back in England?'

'It would seem so.'

'Oh, for goodness' sake, Gina,' Adam said in exasperation. 'Give up on the ice maiden bit, will you?'

He looked at her properly for the first time. Her hair was a tumbled mass of damp curls the colour of black coffee, her amber eyes were sparkling with annoyance, and the T-shirt barely covered her knees. He carried on looking and saw the ice slowly melt. Her arms dropped to her sides and she ran the tip of her tongue over her lips.

He had to bend down to kiss her on the mouth, but she was already on tiptoe. As they tumbled on to her still unmade bed, she was pulling her T-shirt over her head.

He took his time with her, kissing different parts of her, while he slowly took off his own clothes. Today, there was no Megan down below in the studio and no customers in the shop. Gina could make as much noise as she liked and she found she liked making a noise. With Simon, the sound of sex had been an embarrassment. With Adam, it was a delight.

When he eventually collapsed beside her, she was still smiling. 'Sunday lunch,' he said. 'Early. You make me hungry.'

She slid off the bed. 'I'm going to have another shower.' She looked over her shoulder at him and caught him staring at her bottom. 'There's room for two.'

The shower took longer than expected and by the time they were both dressed it was time to find somewhere to eat. The weather was gloriously hot after yesterday's rain, so Adam drove them to the riverside pub where they had eaten before. Unfortunately, everyone else seemed to have the same idea.

'It'll be at least an hour before we can find you a table,' the waitress told them. Too hungry to wait, they were about to leave when a voice called out from the deck overlooking the water.

'Hi, Ads. No booking? I thought you were always so organized.' Gina turned to see Jack Lowry and Megan sitting at a table on the deck. 'Come and join us,' Jack said. 'We've got a table for four. Plenty of room.'

Megan was dressed in a tank top and jeans, her pale shoulders already turning pink in the sun. 'Jack didn't want me to cook,' she said.

'Just as well,' Gina said dryly. Megan had once confessed she didn't know how the cooker worked and had never turned it on. 'It's too hot to cook, anyway.'

Once the food was on the table they started talking about the Cauldwell affair.

'Cauldwell was on television yesterday, speaking from his hospital bed, praising the police force.' Adam smiled at Gina. 'Funny, he didn't mention you once.'

'He obviously doesn't know I saved his life.'

Jack had a good idea what had happened so far, as Adam had been keeping him up to date. 'Cauldwell's milking the whole thing,' Jack said. 'Talking about how he's going to take crime off the streets and make Castlebury a better place to live. All that rubbish.'

'He told us all how he fears for his pregnant wife,' Megan added. 'Evidently, no one is safe with people like Gary walking the streets. I wish there was some way to get Robert Cauldwell off the streets.'

'So you have nothing to incriminate Cauldwell? No hard evidence at all?' Jack asked.

'There is a bit more information,' Adam volunteered. 'I did some checking, and found out one of the houses backing on to the field where the bones were found once belonged to Martin Edge's parents.' They all looked at him and he grinned, pleased with the effect he was having. 'And the parents worked abroad while Martin was at school. So the house was empty most of the time.'

Gina looked down at her uneaten food. 'So the three of them killed the child at Martin Edge's house and dumped her body in the pond.'

'Hang on,' Jack said. 'That's taking a big leap, isn't it? The house is another bit of the puzzle, but not proof of murder.'

'So what do we do now?' Megan asked. 'Even if Gina's right, we still don't have any evidence. We don't know who the Hummer man works for and Nathan Fox is still missing. I know Gina could pick him out if she saw him, even if he was disguised, but we have to find him first.'

'Have you got anything else, Gina?' Jack asked. 'Anything at all, even something that doesn't seem to be important. What exactly did this Nathan Fox say to you when he met you in the park?'

'I said I was going to put everything back in the house, but Fox told me not to. He said to hang on to it until he tells me what to do with it. There is nothing written on the back of any of the photos, the letters don't seem to have any hidden meaning, and we've been right through the diary several times. Just appointments for the hospital, dentist, hairdresser's, things like that. The letters are personal, from Fox to his wife, no invisible writing or hidden clues.'

Adam looked at Gina. 'When was the last time you checked your email?'

'Yesterday,' she answered, much too quickly.

When Adam raised a disbelieving eyebrow, Gina felt a wash of fear. When had she last checked her email? She couldn't even remember. At that moment Jack's phone rang. He waved a hand in apology and stood up, walking out to the street to take the call.

While he was outside, Adam ordered coffee. When the waitress had gone, he looked at Gina. 'You really must get into the habit of checking your email every day.'

Jack came back to the table and saved her having to answer. 'I'm off to Thailand again in a few days, a follow-up to the tsunami.' He looked at Adam. 'Why don't you come with me? There's a lot to write about. People are having to rebuild their lives and the situation out there needs reporting.'

Adam didn't answer immediately. The coffee had just arrived and Gina was staring into her cup as if a tsunami might appear in the dark liquid at any moment.

'I'll think about it,' Adam said. 'It would be nice to finish this Cauldwell thing first, though. I've put in months of work, but got nothing I can use.'

'Fox may still get in touch. I expect he wants Robert Cauldwell out of the way as much as you do, but you have to remember he won't want to get caught up in a police net and pulled in with the rest of them. If he's got any sense he's already left the country.' As they stood up to go, Jack put his arm round Megan's waist. 'Come on, my little lodger, let's go home and feed the cat.'

'I hope he doesn't hurt her,' Gina said quietly.

Adam watched them leave. 'He won't.' When he pulled up outside Gina's studio, he sat with the engine running. 'Do I get to come in?'

Gina shook her head. 'I need to chill out by myself tonight.'

Standing at the top of the stairs watching him drive away, she wondered if he would go to Thailand with Jack Lowry. Probably. The men in her life didn't usually hang around for very long.

32

Once in her flat, Gina couldn't get to the computer fast enough. Why had she lied to Adam, and why, oh why, didn't she check her email each day? She had a new monitor now so there was no excuse. Not too many messages, and most she deleted straight away, but there was one that made her heart almost stop and then race until the blood was hammering in her head. The one she was almost scared to open. The one from Fox.

Meet me at my wife's house Sunday evening. Bring the diary. Fox.

Her watch told her it was ten minutes to five. Not evening yet, thank God. Fox would pick a quiet time, when everyone had eaten their Sunday lunch and had their walk in the park, not many people about and not many cars on the road. God, she couldn't afford to miss a meeting with Fox because she hadn't checked her mail. The thought was appalling.

She didn't phone Adam. Not only would he kill her if he found out she'd been lying about checking her email, but he'd want to go with her, and that would cause all sorts of problems. Fox knew her, he didn't know

Adam, and he'd probably disappear for good if he saw a stranger. No, this she could do on her own. If Fox had wanted to harm her he would have done so already, and this time she'd make sure he told her everything she needed to know to put Robert Cauldwell away for good. She was fed up with all the secrets and lies.

She changed from shorts into slim black jeans and a lightweight sweatshirt. With trainers on her feet and her hair tied back in a loose plait to keep it out of the way, she felt like Lara Croft. All she needed was a gun strapped to each thigh.

She left her flat just before six o'clock and with the roads relatively clear she made good time. She drove past Jessica's house, then parked in a side street and ducked down the alley to let herself in the back gate. If Fox was there already, the back door should be unlocked; if not, she was stuck. Adam still had the key. She could knock on the front door, but that might not be a good idea.

It was still daylight — the sun wouldn't set for several hours — but thick cloud had covered the sun and the back yard of the little house was in full shadow. Gina shivered, wishing she'd worn a jacket. Was she being really stupid, coming here on her own? For the first time it occurred to her that this could be a trap. If the door was locked she would turn around and go home.

The door was unlocked, the house quiet.

Gina opened the door and hesitated, reluctant to step inside. Fox must be in there already if the door was unlocked, unless she'd misinterpreted the message and he'd already been and gone — or hadn't arrived yet.

For Christ's sake, Gina, she told herself, just go inside.

She'd left her bag in the car, putting her car keys and her mobile phone in her pockets, but now she took out her phone and turned it off. The last thing she wanted was Adam ringing her and spooking Fox. She moved slowly into the kitchen, her feet silent on the tiled floor. The room was bare. All Jessica's little touches gone, all the kitchen utensils, even the cooker. A look in the lounge confirmed the house had been stripped; all that remained were the carpets. She wondered how badly the house had been trashed before Aunt Jane came in and cleaned up.

She moved from the kitchen into the hall. The house was too quiet, and there was also a strange, sour smell. Not just the musty smell of an empty house. Something else. She was about to call Fox's name when she heard a small sound. A tiny mewing noise, like an animal locked in a room somewhere. She lifted her head. The sound was coming from upstairs, but she stood still with her hand on the banister rail, suddenly feeling very alone.

'Mr Fox?'

Her voice sounded startlingly loud, echoing round the empty house. Holding her breath, she started up the stairs. The noise had stopped, but the smell was stronger, the silence absolute. If she called out again she would make herself jump. She climbed the stairs slowly, her feet silent on the carpet, her ears pricked for the slightest sound. The stairs took a sharp turn at the top and she stopped, clutching the banister rail, her heart trying to climb out of her chest, not wanting to believe the sight in front of her.

Nathan Fox sat upright on a wooden chair in the main bedroom, facing the open door. He was naked, bound with parcel tape like a mummy. His arms and upper body were taped to the back of the chair, his ankles to the chair legs. The tape over his eyes pinned his ears to his head and his mouth was taped shut. He had been left blind and mute, sitting in his own excrement. Burn marks covered his body, fresh and raw.

'Nathan?' Gina whispered.

She was unsure whether he was alive or dead, but he moved his head when she said his name. She forced herself to take the few steps towards him and rip the tape from his mouth, too scared to be gentle. He licked his lips, bloody where the tape had torn the skin.

'Who is it?' His head moved again as he tried to see with his blind eyes. 'Who's there?'

'Gina Cross.' She wanted to touch him but couldn't. His skin had an unhealthy sheen, slick and oily, and the stink of him made her gag. 'You left an email message.'

'No. No, I didn't.' His voice was weak, little more than a croak. As she tried to pull the tape from his eyes he shook his head frantically. 'Please. Just go.'

'Where's the evidence, Nathan? We need something against Cauldwell.'

He tried to lick dry lips. 'Look in the diary.'

A click behind her had her turning her head. The Hummer man stood looking at her, a gun in his hand. 'Good evening, Miss Cross. Glad you could come.' He walked past her and stood in front of Nathan Fox, shaking his head sadly. 'Tut, tut, we should have put you in a nappy. I thought you'd manage to hang on a bit longer.' He held the gun a few inches from Fox's head and pulled the trigger.

Gina watched the bullet enter just above the bridge of Fox's nose, watched the explosion of blood, watched brains and bone hit the wall behind him, but almost before the scream left her mouth the Hummer man had backhanded her round the face so hard her feet left the floor. She hit the ground with her shoulder, momentum slamming her into the wall, and she stayed there, curled up like a foetus, until he grabbed her plait and pulled her to her feet. She felt a sharp pain as hair was ripped from the back of her skull.

Still holding her by the hair, he put his face close to hers. Incongruously, his breath smelt of mint toothpaste. 'We don't need Fox any more, do we? I left him there to show you what we do to people who don't cooperate. At first he refused to tell us anything, but some people can't stand pain. Now suppose you hand this diary over so we can all go home.'

Gina managed to get her legs to work and stood up as straight as she could, taking the weight off her plait. She didn't feel sick or faint or even sad that Fox was dead, just terrified that she was going to die herself, and even more terrified she was going to be strapped naked to a chair until someone came and shot her.

When she didn't answer, the Hummer man hit her again, quite gently in comparison to the last time, but he had the gun in his hand and she felt the bones in her cheek shift, blood dribbling into her mouth.

'I don't have it here.' She was about to tell him the diary was in her handbag in the car. She would have told him anything he wanted to know, but he didn't give her the chance.

'You're lying.' He twisted the plait, almost lifting her off her feet. 'One way or another, you're going to tell me exactly where the diary is.'

'No, she's not,' a voice said quietly from behind them. Adam stood in the doorway, a gun in his hand.

The Hummer man swung Gina round by her hair and clamped an arm round her neck. She gagged, struggling for breath. She knew Adam wouldn't shoot while she was being used as a shield, so she lifted both her feet off the floor, hoping she wouldn't break her neck or choke to death. She only weighed 110 pounds, but the Hummer man couldn't hold her with one hand and aim the gun at Adam. He let go and she slid to the floor, clutching at her neck, wondering if she would ever breathe again.

She heard a gun go off and saw Adam's body jerk as the bullet hit him, his legs buckling as he fell. Gina stared at him in confusion. That wasn't supposed to happen.

A tall, skinny man came racing into the room. His eyes went from Adam to Gina. 'What the fuck!'

'A problem,' the Hummer man said. 'We got the girl, but the boyfriend turned up as well. The girl's got the diary. She'll tell . . . ' His voice tailed off at the sound of a police siren somewhere nearby, gradually getting louder. 'Grab the boyfriend, it's time we left.'

He dropped the gun in his pocket and caught hold of Gina, lifting her round the waist and holding her tight against him. Although she beat him round the head with her clenched fists and screamed in his ear, he seemed oblivious.

It wasn't until she bit off the top part of his ear that he let go of her and dropped her down the stairs.

'Bitch!' he shouted at her as she tumbled to the bottom. 'Fucking bitch!'

He followed her down the stairs and aimed a kick at her, but the police car had screeched to a stop outside and someone was battering on the front door.

'I'm off!' the skinny man shouted from the landing. He had been in the process of hauling Adam to his feet but now he dropped him, ran down the stairs, jumped over Gina, and scooted for the back door. The Hummer man kicked Gina one last time, clamped a hand over the remains of his bleeding ear, and followed his mate.

Gina managed to crawl up the stairs to

Adam. The front of his shirt was soaked with blood. 'You were supposed to shoot first,' she said through her tears. She stared at his bloody chest, afraid to touch him. 'How bad is it?'

'It's only a flesh wound, I think, in my shoulder.'

Gina called frantically for help and a young police officer appeared at the top of the stairs. He looked through the bedroom door at Fox and Gina saw the colour leave his face.

'We need help here. You can't help that man, he's already dead, but we're still alive at the moment.'

'Sorry.' He turned away from Fox and knelt down in front of Adam. 'His pulse is good. I think he'll be OK. How about you, ma'am?'

'Just cut and bruised, I think.' She opened her mouth experimentally. 'My face feels strange, though.'

Reagan walked into the room. He looked at Fox and then back at Gina. Adam tried to get to his feet but changed his mind.

'Ambulance is here,' Reagan said. 'We'll get you both to hospital.'

'Have you caught them? The Hummer man and the other one?' Gina asked. Her face felt tight and she was having difficulty talking. A paramedic came into the room and she shuffled to one side so he could work on Adam. 'Even if you catch both of them, they won't know anything. They won't even know who employed them.'

Reagan shrugged. 'Good to get them off the streets, though. We've got them both. Which one killed Fox?'

'The one with the cat scratch on his face and a missing ear. The Hummer man. He shot Adam, too.'

The paramedic attending to Adam stood up. 'He's lost a bit of blood but he's going to be fine. The bullet went right through and out the other side.'

Adam looked at Gina. 'I wasn't much use, was I? Too slow in my old age.'

She smiled at him. 'Aren't you supposed to stick your gun round the door first?'

'If I'd stuck my gun round the door first I wouldn't have been able to see what I was shooting at, and I knew you were in there somewhere. I didn't particularly want to shoot you.' He managed a smile. 'Although there are times . . . '

★ ★ ★

Megan and Jack were waiting when Gina came out of X-ray a few hours later.

'No bones actually broken, just badly

bruised ribs and a few stitches in my cheek. I must be tougher than I thought. I feel like an old lady, though. I can't breathe properly, or stand up straight, and I'm not going to be able to run for weeks. I'm going to have to shuffle around like a cripple.'

Megan gave her a gentle hug. 'I know exactly how you feel. Just be glad you're alive. Stay indoors and eat chocolate.'

'How's Adam?' Jack asked.

'Still in surgery,' Gina told him. 'But God knows what he thought he was doing. He had a gun. He should've fired straight away, not got shot himself.'

'Adam's had that gun since he left the army. It's never loaded because he hasn't got a permit.'

So the stupid idiot had been standing there with an empty gun and no way of defending himself. 'Who called the police?' she asked Jack.

'Adam called me on my mobile and said to get the police to the Fox house. He said you were there on your own and not answering your phone.'

Guiltily Gina remembered turning her mobile off, although if it had gone off in the house she would probably be dead by now. She tried not to think about Fox and what they had done to him. His torture must have lasted for days, but now she had no need to keep the things she had taken from the house. Enough was enough. Tomorrow she would post the lot to Cauldwell.

33

The next day Adam was sitting in a chair in his hospital room with no signs of injury apart from a drain tube in his shoulder. Gina looked worse than he did. The side of her face was puffy and beginning to darken, and one eye was half closed. She walked into his room as if she was wading through hot sand, each step a painful experience.

'Ribs aren't actually broken,' she said. 'Just feels like it. Hurts when I breathe, hurts when I talk.' She looked at him accusingly. 'Why don't you look ill?'

'Because I have this amazingly robust constitution.' He grinned at her. 'Want my bed? I'm willing to share.'

She lowered herself gingerly down on the edge of the bed. 'Jack brought me in to see you because I can't drive. Megan can't drive, either, because she never learned, so I'm stuffed, basically. I'm glad you followed me to the house, though. How did you know where I was?'

'I went round to your flat to remind you to check your email and found your car gone. You weren't answering your phone, so I, er

. . . let myself in.' He looked at her accusingly. 'You still hadn't put the deadlock on.'

'Good job I hadn't, evidently.'

'There was a message from Fox on your computer.'

'So you not only broke into my flat, but into my computer as well. Goodness me, when is this invasion of privacy going to stop?' Gina shifted on the bed and moaned. Actually, everywhere hurt. 'Fox didn't send the message. I walked right into their trap because I was panicking about being late and not thinking straight. Fox wouldn't have left his name on an email.'

'Exactly. That's why I called the police.'

Megan put her head round the door. 'Can we come in?' She sat on the bed beside Gina. Jack followed her in, went to pat Adam on the shoulder, saw the drain tube and pulled his hand back.

'I brought you a bag of stuff from your flat,' he told Adam. 'Thought you might need a change of clothes.'

Adam nodded his thanks. 'They're letting me out tomorrow. They've just got to check there's no infection and get the drain out.'

'I so wanted Fox to get away,' Gina said. 'After all the trouble he went to, keeping himself safe for all those years, and then he finishes up with his brains blown out. He was strapped to that chair like a piece of cheese in a mouse trap, just to catch me.'

'Don't feel guilty, Gina,' Adam said. 'Fox was a blackmailer, not a nice person. He had a film for twenty years that could ruin the judge and put the other three away for good, so why didn't he take it to the police? Once the police had the tape, the whole thing would have been over. In effect, it was Fox who killed his daughter. He blackmailed the boys at the school, and they probably paid up the first time, but a blackmailer is never satisfied, and when he asked for more the boys told the judge. Fox decided to take his money and run, but he kept a copy of the video for insurance. When he came back he tried to blackmail them again. That was his big mistake.'

'Even so, no one deserved what Fox got. Now we'll never know what happened to the child, and Robert Cauldwell is on his way to being our next prime minister.' Gina moved again on the bed, trying to get into a more comfortable position. 'Fox told me the evidence against Cauldwell is in the diary. At least, I think that's what he meant, but we've been through the diary a hundred times already.'

'Are you sure there's nothing that seems odd?' Jack asked. 'No recurring numbers, strange names, anything like that?'

Gina took the diary out of her bag and handed it to him. 'We've all looked and looked, but perhaps you'll see something we missed.'

Jack flipped the pages. 'It could be a code of some sort. The hairdresser has a regular entry every six weeks, and shopping, that's pretty regular. She had a lot of hospital appointments, which you would expect, I suppose, if she had cancer.'

Gina pushed herself up off the bed and stood behind Jack, looking over his shoulder. 'Fox was going to try and get back to see her before she died. There's nothing in the diary to say whether he made it or not.'

'If Fox said the evidence against Cauldwell is in the diary, then it must be there somewhere,' Megan said. 'We'll just have to work it out, however long it takes.'

Adam stirred restlessly. 'If Cauldwell and his buddies give us the time. They know Gina has the diary and the two men the police picked up will be easy to replace. They won't give up that easily.'

'I'm going to post the diary and everything else to Cauldwell,' Gina told them. 'He can work out the bloody code. I don't care if I'm giving him his ticket to Downing Street.' She took the small, leather-bound book out of

Jack's hands and stared at it, frowning. 'I wonder if we're making things too complicated. Fox wouldn't bother with codes, and I keep thinking there's something strange about the diary, as if it's trying to tell me something.'

'Like what?' Adam said. 'The damned book hasn't said a word to me.'

Gina moved away from them, still holding the little book, and walked to the window. An ordinary diary bound in red leather — but this diary was different.

How different?

She stroked the leather. Soft and smooth, just like skin. Not human skin — but skin all the same. If it had been human skin she would have been able to strip the skin from the flesh, the flesh from the bones, and see what lay beneath.

She looked up. 'What we want is in the diary, but we were looking in the wrong place. Anyone got a knife?'

Without a word, Jack pulled a penknife out of his pocket and opened the blade.

Gina took a breath and carefully slit the leather. 'Fox was quite right, we already had the evidence. We've had it all the time.' She worked the knife round the edge of the cover and pulled it away from the cardboard backing, holding up a shiny silver disk. 'A copy of the mystery video, I would imagine.'

No one spoke for what seemed a long time, then Adam let out a sigh. 'We've been looking for the damn thing for so long it's almost an anticlimax.' He stood up, nearly pulling out his drain tube. 'We have to get this to the police, right now, before anything else happens.'

'Sit down,' Jack said. 'You're not going anywhere. Besides, shouldn't we look at it first, to find out what's on it? Make sure it's what we think it is.'

Adam sat down again and picked up the holdall Jack had brought in. He unzipped the flap and peered inside. 'I thought you might have stuck my laptop in.'

Jack grinned. 'I know you can't live without it.'

Gina watched Adam slide the disk into the computer. He looked up at her. 'Whatever is on here, I don't think it's going to be very nice.'

'I need to know what happened,' she said, 'but perhaps Megan should wait outside.'

Megan shook her head. 'I'll stay. Gary used to make me watch really nasty films sometimes. Kids, animals, everything. I just put my hands over my eyes.'

Adam pushed the play button.

The little girl's silence was the worst part.

Whatever they did to her she never once cried out. The boys were talking and laughing among themselves, but the child never made a sound. After a few minutes Adam skipped the disk forward and checked again, then moved to the end. Gina watched Martin Edge help the child dress, smiling while he fastened small buttons, and then the screen filled with static.

Adam looked angry. 'You shouldn't have had to watch that.'

'I didn't have to watch it.' Gina said. 'I wanted to find out who killed the child, but the film finished too soon and now we'll never know.'

Adam ejected the disk from his computer. 'We may never know exactly how the little girl died, but we've got the people responsible. Cauldwell, Edge, Trevor Pollard. All of them. The judge won't be able to get them off this time.'

★ ★ ★

Gina delivered the disk straight to Reagan but it was another two days before they were called in to give a formal statement, which gave Adam plenty of time to write his story.

'We have to handle this very carefully,' Reagan told them. 'The prime minister wants to try to defuse the situation as much as possible before it becomes public knowledge. A paedophile in the government ranks isn't good news. We can't charge any of them with murder, because there's no proof, and Judge Pollard will probably get off because we have nothing to connect him directly with the child or the DVD, but having a son who videos children being abused isn't going to endear him to anyone.'

'How was Fox involved?' Gina asked. 'Was he blackmailing them?'

'Yes, but he was in it up to his neck as well. He was the taxi service. He delivered the children to Cauldwell and his mates. The photo of the child was taken by Fox with his own camera. Some extra insurance in case he lost the video. He probably had photos of all the kids. If he hadn't been shot, he'd have spent a long time in jail.'

After giving their statements, a police car took them home. When the driver stopped outside Gina's studio, she got out and looked at Adam through the open window of the car.

'What are you going to do now? Once you get your story to the paper, you're finished here, aren't you? Will you go to Thailand with Jack?'

He studied her thoughtfully, his eyes very

blue. 'Ask me not to, and I might change my mind.'

Gina shook her head. 'I can't, Adam.'

He smiled. 'I didn't think so.'

She turned away, then turned back. 'You could always send me a postcard.'

'I could do that.' The smile turned into a grin. 'Till next time, then.'

She watched the car drive away, took a deep breath and opened the door to her studio. Ready for her cranky clients, Reagan's dead bodies, and whatever else a normal day might bring.

Epitaph

The child stood with her back against the wall. The tall man had helped her dress and she had been told to wait in the room, but the men had gone now. After a while she tried the door and found it was unlocked. They knew she wouldn't leave because she had nowhere to go.

The other man would come for her soon and take her back to the people who looked after her. They would feed her and let her watch television and she knew she should be grateful for such a nice home. For a while everything would be good, then the man would come for her again.

She opened the door and heard the three men downstairs, laughing and talking. She moved along the landing and crept down the stairs, but one of the boards creaked and she stood quite still, her heart beating very fast. She knew if they caught her they would hurt her. She took off her new shoes and carried them in her hand.

The front door was near the room where the men were talking, so she made her way quietly down the hallway and through the big kitchen to the back of the house. The back door was unlocked, but the garden was very dark and it was raining heavily. Within minutes the rain had soaked through the child's thin dress. She shivered. She couldn't go back now. They would know she had been outside.

She tore her dress pushing through the thick hedge at the bottom of the garden. The ground was rougher here, a large open space, a field of some sort full of short, tufted grass.

The child hadn't been outside on her own since coming to England. She lifted her face towards the black sky and let the rain wash her tears away. On the other side of the field were the lights of some houses.

Someone would help her.

She heard a noise from the house, shouting, and someone calling her name, then the sound of the men beating the bushes to find her. She started to run towards the lights, her feet slipping and sliding on the wet grass. The lights were getting nearer but so were the men. She turned her ankle on a tuft of grass and cried out with pain, but carried on running. Somewhere she had dropped her shoes.

The pond took her by surprise. At first she thought it was just a hole in the ground, then she was sliding down a bank into water. Deep water. She had never learned to swim. She had never been near the sea or played in a swimming pool. Deep water was alien to her.

It had been raining for several days and the bank was too slippery to climb. She scrabbled at the sides, digging her fingers into the slick, wet mud.

At first she tried to fight the water, slapping it with her hands and kicking her small feet, but the pond was deep and fighting made her tired. When she tried to shout, the water filled her throat. She thought she saw someone standing at the edge of the pond looking down at her, but when she looked again they were gone.

After a while she closed her eyes and let the water take her.

We do hope that you have enjoyed reading this large print book.

Did you know that all of our titles are available for purchase?

We publish a wide range of high quality large print books including:
**Romances, Mysteries, Classics
General Fiction
Non Fiction and Westerns**

Special interest titles available in large print are:
**The Little Oxford Dictionary
Music Book
Song Book
Hymn Book
Service Book**

Also available from us courtesy of Oxford University Press:
**Young Readers' Dictionary
(large print edition)
Young Readers' Thesaurus
(large print edition)**

For further information or a free brochure, please contact us at:
**Ulverscroft Large Print Books Ltd.,
The Green, Bradgate Road, Anstey,
Leicester, LE7 7FU, England.
Tel:** (00 44) 0116 236 4325
Fax: (00 44) 0116 234 0205

*Other titles published by
The House of Ulverscroft:*

CRY BABY

Fay Cunningham

Gina Cross has a talent: she puts the flesh back on the bones of the dead, working for the police as a forensic artist. Gina is convinced there's a connection between the body of a teenage mother and a friend's missing sister. She enlists the help of investigative journalist Adam Shaw to help her find the missing girl. Their search eventually takes them to the mysterious Willow Bank hospital — which hides a deadly secret. But if Gina and Adam learn the truth about Willow Bank they may have to be eliminated . . .

THE SHADOW OF TREASON

Edward Taylor

Autumn 1944. The Battle of Britain has been won, Allied troops are liberating Europe and the Nazi nightmare is almost over. But two unexpected horrors are waiting on the horizon: Hitler's final fling — the deadly V2 rockets which will rain down death and destruction from Britain's skies — and the dark forces planning a bloody revolution. A young scientist unwittingly holds the means to thwart the plotters but, falsely accused of murder, he is on the run. Fleeing from both the police and the traitors' thugs, his only allies are a showgirl from the Windmill Theatre and her comedian friend . . .

THE CHESHIRE CAT MURDERS

Roger Silverwood

When a wild cat goes on a killing spree in the South Yorkshire town of Bromersley, Detective Inspector Michael Angel and his team's search for the animal becomes desperate. The cougar appears to be under human control and trained to kill to order. When a well-known cat enthusiast, Miss Ephemore Sharpe, becomes the prime suspect, Angel is unable to prove her guilt. However, her possession of an antique, feline pottery figure marks a decisive turn in the enquiries. But as he races to find an explanation, Angel's investigations become more mystifying and dangerous. Can he prevent more mayhem and murder?

MISCHIEF DONE

J. A. O'Brien

When nine-year-old Miranda Watts goes missing, suspicion falls on Samuel Curly, a local man responsible for the abduction of another girl some years previously. When another young girl is found dead the pressure on acting DI Andy Lukeson intensifies, but the trail goes cold when the search for Curly finds him dead. If Curly is truly innocent, as Lukeson begins to believe, then there is someone out there who knows where Miranda is, and if she's still alive . . .